ABANDONED AT THE ALTAR

A VARIATION OF JANE AUSTEN'S PRIDE AND PREJUDICE

JULIE COOPER

Quills & Quartos
PUBLISHING

Edited by Katie Jackson and Jan Ashton

Cover by Pemberley Darcy

ISBN 978-1-963213-59-1 (ebook) and 978-1-963213-60-7 (paperback)

To Lisa Van Nortwick
It is people like you, pausing during the everyday commotion
of life to encourage people like me, who keep my world going.
Thank you!

PROLOGUE

November 28, 1811

It was not usual for a wedding to be so well attended. The breakfast afterwards, yes—and most of the neighbourhood would participate in that event, too.

Elizabeth sighed at the sight of the crowded pews as she peeked into the nave, feeling as though she was put on display for the entire world. It was her mama's fault, naturally, although, really, Darcy shared the blame as well. Had he not publicly insulted her at the first assembly he had attended, for all the country to notice and remark upon, her recent announcement of their sudden nuptials—which her mama repeated to anyone who would listen—would not have caused such a stir.

Of course, there were those who were curious for more reason than simply their initial antipathy. The abrupt public reversal of feeling had also drawn raised brows and not-so-subtle, measuring glances at her middle.

Elizabeth was certainly not 'in the family way', but there was every need for haste. Darcy's sister—whom she had yet to meet—had fallen in love, although she was so young at just sixteen. Her family, convinced that the man was only interested in her fortune of thirty thousand pounds, had separated them, and Miss Darcy was apparently still very much distressed over the loss of her lover.

Currently, she was living with her aunt and uncle, the celebrated Lord and Lady Matlock, at their London residence. Darcy wished to bring her home. His esteemed relations wished to keep her. He had not objected thus far, because he had no wife and felt acutely his own shortcomings in advising her. In Elizabeth, he claimed, he had found her the perfect sister. He simply had not recognised it upon the evening of their first meeting.

"I was a fool," he had said. "Unhappy about my sister, I took out my frustration with life upon Bingley, with you as the target of my displeasure. I should have been cast out of the assembly for my churlish behaviour. You cannot know how I regret it."

He is not marrying me simply to gain a sister for his, Elizabeth reassured herself. The violence of his affections had been a very convincing argument for his depth of feeling. He had also explained that it would be selfish of him to remain at Netherfield for a lengthy wooing when his sister was so truly despondent.

Elizabeth had met Colonel Fitzwilliam, younger son of the earl of Matlock and Miss Darcy's joint guardian, whom Darcy had invited to stand up with him at their marriage. Although Darcy had assured her of his cousin's amiability, she had found the colonel stiff, cold, and formal. If his parents were cut from the same bolt, she could not believe them to be the best overseers of a sensitive girl who was struggling with bitter disappointment. Besides, the idea of a separation, for months, while Darcy remained in Derbyshire, was an awful one.

It would be wisest, they had both agreed, to marry before Miss Darcy was moved for the Festive Season to Matlock, to present the illustrious earl with their marriage as a *fait accompli*, and to have the three of them start life together without delay.

To that end, just over a week ago he had departed Netherfield to procure a licence from his uncle, Bishop Darcy, in town. He meant to speak to his sister while there, to give her the happy news privately. He had hoped she would be pleased; according to Darcy, she adored Pemberley above anywhere else in the world and must be longing to return. He also insisted that he would have his solicitor draw up a settlement that would see Elizabeth protected, no matter that she brought almost nothing to the match. It would be his privilege to care for her always, he said.

He had not come to her yesterday, although she had expected him—had waited up late, while the torrents drumming at the windows told her that his reappearance was unlikely. If he had not managed the journey during the day, it would be foolish to attempt it during a storm, in darkness. Elizabeth was certain that the succession of rain, which had inundated them from almost the hour of his departure, was responsible for the delay in his return. Large sections of the road must be a soggy, muddy wreck.

Nevertheless, she had been quite convinced that, if he had to walk, he would be at the church before ten o'clock, the appointed hour of their wedding ceremony. The day had dawned bright and clear, as if even the weather was ready to celebrate; she *knew* he was as eager to be her husband as she was to become his wife.

She peered again into the nave; there was no sign of either her bridegroom or the colonel. Beside her, her father, so jovial and eager thirty minutes before, looked concerned.

The vicar, Mr Palmer, appeared in the vestibule. "Miss Elizabeth, perhaps you and your father would care to await your bridegroom in a more private chamber? It is chilly out here." He hesitated. "If you would like, you can come around the north side and enter that way."

So that I do not have to stride down the aisle with no bridegroom awaiting me, causing further talk.

"Yes, that is an excellent idea," Mr Bennet agreed immediately.

They tramped around the church to the smaller entrance, used mainly by the vicar, and he let them into the vestry before leaving them to wait alone. There they sat in uncomfortable silence as the muffled sounds from beyond the vestry door grew louder.

"What time is it, Papa?" Elizabeth finally asked.

Slowly, he withdrew his pocket watch, snapping its brass cover open. "Twenty minutes after eleven, but this dashed watch cannot keep time lately. It is probably running fast. I must take it to be repaired."

For the very first time, a cold sliver of fear streaked down Elizabeth's spine. Impossible that Darcy should not be here, not unless something had happened to him. If there was one thing of which she was certain, it was her betrothed's integrity.

An accident. It was the only answer.

Do not panic, she cautioned herself. *You do not yet have any information. A lame horse, a transom requiring repair, a tree downed across a road, all these things might cause significant, unexpected delay.*

Perhaps it was silly, but she believed with her whole soul that he was not harmed. She felt, somehow, that she would *know* if that were the case.

Some minutes later, she heard the murmurs beginning to quiet, and the echoing sounds of footsteps on the limestone floor. Onlookers were, clearly, leaving; presumably her family had departed as well. Still, she would not surrender her hope, even though her father now looked positively haggard.

Mr Palmer entered at last, regarding her with obvious pity. "It is noontime. I can no longer perform the ceremony today. Perhaps we ought to reschedule for tomorrow."

Hope gave way in a flood of anxious worry.

"Let us go home, Daughter," Papa said gently. "I am certain we will have news later, and we should be home when it arrives."

It was plain that he, too, believed some terrible mishap had occurred. Numbly, she nodded, standing.

At that moment, old Mr Goulding entered the vestry, appearing surprised to see them all standing about. "Bennet. Miss Elizabeth. Mr Palmer." He gave a little bow, looking from one to the other of them, shifting uncomfortably on his feet.

"Goulding," Mr Bennet replied, nodding shortly.

The older man scratched his head. "I say," he started, glancing anxiously at Elizabeth and then her father. "I require…a moment, Mr Palmer. Could I speak to you…to relay some news…privately?"

It was so obvious that the 'news' concerned the Bennets, Elizabeth could not hold her tongue. "Is it about Mr Darcy?"

"Well…as to that—" Goulding hesitated, and then scratched his head again. "—was not sure who to tell. Or if I ought."

Elizabeth thought she might scream.

"Goulding, we have been friends for many years. Do tell us what you have to say. It is best we hear it directly," Mr Bennet bade, his voice stern. But he moved closer to Elizabeth, placing a comforting hand upon her shoulder.

Goulding appeared as if he wished to be anywhere else in the world, and, albeit reluctantly, nodded his agreement. "I had a meeting with my solicitor in town this morning…no time to cool my heels at the church, so I was on my way as soon as it became apparent the bridegroom would be late." He began apologies for this, but thankfully Mr Bennet cut him off.

"Please, sir, come to the point!"

"Yes, yes of course. Had barely begun my journey when one of my horses threw a shoe. Was brought to a halt just beyond the lane leading to Netherfield's drive. I was surprised when a few minutes later, as I was out with my coachman, discussing what ought to be done, the fellow you introduced to us at Philips's home last week, Colonel, er—"

"Fitzwilliam," Mr Bennet supplied.

"Yes, yes, that's the name. Fitzwilliam. He came riding by, slowing when he saw us. 'I believe you are heading the wrong direction,' I called to him, pointing back to Meryton. Thought he might be turned around, you know. 'The church is the other way. You have a village full of folks awaiting the bridegroom —your Mr Darcy.'"

Goulding glanced at Elizabeth, and began speaking more quickly, obviously trying to get the tale over with. "He said Darcy was no one's bridegroom. That just because a group of yokels tried to force him into wedlock, he was under no obligation to support rumours and misunderstandings. That a man has every right to come to his senses once he's out from under a siren's thumb." He glanced at Elizabeth again and flushed. "Then he rode off at a trot. Towards London."

"He must be mistaken!" Mr Palmer cried, appearing astonished. But then, before their eyes, his aspect changed—to one of doubt. "Of course...I have never spoken to Mr Darcy myself. Do you suppose, Mr Bennet, that you were confused? About his intentions, I mean?"

"Absolutely not!" her father snapped. "Mr Darcy approached *me*, in *my* book room, and asked for my daughter's hand in marriage. He asked me for a letter granting this permission, so that he could obtain a licence. I *wrote* the letter. He *said* that he would meet us, here, at this church, at ten o'clock today, with licence in hand. I could hardly have misinterpreted *that*, could I?"

"No, no," Mr Palmer said, his voice soothing. "'Tis odd he did not speak to me about the matter, perhaps."

Mr Bennet huffed. "Mr Darcy did not speak to you

because he asked *me* to. He must have met with some accident or unavoidable delay preventing his timely reappearance."

"Must be it," Goulding agreed, although Elizabeth could see scepticism writ all over his face, plainly shared by the vicar.

"Come, Elizabeth," Mr Bennet ordered sternly, although his hand upon her shoulder gave a comforting squeeze. "Let us go home and await word there."

Stricken, disbelieving, heartsick, Elizabeth stumbled from the room.

CHAPTER ONE

November 14, 1811
Two Weeks Before the Wedding that Was Not

From the moment the note arrived from her sister Jane, notifying Elizabeth of the fever which kept her confined to Netherfield Park, Elizabeth ought to have known her own life would change forever. Her failure to recognise this was not entirely her fault; she had lived the previous twenty years in rote sameness, the facts of her life completely fixed: the second eldest of five daughters, her family the chief inhabitants of the village of Longbourn, their estate entailed away to a distant cousin, her portion as minuscule as her prospects. It was a good life, with a good family, but hardly one of *expectation*.

The change had begun unobtrusively with a lease to a neighbouring property—the aforementioned Netherfield Park —by the gregarious Mr Bingley. It had subtly continued when

Jane had fallen in love with him. Fate, albeit still in disguise, had roared to life when Mr Bingley brought his friend to visit, the handsome and wealthy Mr Darcy.

Her first impressions of Mr Darcy had not been encouraging ones. 'Tolerable, but not handsome enough to tempt me,' had been his stupidly announced opinion of her from the assembly at which they met. Neither had she any desire to 'tempt' him *or* his consequence; she knew his type. All Elizabeth had hoped of him was a partner in the reel, and his offensive dismissal had convinced her that he was naught but a pompous aristocrat.

Nothing much had happened to change that opinion, until she had come to Netherfield to watch over Jane.

It had not been a terrible stay, once her worst fears over Jane's illness had passed. Although Mr Bingley's sisters, Mrs Hurst and Miss Bingley, were—in Elizabeth's opinion—as haughty as Mr Darcy, their accommodations were comfortable, Netherfield's cook was superior, and the garden paths were pretty. Mrs Bennet had sent a note urging her and Jane to stay, as she and the two youngest Bennets had contracted fevers similar to Jane's and were confined to their beds. She *said* she feared contagion, although it was likeliest that she feared they would depart Netherfield before Jane received a proposal of marriage from the kindly Mr Bingley.

Since Jane's fever had proved minor, Elizabeth had no doubt that her family's recovery would be swift as well. She was anxious to go home, but wavered—*should* Jane be exposed to additional illness?

While contemplating whether to beg for a carriage to Longbourn or to settle in for a few more days, Elizabeth ran downstairs to the library, anxious to see if anything in the admittedly small book collection might provide amusement for her ailing sister. Disdaining the slim selection at eye level, she had just knelt to read the titles on the lowest shelf, when she heard the creaky door open, then firmly shut. A voice—Mrs Hurst's—demanded, "Caroline, you must gain control of yourself! Stop this, now!"

The sound of sobs echoed throughout the room.

Startled, Elizabeth froze; she did not wish to embarrass her hostesses by revealing herself, but neither did she wish to eavesdrop. Miss Bingley was hysterical, and all of Mrs Hurst's hushing did not appear to be helping. Still, she started to stand, to make them aware of her presence when Miss Bingley blurted, "That awful Elizabeth Bennet! *Why*, Louisa? Why is he in love with *her*?"

Elizabeth plopped back down onto the plush carpet. *In love? Who does she believe in love with me? Is Miss Bingley mad?*

Yet, as she thought it, the image of the tall, handsome Mr Darcy flashed within her mind. *There is only one man who might excite Miss Bingley's jealousy to such an extent, except...he despises me!*

"Listen to me!" Mrs Hurst ordered in a firm, lecturing tone. "You must not tease Mr Darcy about Miss Elizabeth. Why would you so boldly plan aloud his marriage to her? Her eyes *are* her finest feature, so why do you frequently draw his attention to them? Do you wait for him to refute it?"

"What does it matter?" Miss Bingley sniffed. "He does nothing except follow her with *his* eyes, everywhere she goes! He says she is the handsomest woman of his acquaintance—

never hesitating to bestow praise upon her for the slightest goodness while she is practically rude to him in return! Anyone can see her indifference, whilst he slavers after her! 'Tis so unfair! She is a nobody with nothing!"

"Exactly," Mrs Hurst chided. "She is a good-looking nobody. He cannot marry her—she brings nothing to the match. So what if she has sparked his interest? He will resist. But whether he does or does not, Caroline, you have always known he looks upon you almost as a sister and nothing else. The more you tease him, the more insistently he attempts to show you that *your* wishes are futile. I do not believe he means to be unkind. He wants you to stop hoping."

"Do not you think I know that?" Miss Bingley cried. "But to watch him fall in love, right before my very eyes, with an impoverished woman who thinks herself better than him, is excruciating! She has no right to-to belittle him before everyone. He does not see it!"

"Would it be any better if she returned his affections? Be thankful she does not care for him if it is so upsetting, but dear, you *must* prepare yourself for his eventual marriage!"

Miss Bingley sniffed. "You know Charles needs him still —Papa died too soon, and our brother would be utterly lost in taking the reins of estate management, or really, anything of import without him."

"Of course he does—but that is no reason to keep hoping. He will never change his mind, not if Charles relies upon him in every decision for the next decade," Mrs Hurst argued relentlessly. "You are beautiful, with wealth and untold opportunity before you. Take advantage of your connexion to Mr

Darcy, but do not let it destroy you. Above all, you *must* set your heart upon someone else."

"As you did?" Miss Bingley said—not snidely, but rather as if it were a hopeless task.

There was a long pause.

"I chose Montrose Hurst because the match allows me to do exactly as I please. I did not want love then and still do not. Monty does as he wishes, and so do I, and both of us are content. You are responsible for your own happiness, dear. Believe me when I say, it will *not* be with Fitzwilliam Darcy. Find another man."

The silence lasted a few more moments. "I hate the country and, most especially, I hate this place," Miss Bingley said, her voice less tearful. "The sooner we can extract Charles from Miss Bennet's clutches and return to town, the better."

"That would be wisest," Mrs Hurst agreed briskly. "Now, take yourself to your chambers, rest and restore yourself. No more of these tantrums, Sister-mine."

Shortly thereafter, the creaking door opened, then softly shut. When Elizabeth was certain she was finally alone, she collapsed onto the library floor, staring up at the ceiling. What, oh what had just happened?

How could Mr Darcy possibly be in love…with me?

It was not until they shared a house together that Darcy realised the extent of his danger. This, even though his interest in Elizabeth Bennet—unsought, unwanted—had begun simmering shortly after the assembly where they had been introduced.

Or, to be explicit, where at least twenty young ladies had been introduced, the gleam of avarice shining in parental eyes as they chucked their daughters at him. All Darcy had wanted was to set up Bingley with his new neighbours so he could return to town and begin trying to cheer his grieving sister. He had seen no reason to give any of those naïve country lasses hope. Although he *did* need to marry, and had no idea of their fortunes or standing, he had been able to tell at a glance that none would meet his own discerning standards, much less those of his aunt, the fastidious Lady Matlock, nor his uncle, the renowned earl of Matlock —both of whose good opinion he deemed necessary for Georgiana's sake. A settlement of at least thirty thousand, stylish in dress and etiquette, sober in behaviour and breeding, a *ton* leader who would both guide his sister and be a credit to Pemberley— these were Darcy's minimum requirements. Instead, he had been surrounded by loud laughter, light minds, and last year's fashions.

Thus, when Bingley had first urged him to dance with Miss Elizabeth, he had seen nothing but the thinnest veneer of her—young but not too young, tall but not too tall, a dark-haired, dark-eyed…lump. He had delivered an insult rather than an offer, with a precision slice meant to cut away any expectations and leave him in peace.

That the insult might have been spoken loudly enough to hurt the feelings of said lump, he had not considered; he had meant, only, that she—*it*—ought never to look at him again.

He had not, however, expected eyes sparkling with *laughter* as she murmured something to her friend. He had not caught much of what she said except the word 'relic' and the phrase 'decaying dullard'. *Relic? Me? Decaying dullard?* he had thought. She was odd and absurd and tasteless, and he had been left with the feeling she had meant him to hear.

Yet, she had made an impression, if not a good one. Over the next two months, he had not been able to help picking her out of every crowd, and she seemed to be *everywhere*. People were more likely to smile when she was near; they flocked to her like Lot's wife to Gomorrah, asking her opinions, wanting her conversation, her smiles, her attention.

Of course, the more he observed her, the more he became aware of her familial flaws. While she—and her elder sister, it must be admitted—behaved with perfect propriety, her mother was loud, gossipy, and scatter-brained, her younger sisters silly and shameless. The father was a gentleman, but he certainly curbed none of the behaviour in his womenfolk he ought to have checked.

So why was it a struggle to ignore them all, and most especially Miss Elizabeth? It was damnably annoying. Still, he might have resisted—*would* have resisted—had not Miss Jane Bennet fallen ill at Netherfield.

From the moment Miss Elizabeth had first appeared in Netherfield's breakfast parlour—her glorious hair escaping its restraints, her cheeks pink, her eyes brightened by the exercise of walking three miles to reach her sister—his entire body had become an arrow pointing to its own true north. Miss Bingley had rattled on with stinging criticism—would he want Georgiana to tramp for miles through mud, to appear amongst relative strangers, to bring those strangers to their feet with various expressions of astonishment at her appearance? No, of course not!

There was absolutely *nothing* in his feelings for Elizabeth Bennet that he wished *any* man to feel for his young sister.

It was not until that moment that he had realised he *wanted* her—wanted her not simply in his bed, but in his life; he wanted her attention, her regard, her feelings, her *commitment* to him and only him.

Miss Elizabeth's sole aim was to care for a most beloved sister, Darcy could easily see. Had she heard the critique on her muddy hems or wild hair, she would have cared nothing.

Her family was still shockingly inappropriate; her portion, Miss Bingley had hastened to inform him, was non-existent. Miss Elizabeth was not for him.

But he wanted her, and the wanting was a fever far worse than anything that Mr Jones, the local apothecary, could ever treat.

CHAPTER TWO

The Next Day

Mr Darcy certainly did *not* appear as a man in love. Whatever Miss Bingley's feelings on the matter, she must have been quite mistaken. Elizabeth, accustomed to eating later than the family for the sake of waiting upon her sister, had breakfasted alone since arriving at Netherfield three days before. She had been astonished to find him in the breakfast room, still, this morning, and she glanced surreptitiously at the solemn man who shared her table.

Elizabeth could acknowledge that she had, likely, been harsher in her estimation of his character than was fair. It was true that his cutting remark towards her at the assembly had given her a poor opinion of his temperament, his arrogance, and his manners. However, she had regarded him with new insight the evening before. With poor Miss Bingley, he had demonstrated considerable patience with her unending adulation. Really, had the man demanded she kneel before him, she would have offered herself as a footstool. Mrs Hurst was correct; Miss Bingley was losing her dignity over him, and while she was to be pitied, Elizabeth would have been hard-pressed to show the same restraint as Mr Darcy.

She had thought him a tad hard on Mr Bingley, but now that she understood him to be acting more in the role of guardian than simply as a friend, his attitude made sense. Considering her new knowledge of the situation with Mr Bingley's sisters, she thought Mr Darcy had actually exhibited remarkable forbearance with the lot of them. Towards herself, she was not quite so certain.

Was he so accustomed to women instantly falling all over him in adoration? He was wealthy, yes, but so were the Bingleys. From the Bingley sisters' conversation, it appeared they *both* had fallen in love with him. *He* is *more handsome than I first considered, now that I have decided he is not quite so supercilious as I once believed*, she thought with an inward smile. He was also very blue-blooded—Miss Bingley gloated over his kinship to the earl of Matlock, unquestionably a fixture in society's highest circles. There was hardly a more desirable connexion in all of England.

But...in *love*? Would Miss Bingley so passionately sob over the loss of a highborn uncle? Imagine choosing the vacuous Mr Hurst as one's mate, simply so that one might never again feel the pain of unrequited emotion? What was it about this man that inspired such admiration?

It is not his ability to make pleasant breakfast-time conver-

sation. To distract herself from the urge to giggle, she returned to the sideboard to examine the morning cakes.

"The honey cake is an excellent choice," Mr Darcy said, suddenly at her elbow and startling her. "I do not know why so many prefer the plum when honey is served."

"I am in no humour at present to give consequence to a cake that has been slighted by other diners," she replied in mock-sober tones, reaching for the plum. She could not help it, and the giggle escaped anyhow as she looked up at him.

To her surprise, he flushed.

"Point taken, madam," he said, his expression grave.

"Come, now, Mr Darcy, you are noted for your presence of mind. One so gifted must surely appreciate a talent for turning past insults to present pleasure."

"I have been reminded that I made myself ridiculous in your eyes. Should I be pleased?"

"Is not your memory under as excellent a regulation as your pride?"

He shook his head, sighing. "You are determined to prove me absurd."

"Nothing of the sort, surely," she murmured. "Perhaps slightly…inconsistent."

"Besides, you need prove nothing," he said gravely. "Not when I continue to offer up, constantly, new fodder for your amusement."

She smiled again. "I do love to laugh. But I hope I am not so frivolous as to search for faults instead of follies. In this instance, I was not thinking of your feelings, but my own. I completely comprehend not wishing to dance, although an assembly seems an odd outing to attend when one is affronted by the notion. I do not at all understand your need to offer offence along with your rejection. You did not *want* me to like you, plainly."

"Thus, you did not."

"I will not exchange one offence for another by admitting it."

He appeared to hesitate. "Would you be so kind as to accompany me for a walk in the garden? The sun is shining, if it provides little in the way of warmth. When you have finished your breakfast, of course."

Elizabeth was astonished at this invitation. Was it an apology, of sorts? A concession of attention? She did not require it, happy to settle for mere civility; neither, however, did she wish to be unmannerly. "I should not leave Jane for too long," she said, hesitating.

"Your own health ought to be considered. The briefest airing, I promise."

He was trying, it seemed, and it would be rude to suppose it to be mere condescension.

"Thank you, yes," Elizabeth agreed. "I am almost finished with my breakfast." She gestured to the plate she still held, upon which the plum cake rested; but Mr Darcy had evidently had enough of the meal.

"I shall see you downstairs in perhaps quarter of an hour?" he asked, to which Elizabeth politely nodded.

After his departure, however, she returned to her sense of astonishment—at herself, as much as anything. What she ought to have given was proper thanks for the invitation, while declining for Jane's sake—her sister *was* improved, but not nearly recovered. It would have been a perfect excuse for the avoidance of half an hour's awkward conversation.

What was I thinking?

Then, she did something more inexplicable than ever. Returning the plum cake to the sideboard, she instead served herself a slice of the honey cake, reseating herself at the empty table. She took a bite, finding it truly, wonderfully delicious... down to the very last crumb.

What was I thinking? Darcy wondered at himself, much astonished.

You were not, the face in his looking-glass reminded him. He had returned to his chambers to fetch a warmer coat, and now peered at his condemning reflection. *You were ashamed of yourself for insulting her, embarrassed that she so coyly admitted it, and you gave way to wanting. To desire. To the temptation of half an hour of her company without a servant looking on, or worse, Miss Bingley.*

Until last evening, he had suddenly realised, he had simply been more furniture in the room to Miss Elizabeth, or a potted plant, perhaps—and not a very interesting one. Something had changed; she looked at him more frequently, teased him more often, smiled more fully—seemed simply more *aware* of him. He was ashamed to say he had not *truly* noticed her essential apathy towards him until that change—until she no longer treated him as...as a potted plant. Unfortunately, the difference between wanting a disinterested Miss Elizabeth and this new, arresting version was the difference between warming oneself at a pleasant hearth and running headlong into a wildfire.

Along with his extraordinary desire was a new, added intrigue. He wanted to know why. What had happened to make her tease him about his flawed manners, instead of despising him for it?

That is all I need to understand, he told his sober countenance. *A simple walk in the garden, and I shall henceforth leave her severely, permanently alone.*

With a spring in his step, he hastened to Netherfield's marbled entrance hall to await Miss Elizabeth.

CHAPTER THREE

The two were silent as they walked the gravelled path between aisles of shrubbery. It was too late in the year and much too cold for blossoms, but the garden had its own beauty despite grey skies and inclement weather.

Miss Elizabeth, Darcy noticed, wore a warm pelisse, along with a small chip hat adorned with becoming silk flowers—it was obvious she did not fear rain.

"I brought an umbrella, in case of showers," he said, stupidly—unable to think of one suitable topic of conversation, as if he were a green lad who had never before been alone with a desirable female.

"It will not rain. John Stevens has sworn it will not, today nor tomorrow, neither one."

"John Stevens?" Darcy asked, curious. "Who might he be?"

"Oh, he is Netherfield's chief gardener. He has held the position for many years and came with the house. His weather predictions are amazingly accurate. The entire neighbourhood relies upon them."

"Ah. Well, perhaps I shall keep hold of the umbrella, just in case he fails us."

She grinned, undoubtedly finding his faithlessness foolish, looking pretty as springtime in her little hat. "How long have you known the Bingleys?" she asked conversationally.

"I met Bingley at school. Eton."

"Really? He is several years younger than you, is he not?"

"Yes."

She glanced at him with her own curiosity, but she asked nothing.

"Our friendship did not begin conventionally. It is somewhat of a lengthy tale, and probably an uninteresting one," he added discouragingly. He did not wish to spend any of these few moments alone with Elizabeth upon the hated Wickham.

"I would be honoured to hear it," she replied, and he believed there was real interest in her tone. Irresistible interest.

Hardly able to believe he was talking of all this, he cast his mind back to a time he had not thought of in years. "It all began, I suppose, when I went off to school with my good friend, my father's godson." He was struck by a sudden thought. "In a way, one might say that my own father was responsible for the entire situation, by paying for my friend's schooling."

"The situation?" she asked, observably puzzled by this apparent non sequitur.

"I have never before considered it in that light," he explained. "My father and his were great friends—his father held the management of Pemberley, but could not afford to send his son to Eton. If he had not gone to Eton, Bingley and I would never have become acquainted."

"Your friend...he was the one who introduced you to Mr Bingley?"

"Not exactly." Darcy sighed. "He was the one who tormented Bingley until I was forced to intervene."

"Oh, dear." Miss Elizabeth's brow furrowed as her quick mind caught upon a salient point. "I would think Pemberley's land agent to be an excellent position."

"Oh, yes. His wife was to blame, I thought at the time. She was always extravagant. And yet, my friend, I can see now, held some fault. She would never refuse him anything, and I believe she took the blame for money squandered by her son, at least in later years. At the time, I could not conceive of going off to Eton without him. But within a year or two, Wickham and I had grown completely estranged."

"Wickham was your friend?"

Hearing Wickham referred to as his 'friend' touched off his inner fury, but he somehow managed to keep his tone even. "Yes. He fell in with a crowd of boys who were older, and whose main pursuits had very little to do with education. It was difficult, in the beginning, for me to accept. But I cared for little beyond my classes and cricket. He preferred more... worldly pursuits."

"You mean, gambling and girls," Miss Elizabeth said bluntly.

Darcy glanced over at her, and she grinned. "I am, of course, a fragile flower and have no idea to what I refer. I understand if you cannot confirm my supposition, lest you fear I swoon."

He frowned, trying to think how he felt about her words; he was undeniably accustomed to thinking of young ladies in general as delicate—they were *supposed* to be. But of course, a young lady who would tramp three miles across muddy fields and rocky paths to reach her sister's bedside was hardly fragile. No other woman of his acquaintance would ever think of doing such a thing. Why did the idea of it enchant him? Was it so awful to be able to talk to this woman as he might speak to any of his friends, without weighing every word? What did it matter if he did?

I am hardly trying to impress her.

"Yes," he said at last. "Those were his chief amusements."

"He began his pursuit of a life of pleasure early, then," she remarked pensively.

He shrugged. "Many do. There is a pecking order at school, based upon a number of things—birth, wealth, one's friends, one's manners and address. He stuck with me until he was firmly entrenched in the upper hierarchy, and then proceeded to work his way into friendships with boys I did not like and who, as a general rule, did not like me."

"Because they embraced fewer 'general rules'?"

He nodded. "Most definitely. As he grew older, he adopted the worst habits of the crowd he ran with, eventually becoming its leader, as his elder classmates left Eton for Oxford or Cambridge. Our final year was the height of his reign."

"His *reign*?"

"Yes—his tenure as one of the most influential of his class, with a large crowd of cronies willing to follow him into whatever exploits he demanded."

Too late, Darcy remembered her calling him a 'decaying dullard'. Wickham had certainly accused him of the same often enough over the years—that he was staid, stolid, and stiff. Probably, he sounded like a prig. He glanced at Miss Elizabeth, expecting a smirk or some sign of condescension. It was not there. Instead, she looked back at him, her expression serious.

"I suppose, if he used that influence to be helpful, or if his antics were harmless, that might not be a bad thing," she observed. "I gather he did not and was not, since he became a tormentor."

Remembering, he could not keep all of his anger concealed. "Wickham harassed all the first-years mercilessly, frequently, but of course, that happens so often, it barely is noticed—sixth-years expect the services of younger students. Polishing boots, serving tea, clearing up, running errands—'tis required. I was able to protect them, for the most part, from the sort of humiliation he enjoyed doling out. Of course, I could not be everywhere at once, but Wickham knew which lines he could not cross."

"Until he crossed one?"

"Yes. I am unsure as to why young Bingley drew his attention so frequently. Barely thirteen years old, he was a short, skinny, freckled little thing." Darcy clenched his fist in hated recollection. "I believe Wickham resented that Bingley— whose father earned his wealth in trade—was there at all."

"Why should he? He was there because of your father's good will, not because *he* was the heir of a noble house."

"That was all part of it, I suppose. He acted as though he were a son of Pemberley, but his father was a steward, the son of a vicar. Although his heritage is completely respectable, Wickham was revelling in the company of young lords. Perhaps he realised his little kingdom must eventually crumble. It did not help that Bingley was a touch...obtuse. The poor lad could not tell, usually, when to speak up and when to remain silent. That, and his natural clumsiness made him an easy target."

They turned to a pathway that narrowed, walking between tall, trimmed hedges. "It sounds as though Mr Wickham's entire life was a lie," she said, her tone thoughtful. "Somehow, turning what power he possessed upon a boy younger, weaker, and his social inferior provided him with an odd sort of... balance, perhaps, to his feelings of pretence. Something like a proof, to himself, that he really was superior. That he belonged with the nobles he had courted so assiduously."

Darcy glanced over at her again; he had never met anyone of her understanding. Until speaking of this aloud, he had not really recognised it himself. Her words felt like truth. "Probably," he agreed.

"What did he do to cross that line?"

He paused mid-step. He could never say, aloud, to a lady, the foul, contemptible thing Wickham had attempted. Straightening, he began walking again, shoving the filthy memories firmly back into the past. "You may take me at my word," he said quellingly, "it was an inexcusable act, and not one a lady would wish to discuss."

Her expression immediately changed from interested and reflective to closed off, shuttered, as if she had slammed a door between them. "Of course," she answered mildly. "Enough of such topics. How do you find our Hertfordshire weather? I assume Derbyshire is much cooler at this time of year."

Darcy very nearly replied something about precipitation. It was an automatic response; a lady commented upon the weather, and the gentleman answered her with an equally inane, obvious remark guaranteed to send them both into paroxysms of monotony.

Unfairly, she had placed him back into the 'decaying dullard' category—yet another who treated her as a fragile flower. He was surprised at how little she valued the nuances of civility; despite the proprieties she followed in all other ways, her mind brazenly travelled unallowable paths. Proof, then, that she was not wellborn enough to practise a true lady-like manner; her essential self was ungoverned.

He could never trust Miss Elizabeth to remain remote, aloof, and reserved, as the mistress of Pemberley ought to be. As his own mother had been. The perfect lady.

CHAPTER FOUR

"Wickham forced Bingley to swallow spirits, enough to lose consciousness, and was about to brand a highly offensive insult onto a highly embarrassing portion of his anatomy using a hot iron. You may now proceed to swoon."

Darcy could not believe what he had just blurted.

Miss Elizabeth's mouth formed a little rosebud of astonishment—and not entirely, he thought, because of Wickham's revolting villainy. She had not believed he would tell her.

Well, call us both surprised.

"Perhaps I will postpone the swoon, in favour of asking how you rescued him?"

Darcy knew he ought to keep the rest to himself, end the walk, and return to the house. Yet, once again, she was alert, eager, interested in what he had to say—not, he knew, because she enjoyed disgusting details, but because he felt her strong enough to hear them. He should feel appalled.

Why am I relieved, instead?

"It was easily done. The fools knew they were behaving badly—and, I think, were it not for Wickham's insistence and their own drunkenness, most would not have participated. I simply had to remind them that if he died of infection afterwards, they might be accused of murder, and asked them how they would enjoy a vagabond's life, on the Continent."

She smiled faintly. "I suppose that in return for your heroism, you were never again required to polish your own boots."

He gave her a disdainful look, and she laughed—a marvellous sound.

"Very well, I stand corrected. You never *did* have to polish your own boots."

"The very idea," he drawled, and she laughed again, and he felt strangely, improbably happy, strolling in the outdoors with her on his arm.

Odd how he had never before noticed the beauty of Netherfield's garden paths. Even with autumn's fading blooms, the deep greens, nicely laid walks, pretty statuary, and quaint follies were quite satisfying, really.

A small voice within his mind—a sarcastic voice—noted that it was unlikely his current happiness was due to the beauties of nature and architecture.

"How did your father feel, learning that the godson he treated so well, behaved so poorly?"

Abruptly, his feelings of pleasure ebbed, making way for guilt. "He did not know. By that time, we knew his heart was weak. I was afraid of what it might do to his health, to learn that his favourite was a noxious degenerate. I never did tell him, although Father lived five more years. I ought to have told him. I regret now that I did not."

Miss Elizabeth turned a sympathetic gaze upon him. "I cannot imagine bearing such news to my papa about any of my sisters—whether or not she was a favourite. You cannot be blamed for trying to protect him. It sounds as though your friend was like a brother to you, once upon a time. For that old friendship's sake, it would have been difficult."

Darcy tried looking at the tangle from her point of view, but knew it was not an accurate one. By the time he graduated Eton, he felt nothing but disgust for his old 'friend'. "Do not credit me with any remnant feelings of loyalty—those were gone long before he attempted to...*deface* Bingley."

"Ostensibly, you gained Mr Bingley's friendship in exchange," she remarked. "A good bargain, I am thinking. Still, the difference in your ages—I am surprised you remained close. He would have been too young to join you at university."

Darcy smiled sardonically. "My first letter from Bingley arrived during my second week at Cambridge. I cannot tell you precisely what it said—his scores and crosses were too obfuscating. However, I gathered that he was still having a rough time of it, so I wrote back to him—nothing much, really, just a word of encouragement. Thereafter he was a surprisingly faithful correspondent. Truthfully, his hand is abysmal and for all his education, it has never improved—half the time I have little idea what he means to say."

Miss Elizabeth gave him a look which he thought might be called approving. "Do you know what I believe, Mr Darcy? I think that you worried about him, and you wanted to help him.

I am certain your reputation at Eton remained an excellent one even in your absence, and that by sharing a correspondence, you ensured that others knew he retained your protection. I believe that your friendship, once gained, is given forever—as long as one does not grow into a 'noxious degenerate'."

His return answer was a wry one. "By the same token, my nature is a resentful one—my good opinion, once lost, is lost forever."

"It sounds as though Mr Wickham lost your good opinion for good reason," she replied. "I am not sure forgiveness is possible in such a case. You protected your father from heartache—perhaps a fatal one. What harm was there in that?"

Darcy could not tell her of Georgiana—the wound was still too fresh, too raw, besides showing his sister in a poor light. But there was evidence less fraught. "Harm enough. Upon his death, my father left Wickham a significant inheritance, which included one of the livings in Pemberley's gift, should it become available. It became my responsibility to compensate him for it—because of course, the last office the man should ever hold is a clerical one. Who knows what offences he might have committed in such a position of trust?"

She nodded her understanding. "I am certain, from all I have heard of Pemberley, that it was a significant price to pay."

"Three thousand—plus another thousand for the sum Father left him outright. It is all gone, I understand. He has gambled and wasted what, for another man, might have given security for a lifetime."

"So much," she murmured. "To be forced to bestow so

33

much upon one you hated, and all for nothing. It is inconceivable."

"Three years after collecting his inheritance, I received a letter from him. He had learnt Mr Bradley—who held the living once designed for him—was dead. I could not possibly have any other person to provide for, he was certain. He was ready and willing to be ordained, he claimed, if only I would present him the living my beloved father intended he should have."

"What? The nerve of him!"

"Oh, he has no end of that," he said bitterly. "He tells anyone who will listen of my denial. I have heard—well, it does not matter. He is, doubtless, as violent in his abuse of me to others as he was in his reproaches to myself."

"Failing to mention, of course, that he was well paid for giving it up. What an awful person! When you have done nothing to deserve such infamous treatment!"

Darcy smiled at her vehement defence of him, but his conscience demanded a confession. "As to that, he has other reasons provoking his hatred. He erroneously assumed he would have no trouble taking up where he left off at Eton, once we were at Cambridge. However, I did not repeat my mistakes of the past. I did not allow him to trade upon my reputation. I made it known that I despised him. I befriended a few of his blue-blooded Etonian comrades-in-arms, and then forced them to choose between us. There was no contest. By the time he left Cambridge, he had very few he could count as friends, none of whom held any influence."

"Ooh, well done. Remind me never to make of you my enemy," Miss Elizabeth murmured, a twinkle in her eye.

She was so pretty, so…bewitching. "I would never want you to be," he said, the least of what he felt, the most that he could say.

"As long as I do not insist you dance with me," she laughed.

Regret again speared him; had he not been such a clodpoll, he could have had an hour of her time and attention upon their first night of meeting, and several such encounters since.

They had reached the garden's eastern boundary, where the path narrowed into what was merely a trail, leading into the woods bordering the property line.

"Come with me," he said, grabbing her hand in a most proprietary manner, and setting off down the trail at an unfashionably rapid pace.

She laughed again, as if she was game for any adventure, and hurried along with him.

CHAPTER FIVE

ho is this man? Elizabeth marvelled, allowing him to lead her onto a heretofore unnoticed path into wilderness, unexplored and unknown. It was undoubtedly foolish to go, especially so eagerly. Yet, she had continuously tried to put him back into the category where once he fitted so neatly—an arrogant stick-in-the-mud. He continuously escaped.

Mr Darcy did not smile often, but when he did, every inch of her leapt into awareness. It was as if a part of him was panther-like, caged and oh-so-carefully controlled—yet patrolling its parameters, putting out its paw, testing its boundaries. Wanting to be petted.

She wanted to test his boundaries as well, although she did her best to resist. It would help if he would treat her the same as did Reginald Goulding, John Lucas, Herbert Long, or Sidney King—or in other words, as a not overly intelligent infant. Had she a fortune of ten thousand, any one of them might have asked to marry her. These young men, the best her neighbourhood had to offer, would admire her, but would never try to *know* her. They thought they already did.

Mr Darcy pulled her down the path, leading in a definite direction. It did not take long to see his destination. They entered a woodland glade, a smallish meadow surrounded by birch and hazel, with a few gracious old oaks standing sentinel. Mr Darcy removed his greatcoat and hung it upon a convenient branch, doing the same with his hat, as if the tree were a cloakroom. Even, and adding to her confusion, he removed his gloves. Then he gave her a courtly bow.

"Bingley is dancing with your sister, I believe, and has suggested that I cease standing about stupidly, and instead ask the prettiest girl in the room to dance. May I have the next set, Miss Elizabeth?"

She could not help her grin. "That is not a very close approximation of what Mr Bingley said."

"I vow 'tis what I would have heard," he said, smiling roguishly, "had my hearing been in working order that evening. But one cannot expect the hearing of a relic to always be acute."

"One cannot expect a relic to hear anything at all."

His smile faded as he looked down at her. "A relic might also be blind to what is standing before his very eyes."

She felt her cheeks heat, and to cover it, she made a show of removing her coat and hanging it on another limb; on impulse, she removed her gloves as well, and turned to face him.

"Do you waltz?" he asked.

"Jane, Charlotte, and I did once, with Hortense Goulding's dancing master," she said. "I am certain you will find nothing lacking in my execution, with such training as I possess."

Mr Darcy held out his arms, and she walked into them.

He was *nothing* like Hortense's dancing master. Humming a tune in perfect pitch, he might have been in a *ton* ballroom instead of whirling her about a forest glade. Oddly, there seemed nothing remarkable in the exercise. He led flawlessly, lending his partner an expert grace; one could rest in his arms and allow him to control the steps, never worrying that one's feet might be in danger, no matter the uneven ground.

They twirled, the glints of sunshine and meadow prettier than any ballroom she had ever imagined. He wore his poise perfectly, with a confidence fitting him like a coat from Weston. When he dipped her low, she laughed—but he did not; he just held her there, balanced, breathless, his dark gaze imprisoning, capturing her between mirth and a longing she could not explain.

Feeling her hair beginning to break free from its constraints, Elizabeth reached to rescue her hat. Before she could, Mr Darcy brought her upright in a graceful manoeuvre, and, bewilderingly, plucked the hat off her head with an expert twist of a hat pin. Her hair—never easily confined—spilled out over her shoulders with the loss of its last remaining tether. He dropped the hat to the ground, but she found herself unable to worry about its ruin.

"Your hair," he said softly, lifting one strand, stroking gently, admiring it as if a rare jewel. "I have dreamt of seeing it this way."

His dark eyes coasted over her, regarding her as if she was something precious; Elizabeth felt his words in her skin, in her spirit. Speechless, she could only look back at him in wonderment. This was not happening, it *could* not be, and yet, he was near enough that she could feel the heat of his body, hear his soft breaths.

His hand—an unusually calloused hand for a gentleman— dropped the strand of hair in favour of threading his fingers through the masses of it, his warm skin touching her scalp. He watched her, doing no more, but somehow conveying the strange feeling he saw not with his eyes only, but as if an essential part of him was fixed upon her. *Seeing me as no one else ever has*, she thought, although it was a nonsensical one, for she was hardly a hermit. Yet, it was a strangely compelling notion—to be appreciated by one such as he, who had grown to adulthood surrounded by splendour, riches, and the best of everything. That he perceived her beauty, finding her unique and worthwhile, was flattery of a nature never before felt.

For the first time in her life, Elizabeth understood the feelings Lydia seemed constantly to chase. "You do not understand, Lizzy," her young sister had complained, when she advised her away from her flirtations with various members of the regiment stationed nearby. "The notice of a man is a dozen times more exciting than any of your dusty old rules. You have grown old and dusty yourself, if you cannot see it."

She saw it now—how instinctive it was to look up at Mr Darcy and wish for his attention to linger, to want more of it. He leant in a little, and in a flash of quiet wonder, she thought he meant to kiss her.

More surprising still—considering how she had been well

on her way to hating him a day or two before—she wished he would. But as he drew her up to gather her in more closely, the screech of a magpie interrupted the quiet glade, startling them both. He glanced up at the bird, pausing, his face mere inches away from hers, and she waited, unsure, part hoping, part wondering at his boldness—and her own.

He straightened. "It appears that the gardener was incorrect in his weather forecast," he said, his voice formal now. "I believe those dark clouds grow more ominous."

Elizabeth glanced at the sky—which looked exactly the same as it had earlier—and released a tremulous breath. Mr Darcy turned away from her to restore his coat, hat, and gloves. Her own appearance, she realised, was probably unforgivably dishevelled, and she did her best to twist her unruly hair into something resembling its former style. Pretending that she was as self-possessed as he appeared, she pulled on her coat and stuffed her gloves into a pocket, knowing that her hands were far too unsteady to don them. Bending, she gathered up her hat, and was fumbling with its return to a proper position on her head, when a sudden touch at her nape froze her in place.

"Allow me," he said, and moments later she felt gentle hands skilfully placing the hat and pinning it securely. But once he was finished, he did not move, his hand upon her shoulder.

She stood self-consciously still, trying not to wonder where he gained his expertise in dressing women, confused by his abrupt formality, tempered against his almost lover-like behaviour.

A man at war with himself, she suddenly realised. None of

her attractions included suitability to one such as him. Even in her inexperience, she could feel it—the desire, the dismay. Her own disappointment was threaded through it all, and she straightened her spine in response.

Well. I shall take the battle out of his hands.

She whirled to face him. "You need not worry that I shall take your behaviour amiss," she said, shoving those feelings away. "I am certain you did not mean to break into a waltz, apropos of nothing, whilst touring the gardens. Perhaps you are feverish."

The intensity of his expression vanished in a heartbeat, and to her utter astonishment, he grinned. "Perhaps I am. Will you marry me?"

Her brows shot up. She could not have heard what she thought. "Marry you?"

"You do not suppose that I waltz in the woods with just anyone, do you?"

"You are mad, not feverish. I shall call Mr Jones back to Netherfield. Perchance he has a helpful poultice."

His smile deepened. "Possibly, I ought to have begun by explaining that I have grown to admire and love you. I would be honoured if you would agree to be my wife."

"*Im*possibly, I should have said. You cannot mean it."

His grin disappeared. "You question my honour? You believe me a liar?"

Elizabeth was taken aback. *Would* he lie? The very idea of it was preposterous. Had she just been unforgivably rude in the face of a genuine proposal of marriage? She struggled to make sense of the situation.

"I…I am confused. You have to know—you *must* know I bring nothing, or almost nothing to any match."

He retreated once again into grave formality. "And you must know that I am in a position to marry where I choose."

"But…" She found herself without the right words to explain her bewilderment. "You do not know me. Not really. It is…this is…" She hesitated, then, with some reluctance, pulled back a page of her family history to expose it to his view. "My father is a gentleman, from a very old family— there have been Bennets at Longbourn for over a century. When a new solicitor—with an exceedingly pretty daughter— moved to Meryton to take over the practice of an uncle, my father was entranced. Papa had been acquainted with my mother for only a month before they wed. It…it has not always been a happy match."

Her cheeks flushed with heat, as she recalled her mama's manners in Mr Darcy's presence upon various occasions. Mrs Bennet had never got over her bluntness, her habit of saying whatever it was she thought in the moment she thought it. Her mother had not been pleased with his insulting behaviour upon the occasion of their first meeting at the assembly, and felt absolutely no shame in letting him know of her contempt.

Mr Darcy reached out then, softly touching her cheek. "Perhaps we only met a few months ago," he said, "but I had not known you a week before I realised your beauty. You are not your mother's daughter. I have often watched you—at first, yes, wondering at my instant attraction—for it is not common for me to feel so deeply, most especially so soon. I am not in the habit of falling in and out of love, but you…you draw others to you with disarming candour, with genuine interest in their concerns. Your spirit is a generous one. There is nothing mean in your understanding or petty in your temperament. My young sister would do well to become as accomplished as you."

Elizabeth's shock was overpowering, as a conversation from a few evenings ago blazed in her memory. He had claimed not to know more than a half-dozen 'accomplished' women—and she had protested him knowing any. "Accomplished...as *me*? As I recall, you approved Miss Bingley's substantial notions of its definition, few of which I fit."

"And you did not approve." He shook his head. "I was attempting that evening, not very skilfully it seems, to compliment you," he added ruefully.

"I could not agree without *dis*approving of myself, sir. A number of abilities were asserted that I have never acquired. I am no great musician, my French is barely passable, and my drawing, mediocre."

He raised an eyebrow, and some of the intensity was returned to his gaze. "It was not those talents to which I particularly referred. It was the most important gifts—you possess that 'certain something', in your air, in your address, in your expressions. Once my attention was captured, I found I could not look away. I have never met your equal, not amongst all the diamonds of the *ton*."

She gazed helplessly at him, searching for words to explain her confusion.

"I do not know what to say, Mr Darcy. To call my amazement great is to understate it completely. I am flattered, I am bemused, and I am...I am dazzled. I do not know whether any of those emotions could be called a precursor to love. I have not believed you could think of me in such a manner, and thus, I never before considered thinking that way of you."

"Could you begin considering it now?" he asked, and there was an undeniable sincerity, even a yearning, in his question.

Elizabeth could think of but one reply. "Yes."

CHAPTER SIX

Darcy led Elizabeth back to Netherfield, caught between exultation and worry. He had not meant to ask her to marry him—all the same concerns he had had since the beginning advised against it. Yet, he was not sorry he had, nor that she had agreed to think about it. It was surprising, he could admit, that she had not immediately accepted his proposal—not a woman in a thousand would have turned him down. *It is all part of the beauty of Elizabeth,* he decided—she was unlike a thousand others. She wanted a happy, compatible marriage, just as he did. She recognised the foolish marital decisions of her father, and would never repeat his mistakes. It told him just how right he had been—she was a jewel, a diamond amongst paste stones, a miraculous creation, and far too good for the Bennets of Longbourn. He was confident that she would decide in his favour, and once she had, he would whisk her away to a new life where she could, finally, shine.

There was but one problem, however: his friend, young Charles Bingley.

It was ludicrous for Bingley to think of marriage at his age, when he fell in and out of infatuations every other month, it seemed. Yet, Darcy had seen how the man fussed over Jane Bennet as if her slight fever meant she lingered at death's door.

There was nothing wrong with Miss Bennet, *per se*. She was perfectly correct and polished, and nothing like her awful family. It did not change the fact that Bingley could do much better, and had an obligation to raise his fortunes, not drain them with an absent settlement. Such a marriage would be enough of an encumbrance upon Pemberley, much less upon a youth who had not yet purchased an estate. Darcy had no idea, of course, whether or not the young lady returned Bingley's feelings—she had been ill, and hardly able to carry on a conversation, much less a romance. *Nevertheless, I am certain that, should I announce a betrothal to Elizabeth, Bingley will take it as encouragement to pursue one with her older sister.*

He glanced down at the woman upon his arm, her head bent, her silence understandable. He had surprised her; he had surprised himself. A wave of affection washed over him, along with the ever-present desire, and he stopped walking.

"Are you well?" he asked, wanting very much to hear that she was happy, as well as surprised.

Her dark eyes met his, and he could not read her gaze. What would she do, he wondered, if he pulled her in for a kiss, as he so nearly already had?

"I am," she replied. "Jane was improved this morning. I

suppose, especially in light of our conversation, I should send a note home and ask them to collect us."

"'Tis too soon for her to be moved."

Darcy heard his protest escape before his mind acknowledged that it would be much easier to keep Bingley out of his business and away from Miss Bennet if the young ladies were safely out of Netherfield. But he loved seeing Elizabeth often, having her nearby. Besides, how would he hide frequent visits to Longbourn? The answer was, he could not—and he would be unable to visit her near so often as he might wish without announcing his interest to the world.

Elizabeth raised an eyebrow. "The weather appears to be holding. I do not think there is any danger."

"You cannot be certain," he said, and it occurred to him that there was a way to resolve his concerns about Bingley and hers about propriety. "I do promise to remain a perfect gentleman—a disinterested one, if you prefer—until you make a decision. I shall not remove any choice of yours by pressing my suit and creating expectations."

She bit her lip, and it was all he could do to keep from tugging her closer and doing his best to convince her via the passion he held.

"I suppose it would be unexceptional to remain, in that case," she said at last, and he rejoiced in his victory.

That evening was the oddest in Elizabeth's life.

To all outward appearances, nothing had changed. She

spent the rest of the day with Jane, who continued feeling improvement as the day wore on, and said nothing to her sister about Mr Darcy. A small part of it was guilt—she had not meant to spend an hour in the garden while Jane languished— but only a small part.

Until I decide how I feel about this, about him, I am unable to say anything!

She could not forget his admission that his nature was a resentful one. *Mr Bingley admires Mr Darcy beyond anything —it might destroy Jane's own chances, if he resented my rejection and communicated that resentment!*

This line of reasoning, however, brought another question to the forefront. *Would I truly refuse a proposal from Mr Darcy?*

From a purely mercenary point of view, it would be stupidity itself, and her mother would likely never recover if she learnt of it. Of course, her mother would also never know that had John Lucas, Reginald Goulding, Herbert Long, or Sidney King asked her to marry, she would have refused.

Elizabeth had vowed long ago that she would *never* repeat her parents' mistakes. She had tried imagining, to the best of her ability, giving one of those men her heart and body, and could not fathom it. There was no possibility of love between them. To remain unwed, or to suffer every day of her life with dislike, disdain, or disinterest? It was no contest.

At least a year ago, Elizabeth had begun to realise and accommodate yet another truth: the odds of her own marriage were not good. She had of course never been required to decline anyone; she had captured the interest of the young gentlemen in her circle, and she knew it—but she had been summarily disregarded. If those men, knowing her as well as they did, had been unable to overlook her lack of fortune, what were the chances of some hitherto unknown male of the future doing so?

However, those odds had now been defeated—in the form of Mr Fitzwilliam Darcy, a prosperous gentleman from Derbyshire. He had not overlooked her. He had not, in the end, judged her upon riches and relations. The very fact of this weighed heavily in his favour, and she laughed aloud at herself.

My opinion of his intelligence has risen dramatically, simply because he was shrewd enough to offer for me!

"What is so amusing, Lizzy?" Jane asked. "I am glad to see you smile—you have been so quiet today. I wish you would share the joke."

"Nothing terribly humorous, I promise. I am so pleased at your recovery thus far. I wish for you to rest as much as possible," Elizabeth replied, turning her attention back to her sister's countenance, pale in the grey light of late afternoon. "I have not wanted to disturb you."

"You never could," Jane assured. "I am feeling so much better. Perhaps you could write to Mama and ask her to send the carriage?"

Yesterday, Elizabeth would have obeyed with alacrity; now, she was no longer anxious to be away. How her sentiments had changed!

"There is no harm in resting here, is there? At least until Mr Jones feels you are well enough to journey home."

Jane bit her lip. "Miss Bingley and Mrs Hurst will believe

I am remaining here to...to...push myself forward," she whispered.

"If I were you, I would care solely for what Mr Bingley thinks, and I can assure you that he would be most alarmed at the idea of your taking any risks. I might remind you what Mama said about illness in our own home at the moment. I do not wish you to return to Longbourn, only to take ill with something else while in a delicate state."

"I despise being so weak." Jane sighed. "The idea of leaving any negative impression is awful."

"You have impressed Mr Bingley," Elizabeth said, reaching over to squeeze Jane's hand. "Does anyone else truly matter?"

Judging by Mr Bingley's obvious concern and affection for Jane, he would probably support Mr Darcy in whatever marital decision he made. Yet, the rest of the world would agree with Miss Bingley—Elizabeth was a nobody with nothing, and unworthy of him. He was nephew to an earl; how harsh would his familial objections be?

It was not just any earl either, but *Matlock*. Lord and Lady Matlock were in the papers constantly, reported for their celebrated entertainments, his lordship's politics, her ladyship's keen sense of fashion. To receive a coveted invitation to one of Lady Matlock's affairs was proof of entrée into the pinnacle stratum of society. Lord Matlock's vote on any bill was considered its potential for life, or its probable death.

At that moment, a tap on the door heralded Mrs Hurst and Miss Bingley, who had come, they said, to provide distraction for Jane and reprieve for Elizabeth. Elizabeth was suspicious at first of their motives; was this but an opportunity to hint that their unwanted guests should leave as soon as possible? But their good humour and sympathy seemed genuine, and Jane especially was pleased with their company.

Mrs Hurst and Miss Bingley were not 'noxious degenerates', she reminded herself. They were protective sisters, and did not trust their brother yet to know his own mind. They did not know Jane well enough to realise her beautiful character, to understand that Mr Bingley would be the luckiest man in the world to win her. Miss Bingley, further, was jealous only of Elizabeth; unrequited love must be no easy trial. Both Bingley sisters had known Mr Darcy for several years, and, evidently, *both* had fallen in love with him. Was that not evidence of his goodness?

So Elizabeth stayed, and watched, and contributed to the conversation when she could, and in the midst of it all, turned a single question over and over in her mind: *What will I answer Mr Darcy?*

The evening was pure torture for Darcy.

Elizabeth appeared thoughtful, looking at him once or twice for longer than was usual, but taking up her needlework and saying very little. He attempted to write to Georgiana—difficult enough when every bit of his attention wanted to fix upon Elizabeth, but nearly impossible as Miss Bingley interrupted again and again to pay some compliment or other.

He tried to be polite, but truly, could not she tell that her attentions were unwelcome? Why must he continually remind her of his disinterest?

Later, he feared his envy was on too great a display as Elizabeth took Bingley's side in a foolish dispute regarding the boy's carelessness in handwriting. He had spoken to her of it this morning; was this her way of reprimanding him, of refuting his opinions? Then, somehow, they slipped into a conversation that had nothing to do with Bingley's scores and crosses.

"To yield readily—easily—to the persuasion of a friend has no merit with you," she stated, as if changing one's mind upon a whim was a desirable habit. Or was she attempting to judge whether he would change *his* mind about *her*?

"To yield without conviction is no compliment to the understanding of either," he replied, hoping she would see in his answer his intention of remaining steadfast, as well as his aim of giving her whatever time she needed.

"You appear to me, Mr Darcy, to allow nothing for the influence of friendship and affection. A regard for the requester would often make one readily yield to a request."

Does she think me inconstant? Does she worry my family's possible objections might dissuade me? Does she hint that she might yield to my *request? Or are we still speaking of Bingley's silly impulses?*

"Will it not be advisable, before we proceed on this subject, to arrange with rather more precision the degree of importance which is to appertain to this request, as well as the degree of intimacy subsisting between the parties?"

She opened her mouth to reply, and he almost moved to the edge of his seat—would she say that the parties were *very* intimate? Would she tell him the request was of the *utmost* importance to her? Alas, Bingley, with his usual oblivion, interrupted at just the wrong moment; Miss Bingley proceeded to a defence he neither wanted nor needed, and Elizabeth subsided into silence.

The true torment, however, did not begin until the music did. As Miss Bingley played Italian songs, Elizabeth tapped her foot, keeping time with the pianoforte, slightly swaying to the tune, and he could not help but remember waltzing with her in the forest glade. He had never suspected himself capable of such a foolishly romantic gesture—and yet, it had seemed so right in the moment, and a precious memory, still. To be forced to pretend she was nothing beyond an acquaintance was a punishment indeed.

He found himself drawing near her, and when Miss Bingley began a lively Scotch air, could not prevent murmuring to her, "Do not you feel a great inclination, Miss Bennet, to seize such an opportunity of dancing a reel?"

Her foot stilled, and she glanced at him and quickly looked away. "It is easier to imagine you waltzing in the woods, than to imagine that you seriously mean to dance a vigorous reel with me, while no one else is dancing, before all your friends."

"And yet, I would do either and both. Is a reel too much a declaration of my intent?"

She looked up at him again, her discomposure obvious. "I fear it might be."

"Just so you know, I would have asked it whether or not I had asked that other question you have yet to answer. The sight of you, so lovely, so openly enjoying the music—you were made for dancing, Elizabeth. I would never have been able to resist."

She blushed, and it was all Darcy could do to uphold his

usual manner, to keep his expression severe and disinterested as was his custom. At that very moment, Miss Bingley missed a note—something he did not think he had ever heard her do —and he glanced her way. She was staring at him and Elizabeth.

Perhaps I did not maintain my severity of expression quite so well as I believed.

CHAPTER SEVEN

Darcy was annoyed. He had meandered about the shrubbery for half an hour, hoping to casually meet with Elizabeth on one of the garden paths, only to discover Miss Bingley lying in wait for him. Once she had attached herself to his arm, he could not get free.

"I hope you will give your mother-in-law a few hints, when your alliance takes place," she said snidely, beginning, once again, to bring his attention to the failings of Elizabeth's family. He almost hated Miss Bingley, in that moment, for reminding him. But then, foolishly, she moved on to criticising Elizabeth for a 'little something, bordering on conceit and impertinence' she possessed, and he immediately calmed.

What Elizabeth possesses is both spirit and sweetness—two traits you utterly lack. "Have you anything else to propose for my domestic felicity?" he asked, willing enough that she should continue speaking of Elizabeth, so that he could continue on thinking of her, barely noticing the other woman's sarcasm.

"As for your Elizabeth's picture, you must not attempt to have it taken, for what painter could do justice to those beautiful eyes?"

"It would not be easy, indeed, to catch their expression, but their colour and shape, and the eyelashes, so remarkably fine, might be copied."

At that moment, Mrs Hurst and Elizabeth herself appeared from another walk. Miss Bingley stumbled in her words, for she had been caught delivering insults. Rudely, Mrs Hurst dropped Elizabeth's arm and clutched at his, leaving her to trail behind them—for the path narrowed and would not admit four.

He could tell Elizabeth meant to escape—and it was wholly unfair of her to bolt without taking him along, too. In one smooth motion Darcy twisted, lifting Mrs Hurst's hand from his arm to place it upon her sister's.

"The two of you are most charmingly grouped, and will appear to picturesque advantage on the path before us. Do allow us to follow and admire you." With that, he stepped back to Elizabeth and took her arm. She blinked up at him in obvious surprise.

Mrs Hurst and Miss Bingley gawped, but Darcy merely raised a brow to remind them of correct behaviour. There was nothing for it except to resume their stroll. He allowed some distance to grow between them before he spoke.

"How does your sister fare this morning?"

"She is much recovered. I believe she might join us in the drawing room after dinner tonight, if she continues well."

"I am happy to hear it." It was true. He knew Elizabeth adored her sister; it was a possible wrinkle in his plans, for he must get Bingley away from her as soon as he could. Nevertheless, he would never wish Elizabeth grief of any nature. In time, once Bingley had got over his infatuation, perhaps he could bring Miss Bennet to join them at Pemberley. Mr Spencer, his good friend and neighbour, or Mr Tilney, his vicar —either of them might be a good match for her. He could add something to her settlement to make it a spectacular match for either man. *Yes, I shall do it*, he decided handsomely. It would please Elizabeth.

"Her recovery means we ought probably to return to Longbourn soon."

This was less than desirable. "Surely it would not hurt to remain a few more days."

"Jane is worried that it will appear forward of her to remain," she confided. "As if, completely healed, she is using an excuse of illness to continue her acquaintance with Mr Bingley."

Ah! I knew her feelings for him were not so strong as his for her! Aloud he said, "Naturally, Miss Bennet would not behave in such a manner."

"Of course. But she would not have anyone think she would."

"She must consider her own health above silly conjecture about appearances."

"That is what I have told her. My mother and sisters have also been unwell, and I would not want her to risk coming down with another illness while weakened from the first one."

"Neither would I want *you* to be exposed to whatever

ailment possesses Longbourn," he said, and, temporarily out of sight of the Bingley sisters and seeing an opportunity for true escape, veered from the path to one heading in a divergent direction.

Elizabeth shrugged, not appearing to notice their change in course. "I am absurdly healthy, and seldom afflicted."

"There is always a first time. You must not be careless."

She glanced his way. "Would you be an overprotective husband, do you think? I do like my solitary walks."

His good mood swelled with her question. "At Pemberley, I am certain there are many safe paths that would satisfy your need for nature and solitude. Town is another thing entirely."

"I hope you do not consider me so wild that I would ever go about unaccompanied in London. I have visited often, and believe me, I am well aware of the dangers. My uncle keeps us very well chaperoned when we visit museums and theatres. Although his home is in Grace—"

He did not want to speak—or think—of her uncle in Cheapside. "I consider you a perfect lady," he interrupted in tones of reassurance. "You will, at least during the Season, live a less quiet life once you are my wife. A certain amount of entertaining would be expected, especially in town. My aunt and uncle require some of my time—they entertain frequently."

"I believe everyone in England is aware of the Matlock entertainments," she murmured.

"Yes, I suppose so," he agreed. "I am expected to support the earl's political efforts, as well as his balls and parties, and my wife would be as well."

"*If* I agree to become your wife," she said, but her smile was sweet as she said it.

"As one might expect, I find it difficult to consider the option that you will refuse me—but simply because I prefer to imagine all the ways in which I might see to your future happiness instead."

Her expression turned grave. "I only wish to be certain that we would, indeed, be happy together."

His heart lifted at the purity of her motives. "I do not blame you for hesitating, my darling. Please forgive any expression of over-eagerness for my suit."

She squeezed his bicep where her hand rested, and he had to resist the urge to take her into his arms. To distract himself from temptation, he spoke of Georgiana. "My sister currently resides with Lord and Lady Matlock. It is not ideal. They are excessively formal, and she has recently suffered a disappointment."

"A disappointment?" Elizabeth questioned, understandably surprised. "Excuse me. I thought I heard Miss Bingley say she is but sixteen."

"She is." Darcy picked his words carefully, deciding what to say that would not show his sister in the worst possible light. "Last summer, I allowed her to set up a household in Ramsgate—she was most anxious for a seaside retreat. Georgiana looks much older than her years, and although she ought to have known better, her companion did not restrict her society to those entertainments suitable to a girl of but fifteen."

"It can be difficult to govern what, exactly, *is* suitable

during those years between childhood and full womanhood," Elizabeth murmured.

Too late, he remembered Miss Lydia Bennet, also fifteen, was allowed to freely move in society. Well, it was best she understood *his* feelings on the matter.

"My opinion is that, unless it is a family party, nearly every entertainment which places men and women together in any situation, especially those where attachments might form, is *not* appropriate for one so young."

"I agree unreservedly," she said, and he was comforted.

Unable to help himself, he took her hand in his, clasping it tightly, and hating the gloves that separated their now enjoined fingers. "A man who was much too old for her and, undoubtedly, only interested in her fortune, was allowed to press his suit." He would not disclose that it was Wickham, nor how close Georgiana had come to eloping with the churl—he could not allow his soon-to-be wife to think as poorly of her character as this would surely reveal. Neither did he mention anything else of his sister's scheming companion, Mrs Younge, in league with Wickham, for fear Elizabeth think less of his own diligence. "As soon as I caught wind of the matter, I brought her away. But it has been a great sorrow to her."

Elizabeth nodded, her expression instantly compassionate. "How awful, for her first love to be someone so odious. It would be unusual, indeed, if she was able to perceive objectionable motives in a lover at her age. In two or three years, it is to be hoped, such men would appear more obvious."

"Exactly. I wish to bring her to Pemberley, which she has always loved. Lady Matlock feels she requires a feminine influence, and yet—" He hesitated, not wanting to criticise his aunt. Still, if Elizabeth was going to marry into the family, she ought to understand.

"And yet?"

"My aunt is hardly someone in whom a young girl might like to confide. She is excessively fond of maxims and correctness, and very strict."

"Strictness might not be a bad thing, at this point," Elizabeth offered.

Darcy shook his head, not able to articulate the vast combination of decorum, control, and opinion that was Lady Matlock. "I have two aunts," he said, trying to explain. "One governs by insatiable curiosity and a desire to interfere in the lives of all who come near, almost a caricature of Lady Matlock—who simply *knows best*. She is seldom wrong, and yet, I find myself ignoring her almost as often as I ignore the other. It is difficult to always be with someone who is so inexorably *right*."

"Beating one over the head with her truths, so to speak."

"Exactly," he said, pleased with her understanding.

"I have often envied, at least a little, those who can see only black and white, good and bad. It would be so much easier to assign people a character and force them to stay within it. Sometimes it *is* simple—in a case such as your former friend Mr Wickham, for instance. He has proved, time and again, that he will always behave selfishly and callously, without regard to the feelings of others. Most, however, are a mixture and will by turns disappoint us and exceed our expectations. It would be a shame to miss decency in favour of deficits, and yet we cannot always overlook the flaws of others, can we?"

She was wise beyond her years. "Most of us must cope with the good and the bad in those we love, and spend our lives trying constantly to encourage them to the best possible outcomes," he agreed. "My aunts do not share in this struggle, although they are so different from each other."

"Hence your strong desire to remove Miss Darcy from extended family and create a new one of your own."

He stopped in the middle of the path and turned to her, taking her other hand in his. "I did not ask you to marry me, to commit your entire life to me, solely that my sister might have a better one. In four or five years, heaven willing, she will be set upon a life of her own, and we will have the rest of *our* lives together. I am only resolved to act in that manner which will, in my opinion, constitute my happiness and yours. I can be a good husband to you, and make your life a better one than it would have been without me. Had I not considered that to be the case, I never would have asked. It is true, I do not feel that I can remain at Netherfield for months in a protracted betrothal. I would much rather marry as soon as possible. But please tell me that you believe this much: my feelings for you have *nothing* to do with my sister."

He wished to kiss her, to show her his passion, his tenderness, his love and adoration. It was frustrating, watching the conflicting emotions upon her expressive mien as she bit the lip he wanted to pull into his own.

She gave him a shaky smile. "It is difficult, you see. I had assigned *you* a role, a part to play, and it turns out, an entirely wrong one. Forgive me while I work to resketch your character. I do not think it will take the time I originally believed to amend my drawing, however."

He smiled down upon her. "You will remain at Netherfield whilst you work on this new depiction?"

She appeared to hesitate. "I can stay for as long as Jane's health requires," she hedged.

It was not quite the answer he had hoped for. He dropped one of her hands in order to tuck her arm in his and resume their stroll; but then, in a surprising motion, she wrapped her arm around his and leant her head upon his shoulder. Despite his romantic prowess—he was certainly no ignorant young lad —strolling slowly together in this manner was the most intimate act he had ever experienced.

Darcy said not another word for the rest of their time alone together, terrified lest he spoil this new closeness. He somehow knew, later, when she softly sighed, that it was her conscience reminding her that she ought to return to her sister; he turned them back towards Netherfield, completely uncaring about who might spot them in such a demonstrative proximity.

Regrettably, once they were nearly in sight of the house, she straightened. Silently, he took her arm as if they were only acquaintances—mere and barely friends. As if she would remain forever Miss Elizabeth of Longbourn and he, Mr Darcy of Pemberley—the roles their very lives wanted to assign and keep them fixed within.

He hated it, and prayed for a different fate.

CHAPTER EIGHT

lizabeth's intent was to bring Jane, now much improved, into company after dinner. When the ladies removed, she headed upstairs to fetch her, while Miss Bingley and Mrs Hurst went in an opposite direction. Thus, she was a little taken aback when Miss Bingley called for her to wait before she was halfway up the flight. Elizabeth turned, pausing as the other woman climbed to reach her.

"I have wanted to speak with you," Miss Bingley said, her voice low and urgent.

"Oh?" Elizabeth replied, keeping her expression neutral. It seemed this was a tête-à-tête Miss Bingley had not wished her sister to hear.

"Yes. I have noticed you have drawn the attention, however briefly, of Mr Darcy."

However briefly? "We have had a few pleasant conversations, I suppose," she answered carefully.

"I...as-as your hostess, I wished to warn you not...not to raise your hopes. Mr Darcy is engaged to be married." Her words, which had begun in a stilted manner, proceeded forth in a rush. "To his cousin, the daughter of a great property in Kent. It is a family matter, the union of two great estates. I am certain he finds you engaging, but it has been an agreement of long standing, although little known outside of the family."

"Oh?" Elizabeth repeated, much astonished.

"Yes. I just...I just thought you should know." With that, she turned away and scampered back down the stairs.

Could it be? Elizabeth wondered, placing another stitch in the handkerchief she embroidered.

At first, she had easily dismissed Miss Bingley's 'warning' as preposterous, but as the evening wore on, some doubts emerged. Not about another betrothal; obviously, Mr Darcy could *not* be engaged to be married, and still ask for her own hand. Miss Bingley's message had been, beyond question, a scheme to thwart Elizabeth's own interest in him, and it was wisest to discount everything the woman said. Yet, Mr Darcy could not have been less sociable and more unfriendly had he been disgusted by every single person in the room—herself included.

He ignored everyone in favour of his book; he seemed wholly engrossed in it. Only Mr Bingley and Jane had anything much to say, and since it was not at all interesting to any except themselves, the party descended into tedium.

By the time Miss Bingley nervously invited Elizabeth to

take a turn about the room, Elizabeth—looking for any excuse to think of something else besides her own qualms—agreed immediately. Mr Darcy looked up from his book.

"Will you join us, Mr Darcy? I assure you it is very refreshing after sitting so long in one attitude." Miss Bingley's hopeful look revealed her motive to earn his attention, and despite her obvious machinations, Elizabeth felt some pity along with her annoyance.

Remarkably, he immediately agreed. Moments later, the three of them were strolling around the vast room. His hands were clasped behind his back—to prevent Miss Bingley taking his arm? Or herself? At the tip of her tongue was a question for him regarding his potential betrothal to some unknown cousin, solely for the diversion of needling Miss Bingley… except he spoke first.

"Have you heard from your mother yet, Miss Elizabeth? Does illness still prevail at home?"

Miss Bingley glanced sharply at him before turning back to Elizabeth. "Is your mother ill? I am sorry, I did not realise. How unfortunate. Is your family often thus afflicted?"

"On the contrary, it is rare for us. We have been unlucky of late, it seems, and Mama is still feeling poorly. She assures me that it is an insignificant cold, but it has kept her and my sisters confined to Longbourn."

"You must not take Miss Bennet home yet, then," Mr Darcy said. "You would not wish to undo her recovery by exposure."

Was he doing his best to prevent her departure by forcing Miss Bingley's insincere agreement? That woman hastened to give it, whatever her true feelings on the matter.

"No indeed, Miss Elizabeth—we would not have dear Miss Bennet's recuperation spoilt when she is so very fragile. Who knows what might happen, were she to leave our comfort and care so early in her recovery?"

Her tone implied that sending Jane back to Longbourn was tantamount to pushing her into the wilderness to forage for sustenance. It was one insult too many, in an evening filled with them.

"Thank you for your concern. We would not impose upon your hospitality for any longer than is absolutely necessary. Jane will be very happy to be returned home the minute Mr Jones advises."

The subtle rebuke—and Mr Darcy's frown—had Miss Bingley recanting any opinion at all.

"You have been worried, naturally," Mr Darcy interjected, interrupting Miss Bingley's rambling effusions. "I am certain that by staying in one place, Miss Bennet's improvement proceeds at the quickest possible pace."

Elizabeth glanced at him again, and he gave her the subtlest of smiles, so brief that it was gone almost instantly.

But seeing it, seeing how a smile transformed him, caused her an inexplicable breathlessness.

"That may be true," she said, unable to resist the urge to press him a little. "However, it is possible that the familiar surroundings of home might also ease her recovery. It is diffi-cult to know what is best."

"Fear of the unknown can be paralysing," he replied, and suddenly she knew they were not speaking of the question of Jane's stay at Netherfield, but the question he had asked *her* two days before. "Some might choose to remain fixed in a less desirable present, in prejudice against a future they cannot picture."

I can picture it, she thought. *Picturing it is not the problem.* "Is it always fear?" she asked. "Might judgment, sense, and experience advise looking to the past for answers in the present?"

"The past is not always doomed to repeat itself. The participants have a say in their own futures."

There was truth in his words, and yet it was not so easy a problem as he designed it. History had shown, time and again, that the human condition was one of perception—and that humans were inordinately bad at recognising their own shortcomings. She and Mr Darcy simply did not *know* each other well enough, at this point, to make a rational decision.

"And yet, we almost always participate using recognised patterns of behaviour. Would one visit the theatre for a performance of *Hamlet* and expect Ophelia to meet a happy ending?"

He raised his brows at her comparison. "Why would one simply wish and hope for a different part than that assigned by some phantom director, without applying for it? Nor would a person of sense and action mindlessly repeat the lines rehearsed by others who have played the character before. One's own disposition must inform the performance."

There was certainly nothing wrong with *his* performance now! Elizabeth was unaccustomed to a man such as he, able to discuss subjects beyond the weather or the next assembly; even her father was too fond of teasing to often be serious. What would it be like, to have a husband of such intelligence? Life would never be dull again! And yet, it did not change certain facts of existence—for instance, a union requiring the close connexion of two such opposites as Lord Matlock and Mrs Bennet. Elizabeth tried to picture introducing her mama to the earl—and failed utterly. "Not every particular might be within a person's power to change. The expectations of family, for instance, or the circumstances of birth. These are fixed."

His head tilted back, the corner of his mouth tipping up ever so briefly, as if he, too, found the conversation pleasantly unpredictable. "Expectations are also shaped by experience. When they are sufficiently considered, a reasoning person might make alterations to them."

It was true that his sister's experience with an inappropriate suitor had made it desirable for him to wed expeditiously; certainly, he could have offered for the cousin before this, had he intended to, as his highborn relations must realise. It was also true that he was a man not easily moulded by the ideas of others—indeed, to look at him with the Bingleys, one would say that *he* was the sculptor, and *they* were the clay.

Neither am I easily moulded, she reminded herself. Unbidden, a vision intruded, one of his calloused hands upon her skin…touching and shaping. She flushed, his eyes raking over her as she tried—without much success—to quell the rapid beating of her heart at his expression. It was almost as if they were alone in the room. He was easily the best-looking man of her acquaintance; in comparison, John Lucas was a scarecrow, and Reginald Goulding, a toad. It was incredible, almost as incredible as the sentiment he expressed, however veiled—one she would not have believed such a short time ago. *He wants me to marry him, to be with him, to stay with him, always.*

Miss Bingley saw the look as well; her pinched lips and

angry air were clear evidence that she understood the failure of her scheming "Do let us have a little music," she snapped, stalking towards the instrument. "Louisa, you will not mind my waking Mr Hurst?"

CHAPTER NINE

Darcy glanced up again from his book, mostly to reassure himself that Elizabeth—who was wholly engrossed in two letters received from home—was still here in the library with him. There had been a dangerous moment when he thought she might have departed Netherfield altogether, Miss Bingley having coyly suggested that their carriage could be made available to the sisters to remove them after the Sunday service. Miss Bennet had seemed so agreeable to the idea that he believed his cause was lost. Fortunately, Bingley's protests—which he, naturally, supported—came to the rescue. Elizabeth had remained frustratingly silent upon the matter, nevertheless allowing Bingley's wishes to prevail.

It reminded him, again, that Bingley's feelings were much stronger than Miss Bennet's, and he felt a flash of guilt for choosing his own preferences over what was best for his friend. Every moment Bingley was in company with the young lady seemed to increase his affections, if not hers. However, he needed more time to convince Elizabeth, and having her close at hand was ideal to his purpose—for time, it seemed, was not his ally.

The letter he had received yesterday from Mrs Annesley, who acted as Georgiana's companion, had delivered mixed news. At times, she explained, she worried deeply—Georgiana's appetite was off, and she was prone to indulge in weeping fits. Mrs Annesley had apparently almost written to beg his immediate return, but the last few days had been much better, with Georgiana participating willingly in Lady Matlock's planning for forthcoming Festive Season parties. Still, the companion was not completely satisfied with her charge's progress and wished to know whether she could dare hope that Darcy might be returning to town within a week or two.

It seemed more important than ever that he marry, and soon; his ideal spouse sat on the other side of the library's fireplace, a mere few feet away, a slight smile upon her lips.

"An amusing letter?" he asked.

Elizabeth's dark eyes were mirthful as she turned to him. "One I was surprised to receive, for my father is a dilatory correspondent, to say the least. However, my cousin arrived yesterday, and he missed having anyone about who could appreciate his observations on Mr Collins's character."

"Collins is the cousin?"

"Yes. There is an entail upon our estate and thus he is my father's heir, but currently he holds the living for a grand property in Kent—Rosings Park. Apparently, it acts as his calling card, so to speak. He drags out his position and the magnificence of his patroness at the slightest provocation. Listen to what he tells Papa of her: 'I have been so fortunate as to be distinguished by the patronage of the Right Honourable Lady Catherine de Bourgh…whose bounty and beneficence has preferred me to the valuable rectory,' et cetera, et cetera, 'where I shall happily spend the rest of my days demeaning myself with grateful genuflection towards her ladyship,' et cetera, 'that is, until you die and hand over your home to my humble personage'."

"That is a coincidence. Rosings is in my family—it belongs to my aunt. His 'magnificent patroness', I suppose."

Her smile faded as she studied him, as if trying to determine whether he had been offended by her teasing words.

"My aunt must very much enjoy his opinion of her 'magnificence'," he added with a reassuring smile, happy to quickly pass over the subject of her family's future loss of home and position. "Lady Catherine has an equivalent idea of her own virtues. In fact, she admires obsequiousness above all else—he sounds exactly the sort of person she would appoint. You need not worry—should you decide in my favour—that we would spend a great deal of time with her. My patience is not unlimited."

Her smile reappeared. "This must be the aunt whose curiosity invokes her interference. It is an uncommon advantage, to have near relations so droll, and so determined to give amusement, if only one remains determined to laugh. You need not worry that—should I decide in your favour—I would be easily put off by her." The smile faltered. "I hope you do not believe I take lightly the compliment of your affection. I do truly wish for your happiness, as much as my own."

If ever he had needed put into words his reasons for offering for a woman so patently unsuitable, she had just done so. "I would always do my best to increase your happiness," he promised in a low voice. "Doing so would increase mine."

They looked at each other, just looked, for some moments; he could not tell what she thought, but as for himself, he simply absorbed her beauty, his passion close to overwhelming him. A light pink touched the softness of her cheeks, and he longed to kiss them, and then…to see where else she might blush. It was the arrival of a servant to stoke the fire which brought him back to a sudden awareness of his surroundings, and drew her back to her letters. Once the servant departed, however, he discreetly continued to watch. She soon set her father's note aside and opened the second. He saw the look of surprise appear upon her face as she read it.

"Interesting news?" he asked, longing to be privy to her thoughts.

It was a long moment before she replied. "My father's note indicates that my cousin Collins is a toady chucklehead. My mother's commands that I should come home at once, to marry him."

"What?" Darcy had to restrain himself from launching out of his seat, wanting to grab the letter and toss it into the fire. "How could she consider such a thing?"

Rather than appalled, Elizabeth appeared annoyingly contemplative, as if she were only half-listening to him. "Oh, 'tis not at all surprising. After all, he *will* inherit Longbourn one day."

"Why does she not cast her appeals upon your elder sister?"

She gave him a wry look. "She has other hopes for Jane."

He did not need to ask what *those* were. It was perhaps unremarkable for Mrs Bennet to wish for a match with Bingley, but she had very little evidence upon which to base those hopes; she had not been here to witness the sheep's eyes Bingley made over the young lady. By the same token, it made perfect sense for her to desire one of her daughters to marry the foolish vicar. Still, he resented beyond reason which daughter she had appointed to the duty.

"Then the next youngest sister will have to take him," he said, trying to speak matter-of-factly.

Elizabeth continued to abstractedly study the sheet before her. "Oh, Papa would never make any of us marry him, I am certain."

This was unusual. Did not Mr Bennet worry what would become of them all, once he was gone? "Perhaps he *ought* to consider it," Darcy suggested.

She glanced up at him, finally displaying a hint of annoyance. "Would you consider such a man as I have described as husband for *your* sister?"

Of course not, he just stopped himself from saying aloud. But the fact remained: his sister was not in the same situation as hers.

"I am certain that no one would wish an unhappy match for anyone," he said, in what he hoped were reasonable tones. "However, initial impressions might be deceiving. He may not be as bad as all that, if your mother sees some good in him."

"Oh, well then, perhaps I ought to hurry home," she said brightly. "I shall soon discover which of my parents is correct."

He understood sarcasm when he heard it, but jealousy twisted inside regardless. He forced himself to stare back at the page of his book, with no idea of where in the aimless masses of words he had been reading, nor with any ability to translate the hieroglyphics on paper into actual syllables. After a moment, he turned the page, still fuming.

How dare she, even jokingly, imply she might favour another man?

She abruptly stood, striding to one of the alcove windows overlooking the park. He immediately gave up his pretence of reading, setting the book aside with a sigh.

I am preposterous, he decided. His feelings had nothing to do with her tease, and everything to do with the facts: her cousin was, by birth, by familial expectation, and by convenience, her perfect match. The entire world might call it better for her, even—stories abounded of the unhappiness of those who married outside their sphere. Her own parents were, as she had said, a personal cautionary tale. Darcy might resent it, but he ought not to resent *her* for it. All he had achieved was to remind her of their differences, and she was already well enough aware of those.

The library door stood open, a nod to propriety—although the Bingley sisters had gone upstairs to nap, as had presumably Miss Bennet, and Bingley and Hurst were visiting a neighbour. Leaving his chair, he walked over and quietly shut it.

CHAPTER TEN

Elizabeth had known, as soon as the words were out of her mouth, the utter stupidity of her question.

"Would you consider such a man as I have described as husband for your sister?"

The answer was as obvious as the facts of their existence. His sister, according to Miss Bingley, had a settlement of thirty thousand pounds. Such a man as Mr Collins was not worthy of securing a dance with her in company, much less Miss Darcy's hand in marriage. Yet, the whole world would think it was the best that Elizabeth Bennet could do.

Indeed, Mr Darcy was ready to toss Mary at him without a moment's hesitation.

Why should he not think that? He does not know Mary, her naivety, her eager desire to please, nor her abysmal abilities at doing so. Mary was gifted in saying precisely the thing that most unquestionably should remain unsaid, at precisely the worst moment one could say it. Besides, in Elizabeth's opinion, her sister was much too young to think of taking any husband—much less a a chucklehead *Neither does he know whose perceptions I most trust, between my father's and my mother's.*

Abruptly, she felt heavy hands upon her shoulders.

"I am sorry," Mr Darcy murmured. "I do not know your family well enough to understand who might be appropriate for whom. It was a thoughtless remark."

She turned to face him, a little surprised to find how near he was. Once again, the perfection of his features struck her, and amazement that a man so beautiful—never mind his great fortune—would make her an offer of marriage. Now, here he was apologising, when it was she who had made a rather tasteless joke, in the face of that as-yet-unaccepted offer. The urge to touch him was overpowering. She surrendered to temptation, touching the bristled cheek—a growth of beard already showing though he had been clean-shaven this morning. So different, the texture of a man's cheek, and she wondered how the sensation of it would feel against her own smooth one.

"My mother is terrified," she said softly. "Every day, she worries what future the morrow will bring. Any respectable man will do if it means a daughter married, to her mind."

"Your father does not share her alarm?"

"My father possesses a singular ability to avoid thinking anything about the future at all."

She had accepted her father's opinions of Mr Collins sight unseen, she suddenly realised, without considering her mother's in the slightest. Perhaps Mr Darcy was correct—there *might* be some good in her cousin, and Mary *might* like him, young as she was. It was not as though her father was solely right and her mother solely wrong in this. She looked up at him to say so.

His mouth came down upon hers—an onslaught of tenderness and need. He tasted of fire, of sparks shattering in champagne effervescence, of some kind of pull that drew her in, his mouth exerting the perfect pressure. The kiss would not stay in one place—just as he would not—constantly moving out of range of easy dismissal and cooler mind, trailing up her jaw to an exquisite point behind her ear. It ought not to be sensual, such an innocent spot of flesh—but it was, and she felt her arms wrapping about his neck in a vain effort to get closer.

"Elizabeth," he groaned her name as if he were in pain. "Elizabeth."

The kiss returned to her lips, intensifying from sparks to a real conflagration, inciting an agony of desire so powerful, it did not seem possible to exist within it.

Abruptly he reared back.

One moment she was being kissed to within an inch of her life, and the next moment she was standing alone, the library door swinging wide in the wake of his hasty departure, its draught fanning her hot cheeks.

A day after that kiss, Elizabeth was still unsure what she ought to do.

Jane would be shocked, were she to know what had happened, and insist upon returning home immediately. Home, to Longbourn, where her mother awaited Elizabeth with an expectation that she regard the potentially ridiculous Mr Collins as a suitor

Impossible, of course. I think I am in love with Mr Darcy.

At the same time, her mind continued offering up frightening conclusions. Her father's words haunted her. "Elizabeth, your mother was the prettiest young lady I had ever before seen. Quiet, demure, sweet, pleasant-natured—every young buck in the country wanted her. Nothing would do but that I marry her at once and set up my nursery before any other could beat me to the mark. I hurried into it, without a thought, and have paid for that hurry every day since." With every telling, his bitterness was obvious.

Her mother's words were not much fonder. "Mr Bennet paid court to me every day for a month and then dropped his affections like a red-hot poker once his vows were said."

Desire, pure and simple, was all they had shared. Of course, she had not understood it, not really.

She understood now, though she still struggled with all that it meant. She could not decide whether Mr Darcy's decision not to appear at dinner the night before meant he was disgusted with her response to his passion, or embarrassed by his own.

"Lizzy, you are so quiet. You have not placed a stitch on that handkerchief since you sat with it," Jane said, her voice anxious. "I do hope *you* are not taking ill."

Elizabeth tried to rearrange her expression into nonchalance. "I am well, I promise—only wishing that John Stevens had predicted more sunshine."

It was not a lie; she would love to have taken a long ramble through the garden. She almost envied Mr Bingley and

Mr Darcy, who were ignoring the threat of rain, apparently out riding across Netherfield's park. Not much else could be said, for Miss Bingley and Mrs Hurst shared the morning parlour. The pair were deep in a discussion—some might say, a row—and in the moment, not paying any attention to their guests.

Jane nodded, peering at Elizabeth with some concern, obviously not convinced.

Thankfully, Mr Bingley and Mr Darcy entered at that moment, distracting her.

After Mr Bingley had greeted them all—and ensured that Jane moved to a seat closer to the fireplace—he made an announcement. "We are to have callers soon, I believe. From the south hill, Darcy and I spotted a carriage on the lane leading to our drive, and what are the odds but that it is heading for us? I thought it best to return to the house."

"Charles, you ought not to have cut short Mr Darcy's ride over a neighbour's whim!" Miss Bingley chided.

"Nonsense! We have had a brisk trot already, and he did not mind—did you, Darcy?"

"Not at all," Mr Darcy replied politely. But Elizabeth saw him glance her way with an odd expression upon his face.

Was he happy to see her? Or the opposite?

They had not long to wait before the housekeeper announced their callers—Mrs Bennet, with Lydia.

"Mama! I did not know you were well enough to go out!"

"Oh, it was but a slight head cold." She paused, however, to withdraw a large handkerchief and loudly blow her nose. "It has delayed my ability to see my poor sick girl. Kitty is still suffering—her cough sounds like the bark of that old hound of your father's. But Mr Jones says she will be well soon, and it has not gone to her chest. I simply had to come and see how my dear Jane has fared."

Elizabeth blushed for her mother, but Miss Bingley smiled expressively at Mr Darcy.

"Jane, why are you downstairs?" Mrs Bennet demanded. "I am sure Mr Jones said you must stay abed! How careless you are with your health! You must retire immediately!"

"Mama, Mr Jones said she could come down for an hour in the morning if she stayed near the fire—which as you can see, she is," Elizabeth interrupted the diatribe.

Mrs Bennet sniffed. "Hmph. I daresay you have persuaded her to run as wild as *you* do at home, Lizzy."

"Miss Elizabeth has been most attentive in her care of Miss Bennet," Mr Darcy interjected. "Indeed, I have never seen such affectionate concern."

Miss Bingley's smile turned sour.

Pointedly offended by what she perceived as disagreement, Mrs Bennet sniffed dismissively. "Had you raised Lizzy from an infant, Mr Darcy, you would expect she give her mother as much consideration! The girl once swallowed my wedding ring rather than hand it back to me, and her clouts had to be searched for a week to retrieve it! Please remember, I have borne five children—five! What once was high, now droops. What once was flat, now bulges, and not a one of my offspring listens to me, even so." She blew her nose again noisily.

Lydia giggled, Miss Bingley looked cheerfully smug again, while Elizabeth's face flamed. Thankfully Mr Goulding with his son, Reginald, arrived to pay a morning call at that very fortuitous moment. Mrs Bennet could no longer dominate the conversation, for Mr Goulding was more garrulous than she. Elizabeth had known Reginald for years, however, and could tell that he seemed to be growing ever more impatient with his father as the minutes passed—surely, the two had come for a purpose.

"It is said you are not opposed to amusement, and indeed, Netherfield's accommodations are the grandest in the county," Mr Goulding said at last. "It has also been said, by some, that plans might be in the offing to hold an entertainment of some sort, befitting these lovely premises. At least, there are those who speak of its possibility."

"We heard you have promised to host a ball soon, sir, and it would be most unsatisfactory if it was not true," young Mr Goulding—glaringly dissatisfied with his father's vaguer hints —interrupted.

Lydia clapped. "Oh, yes, Mr Bingley! It would be the most shameful thing in the world if you did not keep your promise to hold a ball at Netherfield. It is why we were determined to call today, even though Mama *is* so snuffly!"

Before Mr Bingley could reply to these demands, however, the housekeeper again entered; all eyes turned to her.

"Excuse me, sir," she addressed the senior Mr Goulding. "Apparently your father quit the carriage where you bid him wait, and no one quite knows where he has disappeared to."

The elderly Mr Goulding was a much beloved fixture in the community, although in recent years he had grown increasingly confused and feeble. The news that he was missing visibly alarmed the older gentleman—and annoyed the younger. Mr Goulding stood at once, excusing himself, while Reginald fumed.

"I told you not to bring him. He does not know his head from his toes these days."

Mr Goulding was out of the door before anything else could be said beyond his hasty apologies, his son following at a more aggrieved rate. Miss Bingley opened her mouth, and by her expression, Elizabeth simply *knew* it would be an unkindness, a slur upon a benign, ageing gentleman.

But before she could speak, Mr Darcy quickly stood. "Bingley, you will want to accompany me. If you will please excuse us, ladies, we had better help Goulding find his father. John Stevens has predicted rain this morning, and sooner rather than later."

Mr Bingley made haste to follow him out; the last thing Elizabeth heard him say to Mr Darcy before the door shut behind him, was "Who is John Stevens?"

CHAPTER ELEVEN

Mr Bingley being no longer accessible, Mrs Bennet and Lydia made their excuses and quickly departed. Elizabeth made her own, citing the need to settle Jane back into her chamber, having no desire to hear any snide remarks from Miss Bingley. Once Jane was resting, however, disquiet meant Elizabeth could not return to her book. A few enquiries gave her the information that Mr Goulding's father had fallen asleep in the carriage during the short journey to Netherfield, leading to a decision not to disturb him. The footman and coachman had been tasked with keeping an eye on the old gentleman, but engrossed in conversation, they had failed to notice his waking and subsequent exit.

The Gouldings had only been visiting for a quarter of an hour, and one would think he could not have gone far—but to everyone's dismay, after thirty minutes of searching, he was still nowhere to be found.

Elizabeth found a spot to keep watch from the library windows overlooking the extensive gardens, where the greatest hub of activity seemed to be centred. The rain had begun in earnest now, and she could see a new haste in the searchers.

Suddenly, from the direction of the western gate, she saw the unmistakeable, tall form of Mr Darcy, his arm supporting the bent figure of the elderly Goulding—Mr Darcy's own greatcoat cast over the man's shoulders. There was a certain obvious gentleness in the way he shepherded Goulding forwards, as if he carefully coaxed him along the garden path.

This is the man whom I once believed hateful, because of a thoughtless insult uttered about a perfect stranger. This is the man who kissed me passionately, tenderly, in this very room.

Several people converged on the two men at that moment, and perhaps only Elizabeth noticed when Mr Darcy slipped away from the crowd, his quest now complete.

Taking a chance on his direction, she slipped down the stairs and to a terrace side door, well out of the way of the returning searchers and any footmen stationed at the more public entries. She had guessed correctly; she met him just as he shut the door behind him, removing his sodden hat and staring at the ruined accessory with some disgust. He looked over at her with surprise when he noticed her entrance.

Now that she faced him, Elizabeth had no idea what to say; she only knew she wanted to say *something*.

"I-I saw you returning from the library windows. Where did you find him?"

"In the maze," he said, not taking his eyes from her. "He

was very bewildered, and it took some time to persuade him to return to the house with me."

"I am so relieved you were able to convince him. Everyone has been very worried."

"My housekeeper's husband at Pemberley was thus afflicted. He had worked as our chief stableman for many years, and yet was suddenly, it seemed, no longer able to fulfil his responsibilities and began wandering about unpredictably. We set up a system, people who would watch over him whenever his wife could not, giving him small duties or shared jobs that he often could still manage. We found that the busier we kept him, the better he slept. On the rare occasions that we lost track of him, however, developing a very persuasive manner became a necessity once he was found. He rather liked his adventures, you see, and was not always easily induced to abandon them."

"Were *you* one who watched him?" She could not keep incredulity from her voice.

He shrugged, appearing embarrassed. "Reynolds taught me to ride—taught me everything I know of horses, really. He was always patient with a lonely child who tagged after him constantly, asking endless questions, and he picked me up and dusted me off from too many foolish spills to count. The least I could do was bring him with me on the occasional outing about the estate."

Mr Darcy's inherent kindness to one so many in his position would never even notice touched Elizabeth deeply; it was a side of him she could not have imagined before today.

"Thank goodness you were able to find poor Mr Goulding.

I have never been through the maze, and would have been just as lost as he," she said, casting about for things to say, feeling as if she were grasping at straws in order to detain him.

"I shall accompany you through it, if you would like, once the weather clears," he said promptly, and her cheeks warmed at the implication that she had been giving him a hint. Still, she determinedly cast away her pride.

"I would like that." Her voice emerged almost as a whisper.

"I would, too," he said, his voice lowering a pitch, his eyes steady upon hers.

They stared at each other for what seemed a full minute, as Elizabeth suddenly recalled those kisses. He had told her he wanted to *marry* her! Why had she not said 'yes', immediately? Would she be as silly as her mama if she were to bring it up again, now? It was as if there was a pull between them, drawing her in, urging her to confess every longing her heart held. Only the sound of splashing distracted her from the dark intensity of Mr Darcy's eyes. With a start, she finally realised that there was a large puddle forming on the tiles at his feet. He had not received his coat back from old Mr Goulding.

"You are so wet. I am sorry to have kept you," she blurted, feeling suddenly foolish.

"I am at your disposal, wet or dry," he said soberly, but was that a glimmer of humour in his eyes? He followed his remark with a low bow, which she answered with a curtsey.

Elizabeth grabbed her courage with both hands. "Tomorrow morning might be a good time to explore the maze," she murmured. "John Stevens swears it will be dry."

"Tomorrow morning," he repeated. "Let us say eleven o'clock. Rain or shine."

Rain or shine. She smiled up at him in dawning comprehension. He *would* ask her, again, to marry him.

This time, she knew how to answer.

CHAPTER TWELVE

Elizabeth awoke early to a heady sense of anticipation. She donned her nicest day gown and spent a good deal of time on her hair—and yet still had to wait close to an hour before Jane woke. She spent the seemingly endless minutes forcing herself to finish the novel she had started the day before—but when she closed the cover at its end, she could not have said what it was about, nor whether she had enjoyed it.

Mr Darcy was not at breakfast; he and Mr Bingley had, evidently, resumed their aborted ride of the day before. For some reason, Miss Bingley seemed exceptionally brittle, complaining to her servants about every supposed imperfection. It was impossible that she should know anything—they had been carefully circumspect at dinner and afterwards, the night before. Except…he had caught her eye a time or two, and given her a look that she had felt in her toes. Surely no one else had seen it, however.

Finally, the clock on the mantel struck eleven, interrupting the desultory conversation between Mrs Hurst and Jane. Just as Elizabeth opened her mouth to make an excuse, Miss Bingley spoke.

"I did not sleep well last night," she said. "It is the quiet of the country, I think. It is much *too* quiet, and feels as if the whole world is dead and one is alone in it." She shuddered. "I shall go upstairs, if you will all excuse me."

Mrs Hurst looked at her sister with visible concern. "Of course you must rest, Sister. I shall accompany you."

Moments later, the Bennet sisters were alone in the room. This seemed a bit of a pickle; Elizabeth could hardly abandon Jane without a reason. However, if she did not go, Mr Darcy might believe she had changed her mind. *Should I simply tell her what I hope might happen? Why do I fear that saying it aloud will make it untrue?*

"I thought I might explore the maze this morning," Elizabeth began. "I have not yet seen it."

"I know what you are trying to do," Jane replied, causing a jolt of surprise to run through Elizabeth.

"You do?"

Jane nodded, appearing anxious. "You are hoping to extend our visit at Netherfield until our cousin Collins departs Longbourn, to avoid Mama's matchmaking. I understand it, I truly do. I simply feel that we cannot possibly stay that long. Unless…" She bit her lip.

Elizabeth was curious. "Unless what?"

"If you were to take ill," she whispered, her face turning bright red.

Elizabeth had to stop herself from laughing aloud. To think

of Jane participating in a deception was comical; she must truly *wish* to stay—and, had she been accurate in guessing Elizabeth's motives, she would have conceived a viable plan. However, being confined to a guest room was *not* supportable.

Before Elizabeth could think how to explain anything else, including her intention of meeting Mr Darcy, Jane glanced out of the window, peering up at the sky. "The sun *is* finally making an appearance. But do wear your warmest pelisse, Lizzy. It is November, after all. I truly do not wish you any illness."

She was still flushed. *Does Jane believe I am wandering outside so that a valid pretence might be made for a future ailment?* "I-I will. You do not mind being left alone?" Elizabeth said, still astonished.

Jane waved this off, set aside her embroidery, and both girls departed the drawing room; only one of them, however, had a heart beating so hard, she feared it would pound out of her chest as she walked towards a fate her sister would *never* have guessed.

Darcy had taken great care with the arrangement of his day; his man had communicated to all the inhabitants of Netherfield that his master be left undisturbed—mostly so that Miss Bingley would not take up a hunt for him or make any plans on his behalf. He had set Bingley up to meet with Netherfield's steward, a sensible man who could teach him much. When he slipped out of the house and made for the maze, he was certain he had been seen by no one, and no one would be looking for him anytime soon. It was vital that he have no company for the most important assignation of his life.

He spotted Elizabeth immediately, a bright yellow bloom amongst the blossomless garden. Slowing his pace, he enjoyed the pleasure of his acknowledged admiration. It had been so difficult, trying to ignore her and his need for her, to repress his great feeling. Certainly, he had experienced infatuation before, as well as simple lust. Always, he had been able to impartially evaluate the wisdom of pursuing a connexion; always he had easily avoided anything serious. Always, his own ideas, ambitions, and plans had trumped any thought of marriage—a vague idea of filling his nursery the sole real incentive.

Now his fondest dream was of the day—hopefully soon— when he would be able to claim his bride. Her wit was unparalleled, her beauty a constant. In fifty years, should God grant them the time, he would still be fascinated. The difference between what he felt now and any slight inclination of the past was so immense, there was simply no question in his mind of its rightness. He caught up to her at the maze's entrance.

"Miss Bennet," he said, sounding somewhat breathless to his own ears, although he had not hurried.

"Mr Darcy," she said, turning to face him.

"How is it that you have grown more lovely between last evening and this morning?" he asked conversationally, taking her arm, enjoying her blush at his remark. "I have been wondering—do you wish to be led to the centre, or would you prefer to search without assistance?"

"Oh, by all means, I wish to find my own way," she said, smiling widely. "I do love a good puzzle."

He had known she would not want his help, and other than one very slight hint that shrubbery had overgrown a sundial, hiding a significant clue, he did not give it. Her mind was sharp, and she did not need it. The sweetness of her joy, when she discovered the lovely little pavilion at the maze's centre, was wonderful to behold.

He seated her at the bench located therein, but instead of sitting beside her, he knelt before her.

Her mouth made a little 'o' of surprise; she had expected this, had she not? He had been certain, in the sympathy existing between them yesterday, that she had known what he meant. Had he been mistaken? Was he about to make a great fool of himself?

"Miss Elizabeth," he began, hearing the stiffness in his tone but unable to prevent it. "I dare to hope that your original sentiments, those from the time I first asked for your consideration, have changed. I wonder if you would do me the honour of accepting my hand in marriage?"

CHAPTER THIRTEEN

I t was not at all what Darcy had planned to say—he had imagined teasing her a little about that first, unplanned proposal, and then, when they were laughing together, he would ask if she would care to make a different answer. Instead, he had offered something so stilted, it could have come from his solicitor.

"Yes," she said simply, unsmiling.

Almost, he was afraid he had not correctly heard her reply. "Did you agree? You will?" His eagerness, the utter lack of dispassion in his voice probably made him sound like a schoolboy, but disguising his emotion was beyond him.

Her sober expression changed to an impish grin. "I believe that my first answer was given to a man I understood so little, he was almost a different person. The second is for the one I have come to know since." She placed her hands upon his cheeks. "I would be honoured to be your wife."

It was such an easy distance to her lips. It was so natural to take her in his arms. The feel of her, the taste of her was explosive; that day he had kissed her in the library he had been unprepared for the volatility of taking her into himself in *any* manner. He had found himself wild, the urge to mate almost a necessity—the lone solution, to flee. Once he had, however, he had been ashamed—of both his lack of control, and to have treated her so callously. At seven-and-twenty, he ought to know what behaviour was lover-like, and what was rude or even dangerous. He had told himself that if the opportunity came again, he would show her by every action within his power that he knew the difference.

It was maddeningly difficult, however. She inspired such magnificent passion—and, judging by her response to him, he aroused the same in her. Those responses were sweetly untutored; it was obvious that he held all the experience, and it was up to him to protect her, even from himself.

"My dearest," he whispered, kissing up her satin-smooth jaw, her eyes closed, the lashes fanning her cheeks. "When can we be wed?"

She let out a breathy sigh. "In a few weeks, I would think. If you speak to Mr Palmer, the first banns could be called this Sunday—"

"Impossible," he interrupted.

She looked startled, and it was his turn to sigh. He moved to sit beside her, keeping his arm about her—he could not bear for there to be any more distance between them than necessary.

"I told you of my sister," he said, feeling her nod.

"Her letters, of late, have been…worrisome." The most

recent had been a litany of complaints over the regimented, uncaring, oppressive attitudes of her aunt and uncle towards her, her loneliness and unhappiness, along with her request for an increase in her pin money—which had always been more than ample. And yet, additional cash for shopping, her sole amusement, was the only one of her needs he could meet! Mrs Annesley, too, was hopeful of his immediate return.

"She is not adjusting to town life?" Elizabeth guessed.

"No. She and my aunt have been at loggerheads, and yet, I doubt her ladyship even realises that they are not…in agreement with each other. Georgiana is not proficient in speaking her thoughts, and my aunt is not proficient at listening."

"Do your aunt and uncle realise…her recent disappointment?"

"No. Georgiana's joint guardian—their younger son, Colonel Fitzwilliam—strongly advised against telling them. I have already told you of my aunt's nature. The earl is very political, and his standing in the circles he inhabits means everything to him. He would *not* be sympathetic."

"Surely his reputation does not mean more than his niece."

Darcy shrugged. His uncle's uncertain temper upon issues such as these did not bear testing.

"They only know she has been unhappy of late."

"I am sorry for her."

Her tone was compassionate; so few people would be. He hugged her to him, relieved when she laid her head upon his shoulder. "What I would like to do is leave for town tomorrow afternoon, that I might both procure a licence and go to the earl, to make arrangements to bring my sister home."

"Your relations will not like it." She said it as if it were an understatement. She was probably right.

Again, he shrugged. "They are not her guardians. I shall tell the colonel first—I shall write to him today, in fact. He has always been a good comrade; I cannot imagine him objecting to any idea of mine for her care."

"I meant, they will not like you marrying me."

"I do not live to please my relations. They may like it or they may not, but if they wish to maintain our connexion, they will accept it. I shall not brook any disrespect towards you, and they will understand it quickly."

"What will your sister think?"

"She will love you. Of this, I am certain." He leant down and pressed a kiss upon her lips—just a soft one, not allowing himself more than the briefest of touches. But he was pleased when a certain stiffness in her body eased, and he had to keep talking so that he would not overindulge in the pleasure of her nearness.

"I must also meet with my solicitors and make arrangements for your settlement. Settlements are not the work of a moment and take time to prepare properly; I *will* see you well provided for, no matter the future. This, I promise."

She reached up and stroked his cheek again, her touch feather-light and yet, electric; he closed his eyes to savour the bliss of it. Then, he had to kiss her again, for longer this time. "Even with all that to accomplish, I, with Georgiana, will be back to Longbourn by Tuesday, Wednesday evening at the very latest. If I am diligent, we could be married a week from Thursday. Is that acceptable?"

She did not answer immediately, a little furrow appearing

in her brow. He pulled back to look at her more carefully. Most women would object to his haste, wanting parties and new wardrobes—but she was not 'most women'. "Next Thursday is too soon?" he asked.

She shook her head a little. "Oh no, it is not that. Well, not quite that. It is…it will be such a surprise to everyone. There is no way round it, I suppose."

He tried to imagine the response of her neighbours and found it, on the whole, nothing he wanted to witness; bearing with her mother's overzealous jubilation would be difficult enough. However, it was likewise very possible that the small-minded amongst them—or, in other words, most of them—would exhibit a distasteful curiosity.

He was asking a great deal. Moreover, he meant to convince Bingley to go to London with him. There was a party at the Philipses' that he no doubt wished to attend—but the boy had been putting off meetings with his solicitors in town long enough. Darcy could guess that talk at the party would be of nothing except his own forthcoming nuptials, which he did not wish for Bingley to hear, not yet. If Bingley did not go to the Philipses', neither would his sisters—no one from Netherfield would attend. Likely, no one in town would hear of his and Elizabeth's marriage for some time, especially if, in his haste, he did not hurry to place any announcement in *The Herald*. Deceit of any sort was an abhorrence, but he did not mean to forgo the announcement altogether, just delay for a few weeks. The Bingleys would then remain completely uninvolved; within a week or two, doubtless another 'angel' would be along to lure his friend's heart in a different direction, and the news would not then matter. *He is so very young.*

"I know I am asking for so much," he said, softly brushing Elizabeth's cheek. "I promise, I shall make this up to you. This summer, we could take a lengthy wedding trip to anywhere you wish."

Elizabeth's smile was sunshine breaking through the clouds.

CHAPTER FOURTEEN

Elizabeth had thought she was prepared for marriage, but the sheer magnitude of the decision she had just made was slightly overwhelming. "I shall need to send a note to Longbourn, for them to send the carriage."

"I hate for you to leave," Mr Darcy said urgently. "Surely you can stay a little longer. One more day cannot hurt."

"I do not wish to sound rude, but I would much rather not speak of our engagement while staying as a guest of Miss Bingley. I do not think she will take the news well."

He did not try to deny it. "I have always been as careful as I can be to ensure she knows my feelings will never be engaged. She has known her cause is hopeless."

"Oh, she is well aware," Elizabeth said. "It will not help her cope with this announcement."

Mr Darcy scrubbed a hand through his hair. "I am sorry for it. Her nature is a jealous one, but she has behaved more than usually so. I had hoped that it was merely a shallow sort of envy that she does not possess your beauty and wit."

It was all Elizabeth could do not to laugh in disbelief; Caroline Bingley was an attractive, fashionable, wealthy woman. When she put forth effort, she could also be a witty, entertaining one. That she seldom chose to did not mean she lacked ability. *She has every opportunity to find real happiness, and no reason to envy me!*

Except that I possess Mr Darcy's heart.

I would not trade him for ten times her beauty and fortune.

"Such gallantry deserves reward." She leant over to place a kiss on his cheek, her own first act of affection. He turned his face at the last moment, however, and her kiss landed upon his lips. It was a long moment before she remembered her topic of discussion.

"Tomorrow morning," he said, after one last kiss. "Let me spend a few more hours in your company. I shall have Bingley's carriage take you home then. Netherfield will seem soulless once you depart, but after I speak to your father, we might spend the rest of the morning together. Then I am off to put our plans into motion."

It was difficult to consider a longer separation, much less argue for a position she did not really like. Besides, Jane very much wanted to remain. "Very well. I shall tell Jane tonight. I feel sure she will say nothing if I ask her not to. You can reveal our news to the Bingleys once we are away."

Mr Darcy kissed her again, his delight in her answer obvious. It was a temptation to stay outdoors with him until dark, but she knew their absence would be noted, and Jane would worry. "I had better return to the house," she said at last, unable to prevent a note of reluctance.

"I ought to finish the letter to my cousin, I suppose. I mean to send it express." He sounded no more eager to leave her than she felt at leaving him.

Soon, we shall be no more parted. Thank goodness it is to be a brief engagement!

"Lizzy, are you sure you are well? You were out of doors a long while today. I could have Mr Jones sent for. I did not mean—I hope, most sincerely, that you did not do it because of what I said. I ought never to have said it—or even thought of it! If you truly are ill, I shall never forgive myself."

Alone in Jane's sitting room, Elizabeth knew her restlessness had been too much to hide. Not that she wished, any longer, to keep her engagement secret—she had only been deciding which words to use.

"Please, Jane...do not fret. I am in the pink of good health. It is just that I have intelligence that will astonish you; I have certainly astonished myself. You will never guess who has asked me to become his wife."

Jane swivelled in her seat to face Elizabeth, concern upon her brow. "Mr Collins did not come *here*, did he?"

"Oh, no. I have not yet met him. I am quite safe from *his* proposals."

Suddenly Jane's whole posture drooped, her pretty face paling. "Has...has Mr Bingley asked you?"

Elizabeth might have laughed, had not Jane been so

desperately trying to be stoic. "Jane! Of course not! I am certain you have seen that Mr Bingley only has eyes for you."

Jane's cheeks pinkened. "I…I am trying not to hope. But who else could it be?"

"Who is the other eligible bachelor at Netherfield?"

"Not…oh, Lizzy. You do not mean—you *cannot* mean—Mr Darcy?"

"Is it so unbelievable?" Elizabeth asked, trying not to be annoyed. It *was* beyond belief, almost, especially after their bad beginning.

"Oh! That he should love you is completely understandable! It is—I did not know he…that he had so suddenly grown sensible!"

Dear, loyal Jane.

Her sister hurried to her, with embraces and many expressions of gladness. After a few minutes, however, Jane grew quieter.

"I do not think Miss Bingley will be pleased," she said, with massive understatement.

"No, I do not suppose so. That is why we shall say nothing tonight. Tomorrow, Mr Darcy will see us delivered home, and he will inform the Bingleys himself. It will not then be so awkward."

"I agree," Jane murmured, looking relieved.

"I also might hope that, since I shall marry his dearest friend, you will often be thrown into company with Mr Bingley. I do not suspect it will take a goodly amount of time before they become brothers, as well as friends."

She saw the moment Jane realised what it might mean for her own hopes, to be so closely connected to Mr Darcy. Elizabeth grinned. "I daresay my plan is a better one than yours was," she added slyly.

Both sisters laughed as if it was the funniest joke in the world.

But that night, as they gathered in the drawing room after the evening meal, she wondered once again whether she might have made a mistake. She watched as Jane constantly looked between herself and Mr Darcy with a confused expression on her face.

As well she might be confused, for so am I.

Mr Darcy acted, for all intents and purposes, as though she were not in the room. He was not rude, of course. He was the man who he had been upon her first arrival at Netherfield, if not quite the man from the assembly. He was *not* the man in whose embrace she had been enfolded a few hours before.

Had the letter to his cousin reminded him of all the reasons he ought not to have proposed? Of course, she did not *want* to announce their engagement yet, not until they were no longer Miss Bingley's guests, not until proprieties—such as her father's permission—had been dealt with. Still, as the evening wore on, she withdrew into herself, feeling hurt for no reason she could quite name. Surely there was no cause, engagement or not, that he should absolutely *ignore* her.

If he is embarrassed to acknowledge any slight friendship with me before his friends, why in the world would he wish to marry?

One could assume Miss Bingley might enjoy witnessing

the coldness he displayed towards Elizabeth, except that *her attempts to draw him into conversation were met with an* equivalent chill. Did he hate everyone this night? Had her agreement to marry him somehow brought about this frigid mood? Or was something else wrong, entirely? It all reminded her that she did not know him. Not truly.

Miss Bingley took the pianoforte at last, and Jane gave Elizabeth a glance, questions in her eyes. Watching her sister's bewilderment at Mr Darcy's obvious detachment was painful. Withdrawing into a corner, wishing she was home, Elizabeth contemplated what she could do to remove herself from the situation, and her humiliation, as quickly as possible. She was a step or two from an exit. *Perhaps it is time to retire; I could quietly excuse myself.*

Mr Bingley engaged Jane in conversation—*he* at least was as enamoured of Jane as ever.

Mr Bingley would never utterly ignore his affianced bride, Elizabeth thought. *He would be unable to. It is not in his nature.*

Mr and Mrs Hurst appeared to be involved in some sort of private dispute, speaking to each other exclusively—in tones too low to overhear—from a settee placed somewhat away from where Jane and Mr Bingley sat. The expressions of unhappiness upon both their faces were impossible to miss.

Mrs Hurst chose him because she could not have Mr Darcy, she remembered, shuddering at the thought of such an unfeelingly loveless connexion.

Suddenly, she felt a whisper, so low it was feather soft in her ears. "Elizabeth."

She glanced behind her; it was Mr Darcy, mostly in the

doorway's shadow, hidden from the rest of the room. Determinedly, she turned her attention away from him, back to the music. Miss Bingley was playing a fugue, a funereal piece that only disheartened her more.

The touch upon her spine was almost as soft as his voice. "I am troubled this evening," she barely heard him murmur. "I find I have no ability for playacting. I pretend I am elsewhere —preferably at our wedding—lest I take you in my arms and shout to the world of my happiness. Which shall it be?"

Miss Bingley's music crashed in crescendo, screaming of scorned love. Even though Elizabeth was certain she could see neither herself nor Mr Darcy from this angle, the woman might as well have announced her despair to the room.

"I am not sure the instrument could take any more of Miss Bingley's unrequited passion," she whispered. She did not mean to be unkind, but it was beyond awkward, being subjected to the rawness of the woman's emotions.

Let me never conduct myself thus, she thought. *Let me never be an object of pity. Mr Darcy may behave as he thinks best; I shall act as a lady, no matter the provocation.*

She tried to smile, tried to experience relief at his words. But it still felt wrong. "You must, of course, do as your conscience guides."

"I loathe disguise of any sort."

"As do I."

"There is no reason, I suppose, why the Bingleys should hear of our intentions before your father does."

"That is certainly true."

"Are you angry with me?"

Elizabeth sighed. "I had supposed there to be an option

between disregarding me entirely and declaring yourself before the crowd. Forgive me for being so thin-skinned, and being hurt that you were unable to think of one."

He grew silent; Elizabeth turned her attention back to the raging fugue. Abruptly, he moved out of the shadows, into the lighted room beside her. "Perhaps, Miss Elizabeth, we ought to join Bingley and your sister. It appears their conversation is an animated one."

She peered up at him. His expression was sober; his eyes now appeared troubled, somehow. Nevertheless, he offered her his arm; she allowed him to bring her to Jane and Mr Bingley, seating her and himself—close, but no closer than was polite.

"Darcy! I was just telling Miss Bennet about the time you prevented me buying the lame mare from Somerset! Him a marquess, pulling the wool over my eyes! Ha-ha!"

Mr Darcy smiled tightly at his friend's laughter; Elizabeth saw that he had, evidently, not been at all amused by the marquess's attempted deception. She was not surprised when he quickly changed the subject to more substantial matters— Bingley's meeting earlier today with Netherfield's steward, and his explanation of the man's long-term plans for Netherfield, answering Elizabeth's questions with meaningful responses—and without any condescension. As he spoke of the land, and the people on it, and plans for it, he grew ever more animated.

This was the *real* Mr Darcy, serious-minded but never dull. She noticed Mr Bingley paying distinct attention as she made a particular enquiry, seeming to listen carefully to its answer. Was it possible that he hesitated, at times, to ask his questions? Mr Bingley did not mind displaying his own ignorance over horseflesh, but it did not follow that he was always eager to sound uninformed—especially upon a topic of such import to his friend.

Jane seemed satisfied, at least, now that Mr Darcy was no longer ignoring them all, her expression easing towards contentment. She did not speak overmuch, but Elizabeth saw how Jane's eyes yearned towards Mr Bingley, and her pretty blushes when he paid a compliment to her. Once again, she could imagine evenings of entertainment, Jane and Mr Bingley, herself and Mr Darcy as a lively foursome.

I have been over-dramatic, she realised with an inward smile. *I was seeing problems where they did not exist. Tomorrow we shall go to Longbourn, and Mr Darcy will speak to Papa, and my next life will begin.*

And with these thoughts, she was comforted.

CHAPTER FIFTEEN

Elizabeth and Jane entered Netherfield's grand entrance hall in readiness for their departure early the next morning; in spite of the early hour, Elizabeth expected that at least Miss Bingley and Mrs Hurst would be waiting there to see them off—if not Mr Bingley and Mr Darcy, as well. Somewhat to her surprise, the hall was empty except for a footman, blocking the open doorway and gawping at whatever he saw beyond it.

Elizabeth cleared her throat, and he whirled quickly back to the ladies.

"Eh, excuse me, miss. Someone's come, and Mr Bingley and Mr Darcy went out to see."

Elizabeth peered out, and the footman's interest became understandable; in the drive was a tall, gleaming, high-perch phaeton, complete with brass rails and burgundy leather—a vehicle little seen in the country. Mr Darcy and Mr Bingley were speaking to the driver, who had yet to dismount; Mr

Darcy, she noticed, did not look pleased. She heard the words 'availing yourself of my vehicle' drift towards her before his voice lowered. The phaeton, evidently, was his—but who was its driver?

There was one way to find out. "Come, Jane," she said. "Perhaps we are returning to Longbourn in style."

The gentleman who hopped down from the vehicle was about thirty, and grinned at Mr Darcy in response to his remonstrations for borrowing a vehicle so ill-suited to country roads. He turned to the ladies expectantly, and she saw that his attention was especially drawn to Jane. This, of course, was not unusual; Jane was extraordinarily beautiful. Perhaps it was her imagination that there was something coolly analytical in his gaze.

Mr Darcy performed the introductions, making them known to his cousin, Colonel Fitzwilliam. His obvious surprise when *she* was introduced as Elizabeth Bennet almost made her smile; clearly, he had picked Jane to be Mr Darcy's soon-to-be bride. He was all politeness, but that same measuring glance was now turned upon her...and she felt his dissatisfaction in the comparison.

"Pleased to meet you," he said, bowing. He did not sound pleased.

At that moment, Mr Bingley's carriage drew round; there was some bustle as a servant emerged from the house with the trunk of Bennet belongings, and Mrs Hurst and Miss Bingley finally joined them to offer their farewells.

Mr Darcy himself handed Jane and then Elizabeth into the carriage, but otherwise showed no particular emotion. If she had had to guess, she would have called him distracted.

Unsurprising, I suppose. He must now face a discontented family member. A curl of nerves slid into her belly, but just before he closed the door, he reached in and quickly squeezed her gloved hands where they were folded upon her lap.

Then he shut the door, and the carriage was promptly on its way. Through the carriage window, she watched the party of five unsmiling persons grow smaller and smaller in the distance.

She was not reassured.

"I could understand, I suppose, had you wanted the pretty one," Fitzwilliam said, lighting his cheroot. "Although, since speaking with Bingley, I understand he feels he has some prior claim upon her. Miss Bennet, at least, would bring something to the marriage in the way of handsome children. But the other…"

Darcy went to the library window and drew up the sash against the cloying smoke of the cheroot—and against his own temper. "I find Miss Elizabeth extraordinarily beautiful," he said woodenly.

I, too, did not find her so lovely upon first glance, he reminded himself, resisting the urge to snarl at his cousin.

"Tell me truthfully, Darcy. Did you seduce her? Is this some sort of guilt offering? Because if so, I am sure a generous sum would do just as well."

Darcy whirled. "Shut your filthy mouth," he said through clenched teeth. "You are so far from the truth that I wonder at the functioning of your brain. I am no seducer of innocents."

Fitzwilliam held up his hands in a conciliatory manner, smiling. "I meant no insult. I am trying to understand. I received an express last night filled with words so unlike your own, I was alarmed. To hear that some impoverished girl you met a couple of months ago and with whom you have been in close company for a few days is now your affianced bride? Incredible! I have never heard you make so quick a decision upon anything, much less wedlock. I do not like it."

Darcy had known that his family would make this difficult —although he had believed his cousin would be supportive. It seemed he had made an error.

"You do not have to like it. For that matter, you may trot back to town in my phaeton, and return to draining the cellars of Darcy House at your leisure."

"Do not be so touchy. What is it about her? Why her?"

Fitzwilliam is trying to understand. His opinion will be carried to the earl and Lady Matlock. Darcy was disinclined to defend himself, but felt he owed an effort for Elizabeth's sake.

"She is intelligent. She is kind. I enjoy talking to her, learning her opinions—seeing her perspectives. She possesses an uncommon mixture of archness and sweetness, grace and elegance, wit and wisdom. Her manner is refined. I am a gentleman; she is a gentleman's daughter—we are of the same sphere. We—"

"You are *not* of the same sphere!" Fitzwilliam interrupted. "Darcy, your mother was sister to an earl. Hers is a daughter of a country solicitor!"

"I only gave you that information so you would understand that this is no mere infatuation. Never mind her mother; she does not matter, her family lines do not matter—she will be removed from them regardless. If you would speak to Eliza beth for a short while, you would realise her appeal. She no more belongs in this country town than my phaeton belongs on these country roads."

The colonel shook his head, obviously bemused. "I can sympathise with you, Darcy, truly I can. The last six months have been difficult, and I know you have been very alone in your troubles. You and Bingley have a great friendship, and he has set about procuring himself a country bride. It must seem very convenient, to a man like you, who has a distaste for the social scene, to take up with her sister. But what is all well and good for him, for you—"

"Once again, you speak nonsense. I have been keeping an eye on Bingley's infatuation with Miss Bennet. You *know* him —he falls in and out of love every other fortnight. Most importantly, she does not care enough for him. I shall separate them when I return to town for a licence."

The colonel stared at him with renewed surprise. "So... what you are saying is that you object to Miss Bennet for Bingley. But are you certain that Miss Elizabeth is the woman for you?"

"As certain as I am of anything in the world."

CHAPTER SIXTEEN

After meeting Colonel Fitzwilliam, Elizabeth had not truly expected Mr Darcy to race directly to Longbourn. Nevertheless, she felt something like relief when he appeared on her doorstep within two hours of her departure from Netherfield.

"But where is Mr Bingley?" Mrs Bennet cried, looking none too pleased at his arrival, and Elizabeth saw that Jane had trouble hiding her disappointment.

"Mr Bingley has some business in town to prepare for," Mr Darcy explained. Thereafter, he engaged in some stilted conversation with her mother and sisters, made more awkward by Mr Collins's wide-eyed interest in commandeering it. Finally, Mr Darcy turned directly to her. "Miss Elizabeth, there seemed to be a prettyish kind of a little wilderness on one side of your lawn. I should be glad to take a turn in it, if you will favour me with your company?"

Mrs Bennet started, peering at him suddenly with sharpening calculation. Elizabeth did her best to appear surprised by the invitation. Somewhat to her wonder, her mama did not seem overjoyed. "I suppose you must go, my dear." Mrs Bennet sighed. "Take Kitty with you."

"Mama! I was going to walk into Meryton with Lydia!" Kitty protested.

"Do not ask me to go," Mary put in. "I need to practise still."

"I would be happy to turn your pages, Miss Mary," Mr Collins said. "Such lovely music as emerges from your fingertips!"

"I cannot go if Kitty does not!" Lydia complained. "Mr Simmons is to receive a new shipment, and all the best colours will be gone if I do not acquire ribbons today!"

"Never mind, Mama," Elizabeth interrupted, blushing, before they descended into a row. "We shall stay in sight of the house. No one need accompany us. I think Mr Darcy would enjoy seeing the hermitage."

A few minutes later, Mr Darcy and Elizabeth walked alone together in the mercifully quiet garden.

"I apologise," she said, feeling embarrassed at the complete lack of enthusiasm for his company displayed by her mother and sisters. He had not been particularly friendly as far as they knew, but good manners, for once, would have been appreciated. "My sisters formed their plans earlier today, and are too fond of having their own way."

"It does not signify," he said kindly. For several moments, they simply strolled, arm in arm. She wanted to ask him if he wished to be taken to Mr Bennet to discuss their marriage, but it seemed awkward, somehow, for her to be the one to bring up the subject. However, his next words brought a flicker of concern.

"I have learnt some unfortunate news," he said stiffly.

Your cousin has demanded you to delay our marriage. Miss Bingley's words about a private betrothal to a cousin in Kent repeated themselves in her brain. Aloud, she said, "Oh?" in what she hoped was a tone of polite interest, and tried to prepare herself for disappointment.

"I spoke with John Stevens before I left for Longbourn. He insists that we shall have relentless, unremitting rain from this afternoon, for the remainder of the week, and onwards through Sunday, at least. I wanted to spend the rest of the morning with you. I am concerned about accomplishing all that I wish, and returning in time, however, if the rain turns the roads to sludge, requiring of me a day or more to get to town instead of a few hours."

"You...you wish to leave immediately for London instead?" she asked, relieved at his reasoning. But why was he so formal?

"I think it would be best."

Should I broach the topic of his Kentish cousin? "Do you wish to delay announcing anything? Should we wait until your return to make any plans?"

"No!" he said fervently, and glancing around, pulled her off the path to a spot where they were definitely *not* in sight of the house. "Darling," he said, and his mouth was upon hers. She felt the rightness of his passion, his longing—and let him feel her own. When the intensity of his affection was at least slightly allayed, she sighed.

"I could see your cousin's displeasure in your choice of bride," she said, hoping he would deny it.

He did not.

"Fitzwilliam will come round. It is only that he does not know you yet. He will stay here, at Netherfield, until my return with Georgiana. He will visit Longbourn, and you will become more comfortable with each other."

It was a relief to know that the colonel was going nowhere, she could admit to herself. Still, if all his family had truly expected Mr Darcy to marry another, they might require a lengthy period of adjustment. "Perhaps we are hurrying into wedlock too quickly. If your family needs time—"

"I need *you*," he interrupted swiftly. "I cannot fathom a wait of weeks or months to gain an acceptance I do not care about. They have no say in our lives, our decisions. I am my own man, and do not require anyone's approval—least of all my cousin's."

"Surely a few weeks' delay will make little difference," Elizabeth offered, although she, too, did not want to wait.

He smoothed the hair away from her face, strands he had disordered in his passion. "I know I am impatient," he said. "I have waited seven-and-twenty years to find you. Are my relations' opinions your sole objection to marrying quickly? If so, please do not give it a thought. I respect my uncle, but I do not curry his favour, rely upon his income, or depend upon his advice. They respect me, and *will* respect my choice."

Slowly, she nodded. It was not quite the *only* objection, but certainly the most important one. Having a betrothal period of weeks, or even a few months, while coming to know each other better was an ideal. However, she was willing to commit to the man she had come to believe so quickly as the best man of her acquaintance—and do so immediately. She did not *want* to create a maelstrom of discontent, especially in so renowned a family; she trusted Darcy, however. If he believed an immediate ceremony was for the best, she believed him.

"You know your family. I do not. I am willing to marry quickly if you are," she said, and he kissed her again, deeply, thoroughly, until she required the tree at her back for support to keep her upright.

"I shall go with Bingley to town this morning, and I shall return next week—hopefully by Tuesday, but Wednesday at the latest. May I go now to speak to your father about marrying on Thursday?"

"He will be very surprised." Elizabeth smiled, imagining it.

"I do not see why. He possesses the most beautiful daughter in the world—he ought to be accustomed to men beating down his door in hopes of receiving his approval."

"We shall knock them all out of the way, and speed you to the front of the line," she said, laughing, and he kissed her again.

Hand in hand, they made their way to Mr Bennet's book room, where that gentleman was, indeed, about to be very surprised.

CHAPTER SEVENTEEN

Darcy felt a good deal of guilt as he climbed into his carriage behind Bingley. Another carriage, Bingley's vehicle—containing both of his sisters and several trunks—was already on its way to London.

He had not lied to Elizabeth; John Stevens really *had* predicted torrential rain, and it truly *was* best to get on the road. Mr Bennet had agreed to speak to Mr Palmer about performing the ceremony on Thursday, and everything would be arranged nicely for an expeditious wedding—probably all the sooner because of his early departure.

Still, a pang of guilt reminded him, he had not been entirely honest with his soon-to-be bride.

He hated doing it; neither, however, could he justify hurting Elizabeth's feelings with his own.

In the conversations he had managed with her, he could see how much she adored her elder sister; and truly, Miss Bennet was an admirable young lady. Nonetheless, she was *not* a lady in love. With the evidence of her lack of feeling, combined with her lack of fortune and family, well, it made sense to remove Bingley from the situation as delicately as possible.

I have been kinder to myself than to Bingley, he thought, watching his friend's morose expression with an ever-increasing sense of culpability. *Yet, I am wealthier and more established in society. I can afford the step of taking an indigent bride, whilst he has not yet even gained full acceptance amongst the* ton.

The discord had begun shortly after the Bennet sisters departed, when Darcy had strongly suggested Bingley go with him to town to meet with his solicitor.

"I shall leave for town on Friday morning," Bingley had said. "I intend to go to the Philipses' party before I leave."

Usually, Bingley was easily persuaded in a different direction, but business could not compete with his objective of spending an evening near Miss Bennet.

It had become necessary to convince him that his hopes in her direction were futile. "Of course she would marry you, should you propose," Darcy had explained. "She would have no other option but to do so, in her family circumstance. You remove all her choices by pressing your suit."

"She is not unwilling, Darcy. I can see it."

"It is her mother who is the willing one, Charles." Miss Bingley had joined the critique.

"Dear Miss Bennet is a treasure, an absolute treasure—but believe me, Charles, she is no more interested in you than in Mr Goulding or Mr Harrington," Mrs Hurst had added.

Thankfully, the colonel was not present for the conversation—else he certainly would have added his own disparage-ments, and likely raised Bingley's ire in so doing. Thereafter, Darcy had not been required to say much of anything, except to agree with Bingley's sisters—who took up the cause with a vengeance. They knew their brother well and were careful not to find fault with his beloved, merely emphasising her disinterest.

In the face of so much opposition to his own opinions, the modest Bingley was soon speaking of not only going to town with Darcy, but of closing Netherfield completely. This idea did not suit Darcy at all for his own plans—at least, not yet. Fortunately, his cousin's arrival provided the excuse he needed to keep it open.

"Once I have completed my business in town, I shall return to Netherfield and spend a few days with my cousin," Darcy assured, grateful his cousin had agreed to remain. "Once the colonel is well rested, we can talk of closing the house—perhaps next month."

It was a deceit, plain and simple. He had deceived Bingley regarding his reasons for keeping the house open. In a lesser manner, he deceived his affianced bride and her family regarding the Bingleys' intentions, pretending Bingley was briefly going to town on business.

It did not sit well with his conscience.

Bingley usually chattered away, his volubility making any travel more pleasant. In fact, at the beginning of most jour-neys, Darcy often asked him a question about some appealing topic to start him off. Bingley knew volumes of information on a surprising array of subjects—from the Great Comet, to King George's latest health reports, to various incredible tales from soldiers in Napoleonic battlefields—he was as interesting as he was affable.

This journey, however, Bingley sat staring absently out of the window, his gloom obvious and unrelenting.

I shall make it right, Darcy told himself. *I shall take him to my club and ensure through a few well-placed hints that he receives invitations to various balls and social events. He will meet new young ladies within a very short period.*

Bingley simply needed time out of sight of the beauteous Miss Bennet. Once he regained his senses, he would be on to the next 'angel'; in a few weeks, he would wonder why he had been so obsessed with the young lady.

I shall tell Bingley of my wedding and send notices to the papers once he moves on. After our marriage, I shall explain to Elizabeth...

What, exactly? That his dearest friend was faithless and fickle?

It would not matter, he decided. Once at Pemberley, Netherfield's doings would seem unimportant. Elizabeth's elder sister would come—and he would see her introduced to potential husbands, men she might truly fall in love with. Tilney and Spencer were both good men. There were perhaps others, neighbours such as Lord Roden who was widowed, his children grown; he was robust and not at all ill-looking. Darcy would settle something on her, ensuring she had her pick, restoring her choices to her.

Elizabeth will be pleased to have her sister nearby for always. We will be happy.

With these thoughts, Darcy soothed his ruffled sense of honour. By the time he dropped Bingley at Hurst's Mayfair home, he was certain of his path and looked forward to seeing Georgiana, to surprising her with his joyful plans. He had meant to wash off any road dust, and perhaps visit his club. From there, he could plan out his time in town. But the lengthy journey with the morose Bingley made him long for his sister.

At last, he would have someone with whom to share his wonderful news—someone who would be pleased and excited for him. If it meant facing his illustrious relations sooner rather than later, it was a worthwhile sacrifice. Instead of having his coachman, Frost, bring him to his own house nearby, he asked to be taken directly to Matlock's London home, a couple of miles away.

It was full dark by the time he pulled up before the grand mansion belonging to the earl. But to his surprise, the earl and his lady were not in residence, having departed the day before to a house party. He asked at once for Georgiana, who, apparently, had remained behind with her companion. It seemed to take forever before he was greeted by Mrs Annesley, who regarded him with a bright red nose and an unusually puzzled look.

"Where is my sister?" he asked, suddenly, inexplicably, alarmed.

"Why, s-sir…" She stuttered, seeming to have trouble catching her breath. "I am sorry. I thought she was with you."

CHAPTER EIGHTEEN

Alarm built to panic, but Darcy fought it down. "Why," he asked with forced calmness, "would you believe my sister to be with me?"

Then he had to wait for the woman to work through a series of sneezes before replying.

"I am so sorry, sir. I-I have had a trifling cold. Miss Darcy had a letter this afternoon—from you, she said—saying you would be home today."

Darcy's blood froze in his veins. He had written no letter.

"She knew I was ill, and begged to take her maid and go— only to Darcy House, that she might greet you upon your arrival. I expected her return any time now, or else word from you or her or both."

Mrs Annesley was well aware of Georgiana's history— Darcy had felt it important that she be perfectly in possession of all the facts. He could see in her face what she was thinking.

"I swear, sir, I have watched her carefully. I have seen no sign of the man you described nor has Miss Darcy spoken to a man of his description. Really, she has not been speaking to anyone at all. She has not been in spirits, sir. Yet, I thought it would pass."

"Has she been doing a great deal of shopping?" He asked the question, already knowing the answer.

"Not really, sir. No. Last week, once, a small excursion. But…but I have been ill, and she has not expressed any desire to do so. Mostly, she writes to you and reads your letters."

Darcy knew he had written once in the last week—arranging for her to receive more pin money.

"Have I been a very frequent correspondent?"

Her eyes met his and her reply was very quiet. "Yes, sir. Now that I consider it, an unusually frequent one."

He controlled his panic, but it was not easy.

"Let us search her room, and see if we can find any of these letters," he said, and followed her up the stairs.

The earl's coachman, who had taken Georgiana and her maid to Darcy House, had nothing helpful to report. He had delivered the women to the front gate, and made his way home again with nary a suspicion that there was anything untoward afoot.

A note from Darcy's butler assured him that Miss Darcy had never entered the house.

It was Mrs Annesley who found the packet of letters,

wedged behind a bureau. Darcy opened the first, and had his worst fears confirmed.

It was George Wickham's handwriting, declaring his love, his devotion, and his continued, avid desire to be Georgiana's husband.

Colonel Fitzwilliam found Hertfordshire to be just as dull as he had expected. He was a gregarious man, fond of food, friends, and entertainment. When Mr Bennet had called upon him, apparently at the behest of his wife and daughters, inviting him to the party at the home of a Mr and Mrs Philips, he decided to go. It would give him an opportunity to see more of Miss Elizabeth Bennet, to try and understand Darcy's inexplicable decision to marry her.

The crowd was a jovial one. Everyone was friendly. Nevertheless, he could not help but see the vast difference between his mother's parties and this one.

These people were loud, sometimes raucous. And the Bennets! To be fair, his criticisms did not apply to either Miss Bennet or Miss Elizabeth—but the rest were awful. The giggling youngest sisters—he never could remember their names—helped themselves over-frequently to the punch bowl, with not a word of discipline from their parents. Their cousin, Lady Catherine's vicar, preached in their stead, to no helpful effect upon the sisters in particular, or upon the crowd in general. The mother and Mrs Philips, her sister, laughed more loudly than the daughters; Fitzwilliam overheard them exchange ribald observations more appropriate to a tavern than to a respectable party. Instead of being aghast, their neighbours found them hilarious. And what did Mr Bennet do? Ignored his wife, his daughters, and their ill behaviour in favour of debating with his neighbours upon some agricultural concern.

There was nothing enriching in their conversation, nor elegant in their manners. Fitzwilliam's father would have been astonished and appalled. His mother would be disgusted.

Miss Elizabeth was merrily chatting to a crowd of young people—many of whom were probably her own age, and most of whom were of the male sex. For the first time, another idea occurred to him—the possibility that *she* had seduced *Darcy*.

She looked the very picture of innocence, but one never knew. Darcy had denied any such conduct…but of course, he would, to protect both himself and her. Socially, she was expert, drawing people into her circle, entrancing them with wit and charm. Trapped together at Netherfield, earning Darcy's pity by playing upon his sympathies, exerting a seductress's pull upon a lonely man? His cousin was no seducer, but *could* he be seduced?

Every single man surrounding her could be, that was certain.

Be watchful of your younger cousin Darcy, Fitzwilliam's parents had told him a thousand times. *He is young, naïve, and unlikely to spot those who would take advantage of him.*

The colonel's protectiveness had begun, he supposed, with the death of his own younger brother—the Fitzwilliam son meant for the church—during his seventeenth summer, an accidental death for which he blamed himself.

Darcy, although three years his junior, somehow had recognised that beneath Fitzwilliam's stoic exterior, he suffered. He had insisted his father bring Fitzwilliam to Pemberley for the rest of the summer's school break, and… they fished. Never much of a talker, Darcy's quiet company in the peaceful surroundings were a balm to his wounded soul. Thereafter, he went to Pemberley for every term break.

What had he found? Beneath the stiff, subdued Darcy exterior was no guileless fool, that was certain. Fitzwilliam Darcy had not needed a keeper. He was, however, in need of a friend —one who cared for him, rather than looked to him for support.

I would do anything for my friend, Fitzwilliam thought, with a hated helplessness. How could he possibly extract Darcy from this fix? Even if he could make him see reason soon, the news would be out too soon to make a difference, and Darcy would be trapped forever.

At that moment, Mr Bennet quieted the crowd by tapping his crystal flute. "We are missing some of our most illustrious neighbours tonight, as Mr Bingley and Mr Darcy were required to go to town. I know not with what business Mr Bingley must engage. However, I know exactly Mr Darcy's reasons—he went to procure a licence. He has requested my daughter's hand in marriage. Our own Elizabeth will soon be Mrs Darcy."

Astounding that no one stared in astonishment! How could they all believe a wedding to be so likely? For that matter, why did no one ever appear to wonder if Bennet had named the wrong sister?

Darcy had been under tremendous pressure since Georgiana's near escape from Wickham's clutches. *I have been too busy with regimental business, leaving him to deal with her by himself. Lately, I have seldom visited Georgiana, who mostly sulks and leaves me feeling incapable of managing her situation. This travesty of a wedding is* my *fault.*

He could not bear it. While the crowd cheered and raised glasses and a few ill-mannered whistles were heard, he turned on his heel and departed so quickly, it was not even polite.

He did not care.

He was thankful for the onslaught of rain that gave him a good excuse to avoid everyone thereafter. However, it also kept him indoors, and the lack of company in the unoccupied house increased his gloom.

I hate this place, he thought. *I hate standing by, residing in empty luxury while Darcy makes the biggest mistake of his life!* His dearest friend was entrapped by a countrified seducer, and he could do nothing to prevent the wedding.

The end of the week was long and tedious; on Monday and Tuesday, he whipped the phaeton round country roads ill-designed for the thing, almost spilling it several times, half uncaring that he might break his own neck.

The day before Darcy's wedding, it rained yet again, a deluge, and he passed the time indoors preparing arguments, intending to do his best—futile though it might be—to talk Darcy into paying off the family and leaving Hertfordshire forever. He expected Darcy at any time. He waited. And waited. And waited. His cousin did not arrive.

At first it was only a suspicion, but as the day wore on, he began to hope it: *Darcy has changed his mind.* While his coach *might* have trouble with the mud, there was nothing to prevent him from riding—floods would not keep him away from something he was *determined* to do. Away from whatever seductive influence the young lady held over him, had the man finally begun to think clearly? *Hallelujah, if it is so!*

By the time the express arrived early Thursday morning, Colonel Fitzwilliam was expecting it. Inside, he was certain, would be a letter explaining Darcy's change of heart, and probably a hefty bank draft payable to the Bennets, along with a letter urging them to forget and forgive his error of judgment.

"I will do this for you, Darcy," Fitzwilliam snapped at his absent cousin, as he unsealed the envelope and unfolded the letter-paper. "I will sacrifice my pride, and extract you from this untenable match. It is unlike you to make someone else deal with troubles *you* have made, but in this case, it is probably best that I act as your representative. I shall bring Matlock's name to bear if they make a fuss. I owe you this and more."

But as he read the words penned in Darcy's handwriting, his mouth gaped, astonishment and fury and heartache each vying for position within his tangled emotions. There were, indeed, two letters; neither contained the words the colonel had expected.

Fitzwilliam—

George Wickham eloped with Georgiana. The foul deed took place on Thursday last, the day I returned to town, and I was made aware of their plot within a very few hours of her disappearance. This provided a great benefit, as they certainly could never have guessed that I would be able to give chase so quickly, and although Wickham attempted to expedite their passage, he was somewhat slowed by taking a circuitous course to avoid the most popular stops along the Great North Road. It took me some time to discover their route; however, I was mounted, and they were in a rackety rented vehicle—early in my search I obtained a propitious clue in its looks, being a rather unusual shade of green. I gained an even greater advantage near Stamford, where I discovered Georgiana's maid, abandoned at Wickham's insistence. She was a fountain of information regarding their expected route to Scotland, and I was thus able to quickly overtake the escaping pair just before they made Newark.

When I explained to Wickham the Gordian knot I have made of Georgiana's settlement since his last attempt at elopement, he agreed that she is not the bride he had imagined. He decided to depart for the Continent, forthwith. I do not believe we shall see him in England again.

I write you from Pemberley, where I have brought Georgiana for recovery.

Cousin, I require you to deliver to Elizabeth the letter enclosed, as early as you possibly can. I pray you receive these missives before Thursday. I would have sent it via express to Longbourn, but a bridegroom failing to appear upon his wedding day requires some sort of gentler handling, I think. As well, it would be best if you are able to hand it directly to Elizabeth. We can trust her discretion. Please, with the letter, deliver my most abject apologies, along with the strongest reassurance that I shall come for her as soon as is possible.

I have not slept but an hour or two in four days, so excuse any confusion in this sorry tale.

Join me at Pemberley as soon as you are able.

FD

CHAPTER NINETEEN

"The blackguard!" Colonel Fitzwilliam shouted, wishing very much that he had been with Darcy at Wickham's capture, instead of cooling his heels in this insipid countryside with its vulgar inhabitants. "I would have seen him depart to the Continent missing all his teeth!" Whatever Darcy had said or done in retribution, it was not enough. And how was it that Georgiana had been so stupid? He had explained to her that the man *only* wanted her fortune! Why had she been foolish enough to be deceived by him, twice?

Too, there were the words Darcy did *not* say. *Recovery*, he called it. Was there a possibility the girl might now be with child—*Wickham's* child? She had been alone with the scoundrel for what—three, four days? Knowing Wickham, there was no possibility he had failed to avail himself of her bed. Even if she had not offered it freely, he would still take whatever he wanted, whenever he wanted it. Fitzwilliam felt sick to his stomach.

How the devil was Darcy going to explain this to his bride? Surely, not the truth?

No, no, no, no. He would not freely hand over such delicate information to these people. Georgiana could be ruined forever, with no chance of any *'recovery'; the earl of Matlock's own niece would become one of Mrs Bennet's ribald parlour tales!*

It was a juicy titbit any paper in the country would pay dearly to hear.

The letter for Elizabeth was sealed, but Fitzwilliam did not hesitate, ripping it in his haste to open the missive.

My Dearest Elizabeth,

You cannot know how difficult it is for me to pen these words, which I pray arrive before November 28, the date we had hoped to join our lives together in holy matrimony. Unhappily, I shall be unable to reach you for a marriage ceremony so soon as that.

I told you once of my enemy, George Wickham—the schoolmate who treated young Bingley so dreadfully. I believe I also revealed that my sister, Georgiana, had experienced an inappropriate entanglement. I omitted the added insult; it was Wickham who attempted, last summer, to elope with her. I discovered the plot in time to prevent it last June. Unfortunately, he has tried it again, and was more successful upon his second attempt. When I returned to London to inform Georgiana of our impending nuptials, it was to discover that she had gone away with him. Due to my unexpected appearance in town, and thus learning of the situation so quickly, I was able to thwart his plot to marry her 'over the anvil'—but not, I am afraid, in time to prevent his ill usage of my sister. He is gone, but I do not know if a child will result from her misadventure.

We are at Pemberley now, and I will close by adding that I intend to come to you at the earliest possible date, if you will still have me. Please say that you will forgive me the delay, and even, if possible, my poor, foolish, heartbroken sister.

I know you will have to share some part of this information with your parents, but I pray you will be as kind as you can be in its expression, and as discreet as can be possible in such a situation as this.

All my love,
Fitzwilliam Darcy

"He cannot be serious!" Fitzwilliam cried aloud. "To share such sensitive information with that household of ill-mannered females! Our entire family's name might be damaged, even ruined, never mind Georgiana's! To expose her like this, via letter, is unconscionable! He cannot have been in his right mind. He has not had a sensible thought, I daresay, since he met Miss Elizabeth Bennet!"

He cursed, he paced, enraged at Wickham, ashamed of Georgiana, affronted by Darcy, appalled with the Bennets, trying to decide what to do and feeling very alone in the decision. What reason could he possibly convey to the bride? Handing over Darcy's letter to his betrothed was absolutely out of the question.

He tossed it into the fire.

"There is *no* part of this tale that I wish to explain," he spat at the flames, as they licked the paper into black ash. "If I could toss Wickham into a fiery pit as well, I would do so. This subject ought never to be mentioned again!"

Is that not the answer, then?

What would be the consequences of saying nothing at all?

At first thought, he shied away from the idea. To leave a bride at the church without explanation was a breach of manners so severe, he almost could not believe he was considering it. It was positively shameful, and Darcy would be furious. Darcy in a rage was not a pleasant notion, never mind his own conscience.

But Darcy was not in his right mind. With all his heart, Fitzwilliam believed this marriage to be a mistake.

It would be some time before Darcy knew anything of it. Time was exactly what Darcy needed. Time to reconsider, away from whatever tentacles of desire bound him to the country wench.

He might write to her, it was true.

But by then, I shall be at Pemberley, and able to talk some sense into him. I can bear with his initial anger, as long as he sees reason eventually. After a few weeks away from her influence, he will surely thank *me for having had the presence of mind he does not now possess.*

Yes, it will cause some embarrassment to the lady—but as repayment for whatever arts and allurements she cast in order that she might ensnare Darcy in the first place, it is probably a just outcome. Darcy will undoubtedly furnish Bennet with a hefty sum in exchange for the trouble, which is more than any of them deserve

By the time the colonel called for a servant to help him pack, and had Darcy's phaeton brought round, he was feeling almost virtuous. At worst, it would certainly delay the stupid marriage proceedings. At best, it might render a return to this heaven-forsaken country entirely unnecessary—for the balance of both his and Darcy's natural lives. Chances were very good that once Darcy's reason was again in working order, with his infatuation out of sight, he would barely remember the girl's name.

Colonel Fitzwilliam liked those odds.

CHAPTER TWENTY

L ate in the afternoon of her aborted wedding day, Elizabeth woke to the sounds of her family's daily activity floating up to her. They sounded…usual. Lydia's laughter, Mary's soft playing, a lively discussion between her father and her uncle Gardiner, the clatter of a tray. How could they go along as if everything were the same? As if her whole life had not shattered while the eyes of everyone in her world watched?

She had begged to be left alone this morning, and they had acquiesced. She had slept so little the night before, she had fallen asleep rather easily, despite her mortification and sorrow. But now she was left with a cold, hard lump where her heart had been, and dry eyes stinging with tears which would not fall.

Her feelings veered wildly with terror that he was hurt. *Did I* tell *him I love him? Did I say the words? Does he know I do? Is he well?* Visions of him, bleeding, broken upon a muddy road haunted her.

The odds that Darcy had been in an accident were slim; if that were the case, why would not Colonel Fitzwilliam have simply said so, instead of, essentially, naming her as some sort of harlot? Besides, she did not want to hear news of an accident either; she must hope and pray it was not so. Yet it was a double-edged sword. If he was not injured, then he had decided not to come.

Darcy *might* reappear, with apologies and excuses; she longed for it, yearned for explanation. But Goulding's recitation of Colonel Fitzwilliam's words was imprinted upon her soul.

"...Just because a group of yokels tried to force him into wedlock, he was under no obligation to support rumours and misunderstandings...a man has every right to come to his senses once he's out from under a siren's thumb."

Yokels. Forced into wedlock. Rumours and misunderstandings. Come to his senses. Despite the condition of her heart, Elizabeth had a working brain. As the hours passed with no word from Darcy, the colonel's words became an incessant refrain.

The faded afternoon light showed dull and grey through her open draperies. Rising, she moved to stare out at the farmlands beyond her window, but could see nothing but the remembrance of Darcy's deep brown eyes, hearing the sincerity in his voice as he declared his love. She had offered, over and over, to give him more time before saying a word to anyone. He was the one who had refused. It made no sense! Why would he humiliate her?

I cannot see him doing it. And yet, it is so.

There came a tap on her door; she did not want to see or talk to anyone, and thus ignored it. But after a moment, the door creaked open, and then shut. With a sigh, she turned her head to see her mother—probably the last person in England with whom she wished to speak. Bracing herself, she forced her voice into what she hoped was a reasonable tone.

"Yes, Mama?"

But Mrs Bennet said nothing, joining her at the window without comment. After a moment, Elizabeth returned to her view, and, finally, almost, forgot her mother's presence.

"I wish I knew what to say," her mama said at last, distracting Elizabeth from her numbness. "I did not like Mr Darcy much, not ever. But I was not in love with your papa when I married him. In time, I grew fond of him. He has given me a good life. I thought you could have the same."

"I suppose we were misled," Elizabeth said at last, unable to think of a suitable reply.

"Maybe. I do not see why a man like Mr Darcy could not do his own engagement-breaking, if he were going to. Mrs Nicholls at Netherfield told Mrs Hill that the colonel received an express this morning. I think there is probably more to this story than we understand."

"Should I hold out hope, then?" Elizabeth said, looking at her mama again.

Mrs Bennet shook her head. "I do not know, Lizzy. But you are a clever girl, cleverer than I am, and probably a lot cleverer than Mr Darcy. I am not like you or your father; I never have the right words. But I know one thing—all will be well. *You* will be well. It might not seem like it today, but you don't need that arrogant clunch in order to be happy. You were happy before you met him, and you will be again."

"Are you sure?" Elizabeth choked out the words around the dull ache clogging her throat.

In the next moment, and for the first time in many years, Elizabeth found herself wrapped tightly in her mother's embrace. "Oh, my sweet Lizzy. My poor, sweet girl," Mrs Bennet said, patting her back as if she were in the nursery again with a skinned knee.

And finally, finally, the tears came, and Elizabeth sobbed within the shelter of her mother's arms as if her heart would break.

At her mama's behest, Elizabeth joined the family for dinner.

"You have a right to your tears. Most women would be hysterical. But I don't see you behaving that way, Lizzy, losing your mind over a man. Besides, your cousin, Mr Collins, is yet our guest. I'm not saying as how he's any great prize, but Mary likes him. I daresay if you wanted him, you could have him instead. Mary would get over it."

"I do not think I am quite ready to move on just yet," Elizabeth said and almost—but not quite—smiled. Her mama was still her mama, after all. "Mary is welcome to him."

"She is awfully young," Mrs Bennet sighed. "But I suppose it is an opportunity not to be missed."

Her family must have made an agreement that Darcy's name, and the awful wedding, would not be mentioned. Mr and Mrs Gardiner guided the conversation with ease to light topics of interest; Mrs Bennet's table, as usual, was a fine one. It was almost surreal; it was so very *usual*—that word again— just a typical meal they might have had on almost any evening.

Mr Collins was rather silly, it was true. But he paid Elizabeth some rather lavish compliments that, he said, he had composed especially for the occasion.

For the occasion of my having been abandoned at the altar by another man? By the pained look upon her father's face, she supposed that was exactly Mr Collins's purpose.

I have two choices, she thought. *I can burst into tears, or try to find the humour in it.* And so, she made herself smile, and if it was not accompanied by any happy feeling, neither was it quite so difficult as she had thought it would be.

After dinner, Mary played, Mr Collins composed compliments, her sisters began a game of charades, and the evening passed tolerably well. Before she retired for the night, however, Mr Bennet called her into his book room, and all the heaviness and despair she had been trying to escape settled upon her shoulders. She sat in the chair she habitually sat upon, and he sat in his, and then he sighed.

"It would be better if I had a copy of the letter of permission that I sent with him to town. I ought to have made him sign something, perhaps write a letter to Mr Palmer instead of offering to make the church arrangements myself. But even so, I think we have enough for a breach of promise suit."

"No, Papa," Elizabeth said. "Please, please no. It would only be more humiliating."

He sighed again. "I thought that is what you would say. I shall, of course, respect your wishes. But if I had ten minutes alone with the man, I could dispense all the justice needed, may he rot in hell "

"Do not say that. He may have been injured. Perhaps we shall hear from him, soon. Perhaps he has an explanation."

She saw, by the look on his face, that he did not believe there was any good one. However, and obviously for her sake, he tried. "Your mother says much the same thing. She warned me not to leap to conclusions. He may yet show."

Elizabeth nodded, suddenly weary beyond belief—even though she had slept most of the day.

Mr Bennet shoved his hands through his thinning hair, looking older than she had ever seen him. "I have always said —rather foolishly, I think—that a girl likes to be crossed in love a little now and then. I claimed it gave one a sort of distinction among her companions. However, when it is one's favourite person in the world whose heart is broken, all such silly adages are shown for what they really are: trite, unfair nonsense. I never wanted it for you, Lizzy-girl."

She nodded again, biting her lip.

"Your aunt and uncle will stay until next Friday. If Mr Darcy has not returned by then, they have invited you to go to London with them, to stay for as long as you like."

It was a kindness.

"If he has not returned, or if I have heard nothing, I shall want to go."

CHAPTER TWENTY-ONE

S oon after breakfast the next morning, Elizabeth found herself rather inexplicably alone in the drawing room with Mr Collins. She gave him a polite smile but quickly resumed her sewing—hoping that he would go away. Unfortunately, he did not, but instead took his seat upon the chair across from her.

"I arrived at Longbourn with the intention of finding a bride amongst my cousins," he announced.

She glanced up, surprised. *Dear heavens, he cannot be thinking of choosing me? No, no, 'tis impossible. Mama said he is for Mary.* Determinedly, she resumed her stitching and pretended she was still alone in the room.

"I am grieved by the uncivil way you have been treated by Mr Darcy," he said. "I had been told that he was betrothed to his cousin, the daughter of my esteemed patroness, Lady Catherine de Bourgh. Thus, I was surprised indeed by his offer to you, but was of course pleased by the idea of a connexion to him."

There it was again, a reiteration of Miss Bingley's tale. Was *there another betrothal?* Why *did I not ask Darcy?* But Mr Collins rambled on.

"I promise you, I have stood as a witness to your neighbours against any implication that Mr Darcy did not truly propose. I was here when he appeared in this very room to ask for your company in the garden, and I saw him afterwards closet himself with your father. I did not hear, of course, any of his conversation or the proposal itself—but what other explanation could there be? And so I have informed anyone who infers otherwise."

Elizabeth closed her eyes, briefly, mortified at his every word. But she clenched her teeth and said nothing.

"I admit, I have formed a satisfactory acquaintance with your sister, Miss Mary. However, in the face of your public humiliation, as the successor to your family's lands, it remains my responsibility—and she agrees—to throw the mantle of my honour over you, to protect your reputation and your future. Will you accept my name and my devotion, Miss Elizabeth?"

The near hysterical urge to laugh swept through her, in opposition to her previous embarrassment. It was a surreal mockery of a proposal, in comparison to Darcy's. Still, her cousin seemed to be attempting, in an inept sort of fashion, to do what he felt was right. At last she met his gaze.

"I cannot, Mr Collins. It is out of the question. Pray, do not disappoint my sister Mary by any renewal of these sentiments towards me."

"You believe Mr Darcy might return, then? I urge you to reconsider—I find it very unlikely that, having behaved so disgracefully, he would ever show his face again at the scene of his dishonour."

His words gave her a stabbing pain in the region of her heart, but she could not deny the reason in them.

"I hope that he will come at least to explain himself," she hedged.

He looked at her with some pity. "I cannot help but believe you are making a grave mistake. I suppose you cannot be blamed for making it. His family is of the highest respectability. I can assure you, it is not at all common to hear of such behaviour from him. However, it is my considered opinion that he, remembering all he owes his cousin, Miss de Bourgh, recovered from his momentary lapse in judgment in selecting a different bride, and will instead take up his duty and obligations to her. I am disappointed in him, and so would his aunt be, were she to know of it."

The words hit hard. If Colonel Fitzwilliam believed the same, his response to Darcy's engagement to another made sense. Yet, *why would he propose to me? Why not accept my offer of a delay, if he had second thoughts after doing so?* Still, to Mr Collins, she shrugged.

"Nevertheless, I shall wait to hear," she said.

It was no credit to herself that Mr Collins looked relieved rather than disappointed, excusing himself hastily. But Jane entered the room in the wake of his departure, and Elizabeth almost cringed. She had been avoiding her eldest sister. Last night, she had pretended to be asleep against Jane's softly spoken enquiries. It was unbearable, seeing the sympathy in her eyes every time their gazes met.

Jane said nothing at all to her, however, plopping with rather unladylike heaviness into the chair recently vacated by Mr Collins, leaning back, and staring upwards seemingly at nothing—a very un-Jane-like posture. Elizabeth looked at her sister with some concern, and saw, resting upon her lap, a letter.

"Who has written?"

Jane did not glance her way, but continued her study of the ceiling. "Miss Bingley," she said dully.

Elizabeth felt a frisson of new anxiety. "What did she say?"

Jane did not reply, handing over the letter instead. Elizabeth read it through. A couple of points were made perfectly clear. The first was that the Bingleys had no intention of returning to Netherfield. The second was Miss Bingley's complete ignorance of any engagement or marriage between Elizabeth and Mr Darcy; had she any clue at all, she would not have been able to avoid its mention—even if it had been a gloat over his change of mind. *Especially* at that.

Unquestionably, he had said nothing to the Bingleys of any wedding plans. Rather, Miss Bingley's only mention of future nuptials was her implication that Mr Bingley would soon be joined in a match with Miss Darcy.

This was it, then. Somehow, for some unfathomable reason, after going to the trouble of speaking to her father and promising to go for a licence…when faced with revealing to the Bingleys his decision, Darcy had not been able to bring himself to do it. If he had baulked at telling the Bingleys, he must have quailed at the thought of revealing it to Lord Matlock. There *was* another woman. Colonel Fitzwilliam's singular, rude behaviour the night of the Philipses' party was explained, refusing—albeit without words—to confirm Darcy's engagement. Doubtless all the villagers remembered it too.

Elizabeth glanced at Jane—whose hopes had also been cruelly disappointed with these tidings. She saw, in her expression, that her sister understood what they meant.

Jane leant forwards, tossing the letter into the fireplace; then she took Elizabeth's cold fingers in hers. Together, hand in hand, they watched as it burned.

On Saturday afternoon, Lydia and Kitty returned from a foray into Meryton splattered in mud. "What in heaven's name happened to you?" Mrs Bennet cried. "Your dresses are ruined!"

Kitty looked uncertainly at her sister, but Lydia snapped, "Who cares? I hate this old thing."

Mr Bennet paused on his way to his book room, peering at his grimy daughters from over the top of his spectacles. "If that is the way you will treat your garments, I shall be in no hurry to authorise another purchase," he said sternly.

"'Tis not my fault!" Lydia cried. "That uppish Pamela Harrington was laughing about Lizzy, and so I told her that if I had a laugh that sounded like a braying donkey, I would not risk allowing anyone to overhear it, and then…she tripped."

Lydia smiled beatifically. "She fell, splat, into the mud, right onto her arrogant face."

Elizabeth raised a brow at this account, which did not at all explain why both Kitty and Lydia were half-covered in filth. Kitty bit her lip, but Lydia stood, defiant, chin raised, as if daring anyone to challenge her version of events.

Elizabeth abruptly realised that Lydia had done much more than simply insult the Harrington girl—and Kitty had joined in. *This is my fault. If they are punished, it will be because of me.*

But to her surprise, her father considered his muck-spattered daughters for a long moment, and then nodded. "Carry on," he said mildly, and continued towards his study.

"You are dripping on my floors," said Mrs Bennet. "Do get out of those clothes, girls, and if you track mud all the way up the stairs, it will be you mopping them and not Bess."

And that was all, it seemed, that was to be said. Elizabeth swallowed a rather large lump in her throat, and quickly excused herself before she burst into another bout of hated tears.

CHAPTER TWENTY-TWO

Every day of the week following, Elizabeth waited for a letter from Darcy—convinced in her heart of hearts that it *must* come, despite all evidence to the contrary. She had studied the situation from every angle. Perhaps he felt he could not tell the Bingleys before explaining his marriage to the earl? His very powerful, wealthy family had, manifestly, offered significant objection. Perhaps there really was some sort of dreaded injury. Her dreams, when she managed to find any rest, were filled with terror for wondering.

If he had surrendered to his family's pressure, it did not follow that he would abandon her utterly to face humiliation before her neighbours without a word of explanation.

There was something missing. She knew it must be so.

On Thursday morning, precisely one week after her aborted wedding, Mr Bennet brought Elizabeth into his study. A newspaper lay upon an unusually uncluttered desk. He turned it to face her, so that she could see the article he pointed to

It was one of the many society columns that London thrived upon. At first she did not see what he meant, lost between the reports of Lord Hargreaves dancing the opening set with Miss Sedgewick at Mrs Johnston's ball, descriptions of Lady Templeton's purple silk pelisse, and semi-disguised hints about which ladies had been seen enjoying Sir M's box at the theatre.

The elegant young Miss Darcy, lately a guest of her uncle, the illustrious Earl of Matlock, has been taken by her brother, Mr Fitzwilliam Darcy, to enjoy the Festive Season at their home estate, Pemberley, in Derbyshire, where, it is reported, they are slated to participate in its annual St Nicholas Day traditions, including estate celebrations, and distribution of gifts for those children fortunate enough to live within reach of their beneficence. It is rumoured they will soon be joined there by eminent relations, Lady Catherine de Bourgh and her daughter, of Rosings Park estate in Kent.

Mr Bennet would not meet her gaze, probably so that she would not see his pity.

She remembered Miss Bingley's fugue.

"Well then," she said, forcing a matter-of-fact tone while her heart broke in silence. "That is that, I suppose."

The next morning, Elizabeth stood over her packed trunks, ready to depart for London.

Though wholly expecting that any letter she might have received from Mr Darcy would be a letter of rejection and apology, she would have given anything to read it. It was obvious now that the coveted letter—of explanation, regret, *something*—would not be arriving.

"I think he did write," she said to Jane. "That express his cousin received would be explained. I think, for some reason, he wanted Colonel Fitzwilliam to justify it to me in person, rather than tell me by letter that he had changed his mind. The colonel did not like me, I am sure of that—but I suppose that any excuse, stated aloud, sounded feeble."

"Colonel Fitzwilliam must have been too embarrassed to relay the message. I think you are correct, Lizzy. It is the only thing that makes a particle of sense."

"I do not like the colonel, either, but Mr Darcy ought to have told me directly. The blame must be his. Still, I cannot forgive Colonel Fitzwilliam for leaving me to be humiliated on what was supposed to be my wedding day. He could, simply, have forwarded Mr Darcy's letter."

"I suppose he did not think it out." It was weak, and they both knew it.

"I do not think I can bear to return to Longbourn, Jane," Elizabeth said quietly. "Not for a long while, at any rate."

Jane nodded sadly. "Papa knew you would feel that way. He says I must return home for Mary's wedding. I can stay with you in town for a mere couple of weeks."

"I am grateful he and Mama are letting you go at all."

"Mama required of me the promise to call upon Miss Bingley. It is the reason she allows my departure. I shall leave my card, but I expect nothing."

Elizabeth embraced Jane, who, although dealing with her own grief, thought only of her sister's.

They made their way downstairs; servants were bustling,

the Gardiner children had all escaped the nursery and were making a happy noise amongst the trunks being brought down and general mayhem. Lydia was whirling the youngest of them, while Kitty read a story to the eldest. Elizabeth gave them both a kiss.

"How lucky you are to be leaving this dreary little town," Lydia said. "I have always wanted to go. Please talk Uncle into allowing me to come, too."

"I am older. I should be allowed to leave before you do," Kitty countered.

Thankfully, the Gardiner children demanded attention before the squabble could degenerate into argument.

"Lizzy," Mary called, beckoning somewhat furtively from the doorway. "I have something to show you."

Elizabeth followed a swiftly moving Mary into their father's book room. "We must hurry, before Papa returns," she said.

Mary went directly to the large family Bible, perched, in pride of place, upon its own wooden rostrum. Carefully she thumbed through the pages until she found the one she wanted.

"Look and see," she said, pointing to a particular verse in John, chapter 12—reading 'And Jesus, when he had found a young ass, sat thereon; as is written'…except, a thin line had been inked through the word 'ass' and the initials FD carefully penned in a delicate script in its stead.

"Oh, Mary," Elizabeth said, torn between laughter and tears.

"It is the worst thing I could think to do to him," she said defiantly. "Almost like a curse. No one will ever read it, I suppose, now that I shall be leaving Longbourn soon. But *we* will know it is there."

"Thank you," Elizabeth said, embracing her sister. "You had best not deface any more Bibles, however. Also, I would not tell your soon-to-be husband of this one infraction."

"Oh, but I have already," Mary said solemnly, returning the embrace. "He understood. He said that if I felt I must, I could mark his—but that I had to choose one of the Deuteronomy verses. He never preaches from that. And of course, that I must never mention it to Lady Catherine de Bourgh, but I would not have regardless. This is our secret."

Elizabeth smiled. "I thank you both, then. I am sorry to be missing your wedding."

"It is just as well," Mary said matter-of-factly. "If you were there, everyone in the neighbourhood would be watching you the entire day, to see how you were bearing up at the wedding of your younger sister—as if you would break down in tears at the sight of my wedding clothes or something. In any event, Uncle Gardiner cannot leave his warehouses again so soon. But Lizzy, you must come to visit us. The ass does not visit, my dear Collins says, but once or twice per year, and probably not until Easter."

Mary said this as straightforwardly, as gravely, as if it were usual to refer to a person in that manner, and Elizabeth finally felt true mirth for the first time since her not-wedding day. "I shall come then," she agreed, with equivalent solemnity. "When the ass is not visiting."

Elizabeth had been gone from Mr Bennet's home for four days before a letter arrived, addressed to her in a firm script that could only belong to one man. It was a fairly lengthy letter, judging by its thickness.

The resentment Mr Bennet felt at this intrusion was beyond any description. This was a man who had destroyed, possibly forever, the reputation of his favourite daughter. Here was proof, had he wanted it, of breach of promise—but such a suit would further humiliate Elizabeth. Not for any amount would he increase her pain.

Almost, he tossed it into the flames.

His ethics would not quite permit it. The letter was not *precisely* his—although, since one could make a good case that the betrothal had been broken, it was not precisely Elizabeth's, either.

Neither, however, did he deem it wise to send it on to his dear daughter. There were two possibilities for its contents— excuse, or apology. Had he meant to *actually* marry her, or even to face her or her family like a gentleman, he would have come in person. There was no excuse, no apology adequate for the shame Mr Darcy had heaped upon her, regardless. Whatever his justifications, this letter could only be, ultimately, more hurtful.

The best response must be to return it, unopened, unread. It would be a clear signal to the arrogant Fitzwilliam Darcy— *we do not accept your apologies, nor your excuses. Tell them to the devil.*

Mr Bennet would *not* hurry right out, however, to return the letter. Let the man wonder, for a week or two, how well his snivelling, cowardly words had been received.

CHAPTER TWENTY-THREE

For the first time in his life, Colonel Fitzwilliam was happy to have departed Pemberley. Even though he believed fervently, still, that he had acted in Darcy's best interests, it had not been easily done.

Darcy was ravaged, full of guilt and grief. He had lost weight, perhaps half a stone; he did not speak, not really, ate little, and slept, apparently, not at all.

All he wanted to hear from me was titbits of Elizabeth Bennet. 'How did she respond?' and 'Does she forgive me?' and 'Does she forgive Georgiana?'

Fitzwilliam had choked on the truths he had meant to speak, truths that Darcy was not yet ready to hear. The poor fellow was eaten alive by regrets over Georgiana's situation as it was, and he clung to a fictional image he held of an Elizabeth who could not possibly exist.

His own self-reproach chased him through Pemberley's gates, whenever he thought of the chit waiting at the church for a bridegroom who would not show. In the moment, it had seemed protective, what the earl would have expected of him —utter renunciation. Undeniably, however, it had not been well done of him, and although he despised the Bennet girl for entrapping his friend and believed her family to be the worst sort of country mongrels, never had he wished so deeply that he had his own fortune, and could pay them off to restore his battered pride.

All he had been able to say to Darcy was an emphasis on the ill behaviour he had witnessed at the Philipses' party, imputing it to revelations he had failed to make to the Bennets. The half-truths he had managed would not hold up to more vigorous examination, should Darcy get hold of himself. As for Georgiana, her weakness for the disgusting Wickham was still evident, and it made him sick that he could not see any shred of possibility for her future happiness. Never had he felt such relief as when the letter arrived from town, demanding his presence.

We all require time, he reminded himself. *In time, Darcy will be grateful that he does not have to cope with an inferior, impossible bride on top of everything else. I have to believe that.*

Darcy peered out of his study window to see his sister sitting alone upon a stone bench near Pemberley's almost denuded garden. A glance at the sky showed him the heavy, dark clouds of early December, and he wondered how long before rain or sleet or snow might inundate them, rendering the roads to

London at times impassable, and more importantly, slowing the mails.

If only I had a John Stevens to predict the weather, he thought, with a stab of pain. There had been time, barely, to receive a reply to his letter, but nothing had yet arrived; he knew that every day it did not, his tension would increase.

Fitzwilliam had been required to return to town, but pressing him again before he left for Elizabeth's response to his news of postponing their wedding had not provided any comfort.

"How do you suppose she took it? The whole family is an embarrassment. You have had a lucky escape, Darcy. Forget Elizabeth Bennet, and come to your senses, man!"

As if he would or could! She was his affianced bride, and had every claim upon him. He had carefully taken time to compose words of apology, of grief, of abject vulnerability—the colonel would have been appalled to read the half of it. There was a possibility, he knew, that her father might read it first—but he had put some words addressed to Mr Bennet in the beginning, hoping that as a gentleman he would maintain Darcy and Georgiana's privacy, and permit the wedding to take place as soon as was possible. Every part of him had wanted to leave Georgiana here with Mrs Annesley, return the colonel to town—and from thence, travel alone to Longbourn.

But the girl sitting outside, alone, on a cold winter's day, still needed him. Her first response to her rescue, unhappily, had been fury. Now, he feared, she had turned the hatred and shame inward—yet another victory for George Wickham.

Darcy took another woollen shawl out to his sister, draping it over her shoulders, fearing the cold and damp was too much— even though she was warmly dressed. Silently, he seated himself beside her. Despite his greatcoat, he felt the chill, but he did not insist upon her return indoors.

"There will be no child," she said at last.

He turned his head sharply, but she stared out into the distance, not meeting his gaze. He was consumed with over-whelming relief; so should she be, but of course, he had no idea if that was the case. He wanted to ask her, but also feared her answers. She had actually cursed him for removing her from the despicable villain—this, after Wickham disavowed her in the cruellest fashion, blaming her for everything wrong in his life. Georgiana, in turn, had blamed Darcy for 'ruining' hers.

"You can say it—I am sure you are happy."

He sighed. "I find that I can only be as happy as you are. You do not seem in spirits, to me."

"I do not know what I am. I am happy that the colonel is gone, so I do not have to hear him tell me that now we can pretend nothing ever happened. He said the earl would have taken the child away, regardless—that I would never be allowed to keep it, and that I would be lucky if his lordship did not send me away to a Scottish nunnery."

Darcy raised his brows; he had not been aware of these threats. "The colonel's battlefield tactics do not translate well into family life, I think. I promise it would *not* have been the earl's decision."

"What would your decision have been?" She asked him as if she were merely curious, but something told him that she cared a great deal. Well, he had nothing left in him and certainly no firm answers, nothing except the truth—and she could listen or not.

"I have absolutely no idea. I have been too angry at you to think clearly of the future. You wrecked my wedding day over a man who has betrayed me and used me ill dozens of times."

Her eyes widened, her mouth gaping. "Wedding?"

"It is why I came to London—to fetch you. I found the woman I love, in Hertfordshire, and wanted you to meet her. She agreed to marry me quickly—more quickly, I think, than she thought ideal—so that we could take you home to Pemberley, since you were so unhappy."

"I-I did not know. It seemed as if I would for years be trapped with her ladyship, and her ideas of which tedious pursuits would be most acceptable and which tedious people would be best to cultivate, and I did not think I could bear it for another minute."

He forbore pointing out that there were other ways to change one's living situation besides eloping. He had managed to bite down his fury at the words of deceit she had used to obtain more money from him, to finance said elopement. He even managed to restrain his tongue, when he dearly wanted to ask, 'Why him? Why, of all people in England, George Wickham?'. If he did, he knew she would only turn inwards, cry, and say nothing at all sensible.

Although the colonel's words had probably been meant to frighten Georgiana into better behaviour, he may have been correct. The earl *might* have recommended she be sent away, had there been a child. Neither Darcy nor his cousin had been inclined to inform his lordship of anything except that they had removed her to Pemberley—as was their right as her guardians—but at least a few of the Matlock servants had a tale to tell, if they wished. If the earl heard of this botched elopement, Darcy had no idea how he would respond.

In the absence of these home truths, however, he could not think of much to add. *Wickham has fooled far more sophisticated women than Georgiana Darcy,* he reminded himself. *If she is not so trustworthy as I thought, neither is she the fallen woman society would name her. She is simply...young. Young and foolish.*

The one suggestion Fitzwilliam had furnished was paying someone to marry her, and doing so quickly. Now that there was no child, Darcy thankfully no longer need consider whose loyalty he might buy, but the last weeks of frantic consideration had been fraught with anxiety. He took a deep breath to calm himself. It was probably time to get *some* of his answers.

"Who in the earl's household brought you Wickham's letters?"

She did not attempt to prevaricate. "Davis collected them from him. She would go out to meet him every few days."

Ah, her maid. I would not have paid her off, had I known she was in collusion with the villain. It was strange that Wickham had insisted on abandoning her.

"I think...I think he was...c-consorting with her," Georgiana blurted suddenly. "She wanted money from him for something. I was not supposed to know. I tried not to know, and I did not, not truly. Maybe I am wrong."

She looked at him with a pathetic sort of hopefulness in her eyes, as if she yearned for him to disagree with her. In this, he could not oblige.

"Georgiana." He sighed again. "I know Wickham well. He could not hide his malicious propensities and sordid appetites from a man his own age. I spent years trying to fix his mistakes and undo his harm. If you believe nothing else I tell you, please believe this: George Wickham would 'consort' with *any* female who would allow it, and more than a few who would not. It has nothing to do with love or passion, not for him. For him, it is about conquest, about getting what he wants, when he wants it."

"Father loved him." She tried for defiance, but he heard the uncertainty, the misery in her tone.

"Yes. I never wanted him to know how awful a man his godson had become, not when his heart was so weak. Our father thought him good and respectable, and I feared him learning otherwise. I cannot repent that decision. But I told you."

There was a long pause. "I did not want to believe you."

"Obviously."

She twisted her hands together; the nails hidden beneath her gloves, he knew, were bitten to the quick.

"I would tell you I am sorry, but what good would it do? I have already ruined my life and yours. I cannot undo any of it."

He shook his head. "Your life is hardly ruined—it has barely begun. Once I am satisfied that you are settled at Pemberley, I shall collect Elizabeth and together, we shall begin again."

"She will despise me. She will believe me a...a slut." A tear tracked down Georgiana's cheek, and then another.

It was what Wickham had called her, to her face, preceding Darcy's punch to his

"You have two choices; you may adopt Wickham's opinion or mine. Mine is that you were thoroughly deceived by a pretty-faced rogue, who made promises he had no intention of keeping, and that you have learnt a hard lesson. Wickham is the villain here, and his foul sobriquet belongs to him alone."

Her voice was small. "I hate myself."

He took her hand. "Hate him, if hate you must. Perhaps in time you might spare a bit of pity for the young girl he duped. You, however, are no longer that girl—are you?"

"I do not want to be." She turned her large, expressive eyes, so like his mother's, upon him. "Must you tell her? E-Elizabeth? Could you not give her an excuse…that I-I was ill? Or…was hit over the head and lost my senses? I promise to be the best sister in the entire world to her, even if she thinks I ought to spend my days entertaining people I do not like and netting purses no one wants and is forever plucking books out of my hands in case reading them turns me into a blue-stocking."

For the first time in ever so long, Darcy wished to smile. "I am not marrying Lady Matlock, my dear. I believe you will find Elizabeth to be just the sort of sister you have always longed for. I have already told her what happened. I had to, in order that she might understand why I would not be in attendance at our wedding."

"She must hate me for that."

His smile faded. "If I thought she would ever hate you, I

never would have chosen to marry her in the first place. I love you."

"I do not understand why. I have now made every poor choice a girl could possibly make."

"Your choices *have* been poor ones. I hope you learn from them. But whether you do or you do not, I shall always love you. You cannot change it, or ruin it. It just is."

She regarded him for seemingly endless moments, before easing against him, leaning against his shoulder as she once used to as a little girl; his arm went about her as it had then.

"Will you tell me about her?" Georgiana asked, as the first soft flakes began to fall. "How did you meet Elizabeth?"

CHAPTER TWENTY-FOUR

A week later, Darcy heard melodious sounds from the pianoforte emerging from the music room. It cheered him immeasurably; Georgiana had not touched the instrument since she had been home. Music had been her greatest love since a young girl, but Lady Matlock's methods of strict regimentation, of forcing Georgiana to limit her playing in favour of singing and dancing and drawing masters, had evidently led to her gradual abandonment of the instrument. He had been encouraging her to take it up again, trying to help her find some joy in life. She had appeared to discount his early suggestions, but now—music.

Could it be that she was returning to her old self? He missed that girl desperately, and he hated not knowing what to say and how to say it, feeling his way along what often seemed a treacherous path. He wandered into the music room, seated himself out of her line of sight, closed his eyes, and tried not to think.

Although the music was beautiful, and he was glad to his soul to hear it, he was not very successful in allowing it to soothe him.

Why have I received no letter from Elizabeth? He had written again—twice, expressing the same sentiments of regret and longing. The silence from Longbourn had grown deafening. The question, niggling at first, but becoming an ever-greater possibility, went round and round in his head: *Has Elizabeth changed her mind?*

"Have I put you to sleep?"

He snapped his eyes open to meet Georgiana's gaze; she left the instrument to sit beside him, appearing…concerned.

"I was enjoying listening, but perhaps I dozed off."

She placed a finger on his forehead between his eyes. "There is a furrow here that tells me you were worrying rather than listening, or, if sleeping, your dreams are not pleasant ones." She took a little huff of breath. "You have been picking at your meals. You have not been eating well."

He raised his brows. "You are a fine one to talk."

Unexpectedly, she grinned. "I suppose we are a pair." But then her smile faded. "It is my fault you are unhappy. Christmas has come and gone, and yet you have had no letters from Hertfordshire."

"Do not make assumptions, please. This is not about you, but between me and Elizabeth."

His tone was more severe than he once might have spoken, but he could hardly help it. *Might Elizabeth be ill?* There had been illness at Longbourn while Miss Bennet was recovering at Netherfield. When he had gone to ask Mr Bennet for Elizabeth's hand, they all appeared healthy. But he had not asked, had he?

"I know you are afraid to leave me here, and afraid to take me to town with you," Georgiana continued as if he had not spoken. "If I promised not to plunge into London's seedy gaming hells the moment your back is turned, but instead to stay at home and not leave it unless you or Mrs Annesley accompany me, would you go? I daresay you could quickly discover what has happened, if you went in person."

Darcy turned to give her a look; this new sarcasm was not entirely welcome. Nevertheless, she was trying to be helpful. *Did* he trust her? Probably not yet—or not much—but he *was* convinced, via certain enquiries he had made, that Wickham had departed England. She was doing better, but he would not yet feel right about leaving her alone for longer than a few days. If he went, she must go too.

"The roads will not be in very good order, after our recent storm," he said at last. "It may not be a pleasant journey."

Georgiana shrugged.

There was just one answer, however; he was longing to go, to discover what he could. If Elizabeth's fears had given way to doubt, he was certain that he could change her mind.

"The hour is too late to leave today. Tomorrow is the Sabbath. We shall leave on Monday."

Georgiana nodded solemnly, and he realised, suddenly, that it had been difficult for her to make this offer. She was frightened of what Elizabeth would think of her, about her, and of what her life would become with this as yet unknown person at least nominally in charge of it.

"I appreciate the suggestion, Georgiana," he added. "It is a good idea."

She smiled at that, a little wryly. "That is me," she said. "Your wise terror of a sister."

"Play *Robin Adair* for me, my dear Terror," he said, smiling back. "I have not heard it in an age."

Darcy sat back on the velvet cushions, and this time he was more successful in allowing the music to calm him. She played for an hour more, at least, and it *did* help. But the worry would not entirely disappear.

Do not be foolish, Darcy, he repeated to himself over and over again. *Elizabeth would not toss you aside over events beyond your control.*

On Monday, just before departing Pemberley for London, he received his letters to Longbourn returned via post, sealed and never opened.

Elizabeth had never read them at all.

William Collins was a happy man. Lady Catherine had been proved in her wisdom once again, in suggesting that he go to his future estate to select a present bride. Naturally, had he seen Mary's elder sisters first, he might have wished for one of them—they were, to be sure, fine-looking females. Very fine, indeed. However, the Lord moved in mysterious ways, and the eldest Miss Bennet's illness, preventing him from meeting either sister before an attachment had already formed between himself and Mary, sealed his union with a sort of divine approval, to his way of thinking.

After Mr Darcy's callous abandonment of Miss Elizabeth, he had been horrified when Mary insisted he ask for her hand. Mary had also been certain she would not agree, and that the risk was minimal. Still, a risk it had been—for both of them— and all because Mary required of him the highest standards of gentlemanly conduct. There was nothing he would not do for his Mary, even propose marriage to her rather intimidating older sister. Miss Elizabeth's opinions were difficult to dissuade, her logic impossible to refute. He would like to see one of his Oxford professors debate *her*, and come up the winner!

At this very moment, Mary might be dressing in her bridal clothes—from her aunt Philips's home, across the street from Meryton's church—although he must not think too long on that exciting subject! Probably in a matter of minutes, the Bennet coach taking his family to the church would return to Longbourn for him. Its arrival at the church for the second time was to be a signal, to Mary and her father, that the chapel was ready for its bride.

In his eagerness for the ceremony making her his wife, he could not help pacing the vestibule, peering out the windows from time to time in hopes of spotting the Bennet carriage. During one of those inspections, however, instead of seeing the expected vehicle, he saw a man on horseback, finely dressed, trotting up the drive.

Who could that be? He rubbed the thick pane with his elbow sleeve, trying to gain a better view. When that failed, he walked out onto the portico.

To his shock and surprise, the last man in all the world he had expected to see was dismounting, tossing his reins hastily over the gatepost, and striding up the path towards the entrance.

Mr Darcy! What could he mean by it? But as God is my witness, I will stand for my cousin; I will be the man whom Mary expects me to be.

CHAPTER TWENTY-FIVE

Darcy was surprised to see the stout man who was, apparently, awaiting him on the front steps of Elizabeth's home—his aunt's vicar, he remembered. For a moment, he almost looked about for Lady Catherine, before remembering that this was Elizabeth's cousin. Had he been here when Darcy had spoken to her father? He rather thought he had, and that he had introduced himself, although Darcy had paid as little attention to him as was possible. *Cockrell? Connor? No, Collins, that was it. Yet another unfortunate relation for her.* He gave him the briefest of bows.

"I would speak to Miss Elizabeth," he demanded tersely, not bothering with further formalities.

The other man stared, as if astonished, gawping at him as if he had demanded to see the prince regent.

"Are you deaf, man? Fetch her, if you will," he ordered impatiently.

At this, Mr Collins drew himself up, as if *Darcy* were the one behaving offensively. "I am all the more astonished at what has happened," he replied, "from that knowledge of what the manners of the great really are, which my situation in life has allowed me to acquire. In the example of your lady aunt, for instance, I have witnessed the most elegant of breeding. The behaviour we witnessed from you, and most especially your *family*, is all the more abhorrent, in comparison. I cannot help but conclude that her ladyship would find much to be disappointed in."

Does this worm know of Georgiana's blunders? Darcy thought, appalled. Had the Bennets been indiscreet? How dare they share his sister's shame with this toad! Had Elizabeth spoken of the colonel's revelations?

But then he remembered the colonel saying that 'the whole family was an embarrassment'. Had Fitzwilliam shared his news with more than simply Elizabeth? Had he felt obligated, due to the last-minute nature of Darcy's withdrawal, to justify it to the whole clan? If so, it also explained Fitzwilliam's testiness whenever the subject was broached. He had made an error there, although he could not have known how brash were Elizabeth's connexions.

Darcy thought of his letters, returned unopened, and now it made a kind of sense. These reprobates had set themselves up as judge and jury of a young girl they did not know. Further, Lady Catherine would undoubtedly learn of Georgiana's humiliation as well.

Darcy's jaw clenched at the thought. Nevertheless, he could not believe that Elizabeth would have responded with anything except sympathy and grief, whatever her family's opinions. Probably, they had not allowed her to know he had written at all.

He leant forwards, putting himself right in the man's face. "Let me make myself perfectly clear. I will speak to Miss Elizabeth, and I will speak to her now."

Mr Collins's face went white, and he took a satisfying step backwards. All too quickly, however, he shook off his obvious fear. "It does not matter what threats you invoke upon my person. I have cast the cloak of my protection over her, and shall never bow to your menace."

Abruptly, the memory of a conversation at Netherfield with Elizabeth, before she had accepted his proposal, hit Darcy with lightning force. She had received a letter from her mother, demanding that she come home to *marry* this churl. Rage filled him, his fingers twitching with a desire to inflict violence.

"The 'cloak of your protection' had better never touch Elizabeth, unless you wish your next sermon to be preached from Hades itself. You will inform her I am here. At once."

Mr Collins's entire demeanour shrank in expected dread, but his voice rose into a high pitch. "I cannot. She is not here. But I would not, regardless. She deserves better, and so does Miss Anne de Bourgh, and so I shall inform Lady Catherine!"

The sound of horses coming up the drive alerted both Darcy and Mr Collins to the approach of others. The other man's relief was easily seen and immediate; sidestepping Darcy, he scurried down the steps to meet the carriage.

Eyes narrowed, Darcy watched to see if Mr Bennet was within; but there was no one else in the vehicle when Mr Collins leapt inside before it came to a complete halt.

Moments later, it continued its way around the drive and back from whence it had come.

Impatiently, Darcy pounded on Longbourn's door. It seemed to take some time before an out-of-breath maid answered.

Lax household!

She took his card, her eyes widening at the sight of him. Instead of answering his question regarding the whereabouts of either Miss Elizabeth or Mr Bennet, she dashed away, mumbling something about fetching the housekeeper.

At last, a respectable-looking, elderly woman, much finer and more civil than he had any notion of finding her, came to the door. Unfortunately, like the very best servants, she provided no information upon the whereabouts of the family or the predicted time of their return—but all with the greatest courtesy—and Darcy was feeling rather desperate by the time he received her gracious dismissal.

"Please," he heard himself entreating. Begging, even. "If you can provide any intelligence at all regarding Miss Elizabeth's current location, I would be forever grateful."

She looked at him for a long moment, and for some reason he felt himself weighed, measured, and found lacking. Her lips pursed. "She is with her relations in London," she said at last. "I am certain that Miss Elizabeth must have spoken of them, as they are great favourites with her. I would suppose that if she did, and if you listened, you would not have much trouble in discovering her." Gently, she shut the door in his face.

CHAPTER TWENTY-SIX

Darcy stormed over to Netherfield and discovered another likely reason for the Bennets' hostility: the house was closed up, just as he had strongly advised Bingley to do. Not that they would know his part in that, but they must have been planning to trade on his connexion to Bingley in order to secure a husband for Miss Bennet. It made for a dashed inconvenience, however; he refused to give the inn here his custom.

He made the return trip to London in much less than the usual time, tearing along roadsides and through villages alike, his mind absorbed in the bitterest kind of fury, almost heedless of his mount and the mud.

How dare the inhabitants of Longbourn treat him as if he were some sort of mendicant, come to beg for Elizabeth Bennet's attention? How dare they pronounce their critical opinions of Georgiana as if they were too good for her? How dare the repulsive Mr Collins, his aunt's *parson*, think himself good enough to deliver a set-down to Fitzwilliam Darcy! They ought to have been grovelling at the sight of him! To think that they would reject a gentleman of his stature and wealth—*returning* his thoughtful letters—the very idea was insulting and revealed their idiocy!

Recalling the upper servant who had presumed to question him—albeit without words—on his knowledge of the Bennets' relations in *trade* filled his heart with outrage. Why *should* he know them? It was not as though he could be expected to acknowledge a lowly tradesman who hung his shingle in Cheapside. *And if they are such 'great favourites' of Elizabeth's, perhaps Fitzwilliam is correct in supposing that I ought never to see her again!*

Finally, however, at that particular train of thought, his heart rebelled.

This had nothing to do with Elizabeth. She was all that was good and honourable; he *knew* it and would not, could not believe otherwise—especially without even speaking to her. She had not received his letters—probably did not know he had written. Her awful family, out of a condemnatory pride, was keeping her from him.

A niggling feeling of guilt kept trying to worm its way into his mind. How the Bennet contingent had spoken to *him* was no worse than *his* opinion of *them*; Elizabeth had, at least once in their private conversations, begun to speak of her uncle, and he had purposely prevented her from doing so. Nevertheless, he could hardly be expected to *rejoice* in their differences in station.

Besides, neither guilt nor outrage would help him to find his bride. He *would* find her, but he cursed the time it would take to search all of Cheapside for a man whose name he did not know

Georgiana heard of her brother's return to their Mayfair home with a sense of astonishment mixed with dread. He had meant to stay in Hertfordshire for a few days, at least, possibly up to a week—making arrangements for his approaching wedding. Due to what had happened last time, he had said he did not feel he could push Miss Elizabeth to marry quickly, by licence; that he would speak to her vicar and arrange for the banns to be called, with hopefully a wedding by the end of January, if she would agree.

But now he was home. *Soon, far too soon.*

Guilt was an ache in her belly and acid in her throat. Since returning to Pemberley, she had done her best to fashion the memory of George Wickham into the person whom she had once loved. She had failed utterly, her image of him refusing to remain the courtly, handsome suitor of Ramsgate.

I was so angry, so disappointed when my brother broke off our first planned elopement. George, via Davis, had quickly re-established contact. He had not accused her brother of lying, no; they both knew Fitzwilliam Darcy to be honourable and upright. Rather, George assured her that there were two sides to every story—that Fitzwilliam's jealousy of their father's preference for George made him interpret the will in the harshest possible light, that she ought to feel pity for her brother, and be the one to help repair their childhood friendship.

If she were truthful, she could admit her childish view of George had begun to shatter on the first night she spent in his bed. It had been painful, and thankfully over with very quickly. George had rolled off her and then assured her she would 'improve with practice'. She had cried herself to sleep, which only made him angry.

Oh, she had tried, tried so hard to please him—even seeking advice from the hateful Davis, who had assumed airs of both pitying condescension and spiteful resentment, once they were on the road. George would alternately lavish adoring devotion and belittling distrust, keeping Georgiana balanced upon the edge of uncertainty, always.

It was really not until she was returned to Pemberley— beautiful, peaceful Pemberley—that she had begun to see those interludes in a different light. The cheap taverns where she stayed with George had been stenchy and uncomfortable. The other patrons were intimidating, frightening, and although George told her that she was a spoilt coward, she *knew* his friends were not upstanding citizens. They joked about their exploits, few of them legal, and George *admired* them for it— insisting, humiliatingly, that she learn to pick a pocket or two at crowded inns to 'earn her keep'; no one would ever believe *she* was the thief, with her 'haughty' manner. He refused to allow her to spend *her* money—he had taken it all—and would grow furious if she asked for any, berating her, telling her that she loved wealth more than him, accusing her of wanting to leave him, of craving a return to her arrogant brother and coveting the life of an overindulged infant.

By the time Fitzwilliam had burst upon them at that Newark inn, she had become so accustomed to protecting

George, to sacrificing for him, to proving herself *worthy* of him, that she had tried to remain—despite his vicious, open rejection. To remember how she had begged George to stay, to *keep* her, now overwhelmed her with shame and humiliation.

Her brother did not come down to dinner, instead sending a message that he was busy with correspondence and would take a tray in his study. After picking at her food for as long as she could stand, Georgiana abandoned her partially eaten meal. She must know, had to understand, the extent of her guilt. By the time she knocked lightly upon her brother's study door, she was sick with it.

"Enter," he called curtly.

He looked up, surprised, when she did.

"You did not join me for dinner," she began, hardly knowing how to ask what she needed to learn. He might tell her it was none of her business.

"I have a tray," he said, managing to sound both harsh and weary. "And letters to write."

She glanced at his untouched tray, the blank letter-paper on the desk before him, and plunked herself down on the nearest chair. This was Fitzwilliam, and he would neither rage at nor belittle her. Something told her that if she waited until he was better rested, he might, stubbornly, admit nothing. He probably would refuse to say much, regardless.

"What happened in Hertfordshire?"

Then, to her astonishment, he told her.

CHAPTER TWENTY-SEVEN

Darcy could not say why he failed to spare himself the degradation of revealing what had happened in today's catastrophic attempt at reunion. Perhaps it was the sincerity of interest in his sister's tone, or perhaps he was so tired of talking to his reflection that he availed himself of the first pair of listening ears.

At least she did not begin a rant on the subject of the inferiority of Elizabeth's family, as his cousin would have. *He* was the only one who had a right to those opinions.

"How will you discover her uncle's name and direction?"

He shrugged. "My solicitors will do that part. I do not imagine that it will be overly difficult for them."

"No, but it will take some time. Do the Bingleys know it, do you think?"

He opened his mouth to deny the possibility, but could he be sure?

"I am uncertain," he admitted. "Mrs Hurst first mentioned them, or I would not know anything—she said he lives 'some where near Cheapside'." He hesitated. "I divulged nothing of the advent of my wedding to them—Elizabeth has an elder sister, whom Bingley was very taken with. I thought it best to remove him without implying that our connexion would soon be furthered."

"You did not like her sister?"

"I did. She is a sweet girl who conducts herself well. Bingley is very young, however. He is forever falling in love, and then out again."

"One of these times, he must fall in love and stay there. Why not when he has met a young lady of whose comportment you approve?"

"I did not think she was especially taken with him. The Bennets...their financial circumstance is limited, their estate entailed upon Mr Collins. He claims he wishes to marry Miss Elizabeth, and certainly he would have her parents' blessing."

"Mr Collins...Lady Catherine's vicar?"

Darcy's lip curled in contempt. "The very same. Miss Jane Bennet is obligated by those considerations to show an interest in any eligible male. I would see Bingley more happily settled than that."

"She only wants his money, then?"

"She—" he began, and then paused. "That is the harshest way of putting it. Due to a chance fever, she stayed several days at Netherfield, and I had ample opportunity to observe her. Her look and manners were open, cheerful, and engaging, but without any symptom of particular regard, and though she received his attentions with pleasure, she did not invite them by any participation of sentiment."

"And due to financial considerations, Miss Bennet must answer all marriage proposals, no matter who from, with a resounding 'yes'."

"I do not say she is as mercenary as you imply, but she would be under tremendous pressure to comply with any good offer."

"Miss Elizabeth is not bound by those same considerations? How do you know whether her sentiments 'participate' with yours?"

"I am not stupid. I can tell when a woman is truly in love."

"But Mr Bingley *is* stupid? He cannot tell?"

"He is young," Darcy snapped, wishing she would go away now.

"How old is Miss Elizabeth?"

"Just turned twenty."

"So, younger than Mr Bingley. But still you are certain *she* is not stupid?"

"Your sarcasm is most unappreciated."

Georgiana sighed. "I do not mean to be sarcastic. It just seems as though you have made quite a lot of assumptions. However, I am the one, certainly, who has been proved well and truly stupid, and have little right to comment upon the intelligence of any other. Perhaps Mrs Annesley and I shall call upon Miss Bingley and Mrs Hurst tomorrow, and discover what they do or do not know?"

Darcy gave his sister a long look. It was very soon to trust her again, and Fitzwilliam would not like her leaving the house without him, but the idea of going himself to pay a morning call upon the Bingleys, of enduring Miss Bingley's attentions, was an awful one. Besides, the colonel was not here to help as a chaperon, was he? And there was Mr Collins, Elizabeth's family's choice, waiting in the wings and hoping, obviously, for an opening, a chance to purloin his bride.

"Perhaps you shall," was all he replied.

Georgiana had always liked Miss Bingley and Mrs Hurst; they showed her a great deal of affection. She enjoyed the fawning, she could admit, even if it was excessive at times. But the best part of their acquaintance had always been that she was not required to make much polite chatter—never a talent of hers—for they assumed the bulk of the task.

It was no advantage this time. They rattled on, quite willing to both ask and answer their questions, giving her no openings for a topic of her own.

How was it that I never noticed this? They assume I am a child, with not a thought of my own to converse about. It is my fault they think it.

Mrs Annesley nodded encouragingly at her. Georgiana had hated the woman barely a month ago, thinking her strict and rigid and old-fashioned, and then had shamelessly lied to her in order to elope. When she was first returned to Pemberley, she had assumed that the subtle punishments of belittling insult once inflicted by Mrs Younge would begin. They never did. Mrs Annesley was a gentle soul wrapped in a refined exterior, who had managed to convey her disappointment without rancour, administering kindness instead of the deserved fury. Georgiana had begun, tentatively, to confide in her, finding her advice sensible.

Finally—albeit awkwardly—she managed a casual question to the sisters regarding the Bennets' stay in their home during her brother's visit to Netherfield. It was akin to dumping a bucket of cold water upon her hostesses. Mrs Hurst recovered quickly with a frown, but Miss Bingley sputtered with discomposure, "Why do you ask after that—that—?"

Georgiana saw at once, by those words and their sour expressions, Miss Bingley's hatred and Mrs Hurst's disapproval. She was also quick to understand that she would get further in seeking information if she appeared to share the sisters' opinions.

"My brother mentioned a Miss Elizabeth Bennet once, briefly, and there was something I did not understand in it, which sparked my curiosity. Distaste, perhaps? Was she vulgar, I wonder?"

It was certainly shades on the truth, but Georgiana did not hesitate to speak them. *There are advantages to being not so virtuous as my brother.*

"She is nothing but a country upstart," Miss Bingley spat, though she subsided when Mrs Hurst gave her a pointed look.

"My sister exaggerates. While we were not, perhaps, much impressed by Miss Elizabeth, we likely did not see her at her best. She was quite worried over her elder sister at the time."

Ah, she is cautious. She saw something in Fitzwilliam's behaviour that revealed his feelings, whether he knew it or not. They do not like her, undeniably. Jealousy?

"I understand from my brother that they are in town. Do you know where they reside?"

"Somewhere near Cheapside. It is not a good address," Mrs Hurst answered quickly.

"I told you they would not know it," Mrs Annesley chided Georgiana unexpectedly. She turned to the Bingley sisters. "Miss Darcy and I had a discussion about this. I have lived in town for several years—with Lady Matlock's niece, you know. There are *many* fine addresses near Cheapside. Not so close, you understand, to the world of trade, although I suppose that, as the crow flies, it must seem near to those less familiar with town. I am certain the Bennets' relations must live in one of those superior addresses, and not in sight of *warehouses*." She pronounced the final word with a distinct disapproval.

"I have Miss Bennet's card," Miss Bingley eagerly rejoined. "She wrote her uncle's address on it in her own writing. Believe me when I say their address is in the thick of commerce."

Mrs Annesley stared with a doubtful expression that was, evidently, too much for Miss Bingley to resist. Abruptly she stood and flounced from the room, returning presently with a small card, which she handed over.

Mrs Annesley glanced at the card with an appropriate air of polite disinterest before returning it to their hostess. "Hmm. It seems I was incorrect, Miss Darcy. This address is very much in the heart of industry."

Miss Bingley appeared pleased, but Mrs Hurst had grown quiet. Mrs Annesley expertly turned the subject to their opinions upon the fashions illustrated in the latest issue of *La Belle*

Assemblée, displayed prominently on a side table. Both sisters entered with gusto into the discussions upon sleeves, and the visit ended very cordially.

Once safely ensconced in the Darcy carriage, Mrs Annesley sighed. "It was rather ham-handed of me, I think, to gain Miss Bennet's direction so clumsily. I could not see any other means of learning it. Had you asked for it outright, I believe they would have demurred."

"It was brilliant," Georgiana replied. "I do not care if Mrs Hurst suspects we had purposes other than passing judgment upon the neighbourhoods of London. The important thing is that now we know where to discover the Bennet sisters! Do we not?" She glanced across at her companion.

"That we do." Mrs Annesley smiled gently, and Georgiana felt a wave of gratitude towards the older woman, who had been so unexpectedly useful. The feelings were unfamiliar, but then, no longer was Davis whispering words of annoyance and suspicion regarding the companion. She had practically taught Georgiana to hate and distrust her.

Why did I listen to her? Why could I not make decisions about whom to depend upon for myself? Ruefully she recalled how Davis had known exactly what to say, how to intrigue her regarding men and their mysteries, and how wise and clever she had seemed—until after they had left for Scotland.

Had she not been so sympathetic, I never would have listened so easily. I was betrayed by those who I believed were my friends.

Her conscience would not remain in silent agreement with this conclusion, however.

Instead, it brought to her recollection how often George

acted cruelly and hatefully. A niggling voice reminded her that every animal at Pemberley was better cared for than how he had treated her. *You not only allowed it, you encouraged it, by remaining loyal to him, by ignoring his every bad behaviour, by doing exactly as he instructed you, every step of the way.*

CHAPTER TWENTY-EIGHT

Darcy did not know what to expect when he alighted from his carriage at the address in Cheapside his sister and her companion had managed to acquire.

It was not this.

Whatever he was, Elizabeth's uncle was no mere attorney. His home was a grand structure of four storeys, adorned by colonnettes, fluting, and compound Corinthian piers below an ornate cornice. Its elaborate stonework and many windows mirrored its prosperous surroundings.

After presenting his card to a neat maid, he was politely shown into a high-ceilinged marbled hall; he stood beneath an exquisite chandelier with countless prisms and dozens of candles, while masterful portraiture stared at him disapprovingly.

And then, he waited. And waited.

There was no chair, and after some moments, Darcy began feeling as if he were some itinerant peddler with inadequate wares. His teeth clenched; if this was a show of disdain, it was a surprisingly effective one, and he felt all the humiliation of it. This was the family who had rejected him and his sister on the basis of her errors, and now they attempted a direct affront. His anger at the insult was great, but his need to see Elizabeth again was much greater.

Finally, the maid returned. "Mr Gardiner will see you now. If you would please follow me."

He had no real choice, as it was clear that he would not be allowed to see his bride without talking to the man. It was frustrating, if not unexpected. He could not deny the elegance of his surroundings; everywhere he looked, he saw tasteful furnishings of gleaming woodwork and marble chimneypieces —the type of elegance which came at significant cost. The rug beneath his feet was so thick, his footsteps made no noise. He was shown into a large study. Mr Gardiner looked at him from across the polished surface of a vast desk, and slowly rose.

He was not a tall man, but broad of shoulder and muscled beneath his well-tailored clothing. He was also surprisingly young to be the master of such a property. There were lines at his eyes and mouth, as if he smiled and laughed often. He showed no such cheerfulness now; his look was an impassive one, but cold.

Darcy was not offered a chair.

"I cannot help but wonder at your audacity," Mr Gardiner said, once the door shut behind the maid. "It is why you were not summarily ejected from my home once I heard you were in it. I eagerly await learning what possible reason you could have for showing yourself here."

"Surely it is no mystery," Darcy said, as a new idea *very*

belatedly occurred to him. *Elizabeth, not wanting to betray Georgiana's elopement, must have given her family no suitable reason for the swift halt called to our wedding ceremony.* It would be another explanation for the overt hostility, the returned letters—though *his* missive sent via the colonel for her had made it plain that her father was to be told.

The sudden notion guaranteed that his tone was much less indignant than it might otherwise have been. Nevertheless, he would have his way in this; these misunderstandings must be overcome. "I have come to speak to my affianced bride."

"Astonishing," Mr Gardiner replied. "I understand you have a sister, sir?"

Darcy stiffened. *What is he about? Does he know, or not?* Considering the ceremony over the anvil so recently averted, raising the topic of Georgiana was highly unfeeling—but could also be considered proof, he reminded himself, that Elizabeth had kept his sister's secret. "Yes."

"Tell me, Mr Darcy, how *you* would feel about the man who left your sister waiting at the church for hours, in the hopes that her bridegroom might appear on her wedding day?"

What was this? Fitzwilliam had failed to mention that his letters had not arrived before the morning of the wedding, nor their lengthy wait at the church for him to show; it must have been a terrible mystery for them both. *Oh, Elizabeth! I am so sorry, my darling!*

All was explained. If Elizabeth had not fully enlightened them as to the real reasons for his failure to appear, her family must not have accepted a lamer justification. Fitzwilliam might even have *urged* her to a secrecy that led to this misunderstanding. He had been very unhappy with Darcy's candour.

"I take it that Miss Elizabeth did not share with you the details surrounding my absence?"

The man stared at him with an expression of incredulity. "Just how was she supposed to accomplish that? After raising her hopes, speaking to her father, and lying about your intentions, you disappeared, never to be seen again. Blast you, I would put all of my considerable resources towards a breach of promise suit, were she not already mortified beyond what any young lady should *ever* have to bear!"

Darcy could only gape at him. "What? But I wrote to her!"

"I can assure you, she received no such communication."

"But...I sent it—care of my cousin, Colonel Fitzwilliam. He said—he said—"

"What your cousin did or did not receive is a matter of conjecture, but what he *said* is on the lips of every person in Meryton, as well as the immediate countryside. As he departed the area on the morning of Elizabeth's supposed wedding, the *only* remarks he made were to one of their respected neighbours who wondered why he was not at the chapel. Your cousin *said* he would deny the 'yokels' trying to force *you* into wedlock, that it was all rumours and misunderstandings, which *he* was under no obligation to support. I believe a direct quote was 'a man has every right to come to his senses once he's out from under a siren's thumb'. Meanwhile, my niece waited at the church for hours, with the entire neighbourhood witnessing her humiliation."

"The devil you say!"

"I do say. Elizabeth would not truly believe it for some days, hoping and expecting to hear from you. Instead, she heard reports suggesting you would soon be engaged to a Miss de Bourgh. My niece makes her home with me now, having chosen to leave Longbourn rather than become the object of pity and scorn by her neighbours."

"This is impossible!" Darcy cried. He felt sick. "My cousin would not betray me like this, nor behave so callously to a lady." But doubts raced through him, and Gardiner's frosty expression told him otherwise. More must be said before this meeting degenerated into a squabble regarding who said what and when.

"Sir, I can assure you this has been a terrible misunderstanding," Darcy implored earnestly. "I have *never* been engaged to Miss de Bourgh, nor created any expectations in her whatsoever. A family emergency arose, requiring my immediate attention. I explained all of it in a letter sent to Miss Elizabeth, but due to the delicate nature of the issue, and the approaching date of our wedding necessitating the utmost haste, I requested that Colonel Fitzwilliam deliver her letter in person. I am shocked and appalled to find she has never received it. She is due my deepest apologies, and I pray she will accept them."

"And you are just now finding time to deliver them?"

"Indeed not! I have sent letters to Longbourn, and they were returned. I visited there myself, and was turned away at the door by Mr Collins, Mr Bennet's heir. It was he who informed me that Miss Elizabeth was in town, but it took me some time to discover your direction."

Mr Gardiner's brows rose, his surprise obvious; Elizabeth's family must not have mentioned these attempts at contact to him. Darcy pressed whatever little advantage it gave him. "Please, allow me to speak to her. I vow I can explain."

For some moments, they stared at each other; it was obvious that Mr Gardiner was not fond of the idea, nor of him. All the same, Darcy would not back down. He could not afford to think of the colonel's potential duplicity at this moment; the situation called for all his dignity and address.

Finally, Mr Gardiner seemed to conclude that there was nothing else for it. "Elizabeth is not at home, and I do not expect her for another two hours, at least. However, if you leave me your direction, I shall send word when you may return and speak to her—assuming she wishes it. I shall not force her."

This was not ideal; Darcy could just imagine sitting with Elizabeth beneath this man's watchful eye with the barest modicum of privacy, unable to say half of what needed saying. Also, he must show both Elizabeth and her family the respectability he offered, as attested by his Mayfair home. If he could change the venue of the conversation, he was certain he could change its tenor.

"Perhaps you would be willing to bring her to my home? Please, accept my invitation to dinner tonight—you and your wife, as well as your niece. At any time this evening which is convenient to you."

Mr Gardiner raised a brow, and his next words showed his abilities as a tactician. "Taking the battle, as it were, into your own territory?"

"A territory which, by all rights, should have been Miss Elizabeth's long before this."

The rejoinder did as he intended—reminding the man that it was not simply Elizabeth's feelings at stake, but her future.

And my own.

CHAPTER TWENTY-NINE

The house bespoke money, old money—the kind of wealth that meant a royal lineage commingled with blue blood going back generations. It was especially manifest in this luxury residence on Grosvenor Square, where even the breezes did not dare waft air tainted by the usual London pollutions.

Elizabeth stared for a moment at the entrance—a canted bay rising through the first and second storeys, supported by two massive, marbled columns—wishing desperately that Jane had not had to return home to Longbourn, and could be beside her to lend her confidence.

It was not merely the obvious affluence; it was the hushed atmosphere, bestowing some sort of structural reverence upon the entire square. Her uncle's home was grand, but this one required more than money to exist. It required power and privilege to maintain a home in this particular neighbourhood— and this home was not Mr Darcy's finest one.

"We do not have to do this," her uncle reminded. "I can have the carriage returned to Gracechurch Street, and us in it."

She smiled at her concerned relations. "Oh, no. He will at least explain himself to me. I am owed it."

This was a truth no one could deny, but there was a part of her that did not wish to hear it. What were the odds that it was a worthy excuse, enough to vindicate his cruelty? Granted, according to her uncle, Mr Darcy had not meant to leave her waiting at the church; nor was there any supposed engagement to Miss de Bourgh. Did all the cruelty belong to Colonel Fitzwilliam, then? Or was 'the letter' he had been tasked to deliver filled with explanations so weak that the colonel could not bear to put himself in the middle of the situation, as she and Jane had long since surmised? Anger was easiest, but heartbreak continued to devastate her. She hoped the truth would free her to move on.

They were greeted at the door by a liveried servant, followed closely by Mr Darcy—almost as if he had been waiting at the windows for any sign of them. He was, unfortunately, even more handsome than she had remembered. He was also an imposing figure, sober, dignified. For just a moment, however, his eyes lit, and he seemed to hesitate for an instant before speaking. Her own tongue was tied as well.

She had her anger, still, but she had not expected the strength of the other feelings flooding her—memories of holding him, being held by him. *Mere desire*, she tried to tell herself, but she knew it for a lie the moment the thought formed. It was *connexion*—an electric recognition that tingled throughout her whole body. Did he feel it, too?

But after those first few seconds, the hauteur he habitually wore in company returned; he reminded her in all ways of his demeanour that first evening of their engagement, when she seemed a nobody or nothing to him before the Bingleys— impassive, distant, dignified.

He never informed them of our engagement, she reminded herself.

Mr Gardiner smoothly performed the introduction to his wife, and Mr Darcy bowed to both ladies. "Perhaps you would come with me to the dining parlour," he began, but Elizabeth knew she could not do it. She could not sit over a meal and pretend to eat and spew pleasantries until he decided enough attention had been paid to the proprieties, and he could proceed to explanations.

"Please excuse my impatience—" she began, but was interrupted by the sudden entrance of a tall, well-formed young lady, who appeared both determined and somehow fragile.

"Please do not blame my brother," she blurted, looking directly at Elizabeth. "I beg you, do not blame my brother for any of it. I—"

"Miss Darcy." An older woman emerged hurriedly from behind her, stopping the younger one's speech. "It would be best if you allowed your brother to render any explanations as he feels are necessary."

"But she should—"

"*Please*, Georgiana," Mr Darcy interrupted. "Mr and Mrs Gardiner, Miss Bennet, my sister, Miss Darcy, and her companion, Mrs Annesley." He scrubbed a hand through his hair, and suddenly he did not appear so very aloof, so much a stranger, but only tired and worried. As for Miss Darcy, Elizabeth noted that—despite a certain maturity of figure—in her obvious unease and lack of subtlety, she gave an impression of extreme youth.

After these introductions, Mr Darcy turned to the Gardiners. "I wonder if it would be possible for me to speak privately to Miss Bennet, regarding those explanations she is owed?"

Mr and Mrs Gardiner exchanged a glance, and Mr Gardiner opened his mouth to speak.

"Just tell them all everything, Fitzwilliam," Miss Darcy interjected fretfully. "Her family should know. If you do not, I shall."

He briefly closed his eyes, and when he opened them, Elizabeth saw his resignation. "Perhaps you would all join me in the library, then." He turned to Miss Darcy. "Please, go and inform Mrs Fowler that we shall require a delay to our meal."

Something to do with his obligations to his sister, then, must have been the reason for his absence. It did not make Elizabeth feel any better. His family must of course always be of great concern, but if her complaints meant he would drop his own wedding day with but a note to his cousin, they had been doomed to unhappiness from the outset.

The younger girl began a response to her eviction—probably a protest—but something in his expression must have, finally, quelled her. Closing her mouth, she meekly departed to do as he bade, her silent companion trailing after her.

With Mr and Mrs Gardiner, Elizabeth followed Mr Darcy up a great oaken staircase with massive balustrade; a footman leapt to open the double doors leading into a large chamber, and closed it behind them. Two sides of the room were shelves lined with books, another was a wall of windows covered by velvet draperies, and the last housed a great chimneypiece of black-veined marble. He led them to two leather sofas that were arranged before the flames. Elizabeth noted that the furniture here was somewhat worn, the leather soft, not possessing gleaming fabrics in the latest style, showing the wear of obvious use. The cushions were still plump, but a depression had formed in the seat of the one nearest the fireplace, and she caught herself wondering if this was a favourite spot for him.

She sat well away from that cushion, as if to protect her heart from the informal image. Her aunt and uncle took up sentry positions on either side of her.

Mr Darcy seated himself directly across from her, looking only at her, as if he were drinking her in.

Stop it, Elizabeth. It was foolishly sentimental imaginings such as these that had led to her public humiliation. She wanted her answers, but must make clear that he had not ruined her entire life, in case it was some finally remembered sense of honour which led him to recall her existence.

"It seems likely, from Miss Darcy's words, that your sister required your attention on the date that was set for our nuptials. Possibly that is why you failed to return for our wedding. My uncle informs me that you wrote a letter to your cousin, Colonel Fitzwilliam, which you assumed had been delivered to me before the ceremony. I wish to know one thing: why would you send such a letter, a letter calling off my wedding, to *him*? It was very obvious to me that he did not like or respect me. Could *you* not see that? He did not hide it particularly well—or even try. I might also, perhaps, wish to be informed why, with so little endeavour at civility, I was thus rejected by him. But I suppose that issue is of small importance, at this late date."

Elizabeth's aunt placed one hand upon her knee; it was a gesture of support, but also of warning—it was probably time to stop speaking now, allowing Mr Darcy to respond. Of them all, Mrs Gardiner had expected that they would hear from him; she knew of the Darcys from her youth, and had declared it impossible for such behaviour to stand without explanation from him. She did not at all blame her niece for her resentment, but sensibly, could not wish for fury to interfere with those answers Elizabeth was owed.

"I do not call it a matter of small importance at all," Mr Darcy replied, his eyes still resting upon her. "You have every right to know. As for his reasons, I have sent a note to my cousin, asking him to explain himself at the earliest possible moment, upon his honour as a gentleman, else never enter my home again. I do want you to know, Elizabeth, that in addition to the letter I asked Colonel Fitzwilliam to deliver to you, I did write to you directly, more than once."

He slid a small stack of envelopes across the low table towards her. "Full explanations for my absence are contained therein. I recently received my letters returned to me unopened, and it was not until then that I suspected something was truly amiss between us."

They both stared down at them, as if it were easier to look at the tattered envelopes than each other. He took a deep breath before continuing. "The gist of it is, I went to town to collect Georgiana and bring her to our wedding, but found her gone—eloped, with a man I particularly hated and who had cause to hate me. That man I once told you of, who treated Bingley so cruelly—although I did not make known to you then that he was the same one who had pressed his suit upon my sister at Ramsgate."

Elizabeth gasped. Mrs Gardiner took her hand, and she clutched it. "Not…not Wickham?"

He nodded once, sharply. "I had missed her by a mere two hours," Mr Darcy continued, his voice unemotional, "and felt there was a reasonable chance that I could follow, that the life of misery and heartache she foolishly had chosen could be prevented, if I acted quickly. Act, I did, catching up to the eloping pair at Newark.

"As for why I chose to send your letter to Colonel Fitzwilliam, he is Georgiana's joint guardian. It was necessary to inform him of her situation, at once. It did not seem right to me, at the time, to send such awful news to you by a letter alone. I imagined that he would behave as a gentleman ought, however, and deliver it to you with my wretched news. I am sorry, unutterably sorry, to find I was wrong."

Astonishment, apprehension, and even horror oppressed Elizabeth, but before she could begin to express the perturbation of mind his words had excited, the library doors slammed open.

"What the devil is this about, Darcy?" Colonel Fitzwilliam growled the question, holding out a sheet of letter-paper before him.

CHAPTER THIRTY

Inwardly, Darcy cursed. It had been so difficult to rein in his feelings at the evocative sight of Elizabeth in his home, at long last. Yet, he had seen the hurt and anger in her visage, and knew he should proceed carefully, giving her every proper attention due her as his bride. At his explanation of Georgiana's attempted elopement, her eyes had just begun to soften with acceptance that the situation truly *had* been beyond his control. She had been ill-treated, and now, at the worst possible moment, entered the cousin who was to blame.

It took that cousin another moment before he realised they were not alone, but Darcy stood immediately as the colonel's lips formed a sneer.

"Not another word, Fitzwilliam," Darcy said. "You and I will speak privately."

"Why are you so concerned about privacy now?" the colonel snapped, giving a contemptuous look at Elizabeth and her family. "I can tell you have been blathering the family business to anyone who will listen."

"Once again, I see your temper has got the best of you. If you have any claim at all upon honour, you will leave us at once."

"Do not talk to me of honour! I received this uncivil note from you threatening to destroy *our* entire family, all over this-this girl from Cheapside! Would you *listen* to yourself? Why in thunder would you chain yourself to a woman whose family you did not deem good enough for Bingley?"

"What?" Elizabeth cried.

The colonel faced Elizabeth. "Darcy confessed to me that he would do everything in his power to separate Bingley from your sister. No, I should not have left you standing at the church—but you ought to have never been in it! My motives for my actions in separating the two of you were and are the same as his for saving Bingley, and why should I apologise for them? Why am I suddenly the villain of the piece? Even he must admit that *your* births are better than his friend's...and yet he cannot see that he is sacrificing himself and his future. You are a gentleman's daughter, yes. But who is your mother? Who are your uncles and aunts? Do not imagine me ignorant of their condition." He gave the Gardiners a derisive glance that made Darcy wish to punch him.

But Mr Gardiner had already stood, making haste to shepherd the ladies from the room. Elizabeth would not look at Darcy.

"Please wait, sir," he begged. "If you would allow me to—"

"You have a situation to resolve," Mr Gardiner interrupted

with a coldness that brooked no resistance. "I will not have my niece anywhere near such low discourtesy as she has already been subjected to. Whatever you wish to say of the circles I inhabit, none of my associates would have treated her like *this*."

The undelivered letters he had written to Elizabeth, Darcy noticed, had been left behind in plain sight upon the table. He snatched them up. "Please, Elizabeth, take my letters," he implored. "Read them. If only you could understand how much you mean to me!"

Briefly she hesitated; was she tempted to take them from his outstretched hand? But when she turned back to face him, he saw naught but grief and rejection in her expressive eyes. "I understand much more than you ever wanted me to, I think," she said, her words a mere whisper, as she allowed Mr Gardiner to guide her from the room.

The hardest thing he had ever done was to watch her go. However, in this Gardiner was correct—to further expose her to the colonel's disregard would be unconscionable.

Darcy stared with narrowed eyes at his cousin; Fitzwilliam's anger at Mr Gardiner's words had been obvious as he watched the party leave, and the air grew thick with silence between the two men who remained.

Sorrow, disbelief, and fury churned in Darcy's gut, a toxic brew threatening to fell him.

"I cannot fathom your thinking, Fitzwilliam. I knew you were unhappy with my choice—but I thought that you respected me enough to lend your support and friendship."

"I am! I do! It is for your sake that I did it, though you hate me for it! You have been fooled, or played for one. Her family is low, vulgar—"

"Enough! Do I have eyes in my head? Do you think me incapable of seeing what—who—is in front of me? Am I blind, as well as foolish, that I cannot judge them for myself?"

His cousin opened his mouth to reply, then closed it again, scrubbing his hands through his hair. "I did wrong by leaving her at the church," he said after a pause. "It was not well done of me, I admit that, and if I had the money to offer recompense, I would."

"Money? You think this is about money?" Darcy laughed with acid resentment. "Who is blind now? They had the evidence for a breach of promise suit lying on that table— pages and pages of promises. They would not take those letters, not when I begged."

"Perhaps the man did not realise—"

Darcy stalked the length of the chamber, his sense of frustration, grief, and betrayal building with every step. "Do not be stupid as well as blind. Her uncle Gardiner lives in surprising wealth, none of it handed to him. To be sure, he is clever and resourceful. I have hurt, however mistakenly, two favoured members of his family. He would never allow either of us to buy our way out of the dishonour you have heaped upon us both."

"Darcy, come now, you must be reasonable," Fitzwilliam pleaded. "You cannot believe that Matlock would welcome such a bride. Why, imagine his displeasure! It does not bear consideration. He would never forgive it."

Darcy stopped pacing to stare at him, shaking his head in

disbelief. It was all growing clear to him, finally, and long after it was too late. "I should have known," he retorted. "When Alexander died, I could see that you—"

"Alexander?" At this unexpected mention of his dead younger brother, Fitzwilliam paled. "What has he to do with this? Not a thing! You are turning wide of the point, sir!"

"I beg to differ. Did not Alexander beg your company before he departed that wretched day? Did you not refuse him because of your sore head, born of making merry with your friends the night previous? Had you accompanied him as he asked, *would* he have drowned?"

Fitzwilliam's face went from white to dark red, his fists clenched as if restraining himself from speaking with them. His voice, when he answered, was choked. "What of it? I suppose you have some purpose in dredging up my old guilt?"

"I do." Darcy rounded on him, using his greater height to advantage, his gaze boring into Fitzwilliam's. "It has always been obvious that you blame yourself. How many times since his death have I witnessed you licking the earl's boots in your eagerness to satisfy his every wish and agree with his every opinion, no matter how outrageous? You still attempt to earn an absolution no one can grant you. I see it now. Our friendship—or what I *thought* was a friendship—was doubtless but another of Matlock's demands, that he might attempt to influence me through you. Will you deny it?"

Fitzwilliam's eyes blazed, and Darcy wondered if the colonel would offer a challenge in response. Almost, Darcy wondered if he was goading him towards it. Certainly, men had fought over less.

"Of course I deny it! Now I am certain you have lost your mind," Fitzwilliam said sharply, before cutting off his belligerence with visible effort. In a much quieter voice he said, "I have always been your friend."

Darcy shook his head, incredulous. "A *friend*? Would a friend lie to me? Would a friend utterly fail to behave as a gentleman, leaving the only woman I will ever love believing I am untrue? Would a *friend* slice my heart out through my back, and while I am bleeding before him, explain I ought to care what his *father* thinks? From the first moment, I may almost say, of sharing with you my decision to marry, your arrogance, your conceit, and your selfish disdain for the feelings of others have demonstrated *your* meaning of the word 'friendship'. I want no part of it. You will leave my home at once. Do not return."

"Darcy, please, you cannot mean—surely you can see w-why—" Fitzwilliam stuttered, but Darcy did not wait to hear more, and strode to the doors.

"Michael," he called to the footman waiting there. "Please show Colonel Fitzwilliam out."

The colonel gawped at his ejection, but tried again. "Understandably, you are too angry at the moment to be reasonable. I am still Georgiana's guardian, however," he beseeched. "You cannot disregard my wishes when it comes to her—we still have much to discuss."

"Take it up with my solicitors," Darcy said coldly. "He who has the most money to argue with them, may have his opinions most heeded."

The sturdy footman entered the room, wide-eyed, but willing. The colonel stared at the two of them, as if weighing whether he could take on them both. Good sense won the day, and instead, he stalked out.

Elizabeth did not speak all the way home. When they arrived in Gracechurch Street, Mr and Mrs Gardiner both begged her to join them in the parlour, where a meal might be brought in place of the one they had missed at Darcy House. She excused herself, however, as having no appetite, and quickly found her own room. She believed perhaps that tears might help, for once, to free the excess of pure emotion trapped within her chest. But lying here, staring up at the ceiling, she knew nothing would erase the dull ache.

No matter how Mr Darcy had wished to hide it, she had seen the truth upon his face. Colonel Fitzwilliam might despise her—*did* despise her, in fact. But he had not lied about separating Mr Bingley from Jane. She perfectly remembered the letter Miss Bingley had written to Jane, with not one mention of a wedding—ruined or otherwise. She had not known. He had not *wanted* the Bingleys to know, because if they did, Mr Bingley would have pursued the connexion with Jane.

A connexion with Jane was, somehow, unacceptable.

If Jane—gracious, lovely Jane—was not 'good enough' for Mr Bingley, what did that say about Mr Darcy and Elizabeth?

I was convenient, she thought. *There was a physical attraction, and all of his worries about Miss Darcy, and he impulsively proposed. Now he is home alone with his troubled*

sister, and I am still, in his mind, the easiest answer to setting
up his nursery and coping with his sister.

Marriages had been based on far less, often enough.

Nevertheless, Colonel Fitzwilliam, hateful and despicable
as he behaved, had produced an undeniable logic. The foundation for this 'courtship'—desire and a sense of convenience—
was unlikely to last much beyond the first year—or the first
ton social event when the earl made his contempt known for
Mr Darcy's country bride. If Mr Darcy believed Jane and
Bingley were a mismatch, what would it be like when he
realised his own?

A lifetime of misery.

A tap on the door broke into her desolate thoughts, and her
nine-year-old cousin, Eleanor, slipped into Elizabeth's room.

"Cousin Lizzy?"

With a sigh, Elizabeth sat up to face the eldest Gardiner
child, a pretty, slender, sensitive girl who reminded her often,
at least in temperament, of Jane.

"Yes, dearest?"

"Mama wants to bring you a tray, but Papa wishes for you
to be left undisturbed. Mama says you are sad and we must all
leave you be. I promise, I shall not stay. It is just that I have a
biscuit that I was saving from earlier. Sometimes, when I am
feeling particularly wretched, I find a biscuit can help." She
held out a small, napkin-wrapped parcel.

Elizabeth found a smile for the child and held out her
arms. "Would a hug come with that biscuit?"

Eleanor hurried to her embrace. "You are my favourite
cousin in the whole world," she declared, squeezing with all
her slight strength. "Well, and Cousin Jane too, because she is

so patient showing me new stitches—but you read the very best stories, because you do all the voices properly. And you sing me lullabies so beautifully, I-I don't ever wish you to be sad. Mama said your nice dinner out was ruined, and I am so very, *very* sorry."

As Elizabeth felt those thin arms around her, she swallowed down her heartache. The Gardiners were the kindest, loveliest family in the world, and clearly this sensitive child had picked up on her parents' distress, not just Elizabeth's. No one knew what to do, how to help. Nor was there much help they could extend. But wallowing alone was not the answer. There was time enough for her own sorrow—years of it—without wrecking the happiness of everyone surrounding her.

"I do not wish to be sad either, sweet Eleanor. I am certain this biscuit will cheer me, but perhaps I should first discover if Cook has conjured up anything to replace our ruined dinner."

Eleanor perked up immediately. "Oh yes! She has! A lovely soup! Would you like me to bring you a tray?"

"There is no need for that," Elizabeth said, smiling at the sweet offer. "I shall go downstairs now, if you will accompany me. Perhaps, while I eat, you would tell me of the next chapter in your novel. Or have you finished *Eleanor Goes to London*? I remember you said it was close to completion."

As the two made their way downstairs, Eleanor chattered brightly about the illustrations for her book she intended to draw of the Bartholomew Fair—an event she had been allowed to attend with her papa for the first time in September. Obviously having heard her daughter, Mrs Gardiner quickly joined them at the bottom of the staircase, her gaze questioning.

"I have decided I am hungry after all," Elizabeth answered her look.

Smiling sadly, the compassion of a thousand unspoken words in her eyes, Mrs Gardiner took Elizabeth's other hand in hers, and together they went to find the promised meal.

CHAPTER THIRTY-ONE

The next day, Mr Darcy came at the earliest acceptable hour for morning callers. His entrance, as well as the flowers he brought, were refused.

"I do not wish to speak to him again," Elizabeth explained to her uncle and aunt. "It is obvious that we will not suit. Unfortunately, I still have feelings for him. It would be best to allow those feelings to starve into nothingness."

"You are certain they will?" her aunt had asked.

"Of course they will!" her uncle assured.

She was not quite so positive, but she would begin as she meant to go on.

The following day, Darcy came again, meeting with the same rejection. And the day after that and the day after that and the day after that. It was beyond distressing, but since he did nothing except meekly accept his rebuff and go away again, there was not much to be done about it—especially because Elizabeth rebelled against any idea of Mr Gardiner's confronting him, which he was more than ready to do by the fifth dismissal.

"His sense of honour demands that he call. He will do it until his conscience assures him that he has made every effort to right whatever wrongs he feels guilty of committing, and then he will go away," Elizabeth insisted. "The best we can do to encourage that effort and that final departure is show our unwillingness to even speak of it."

"It is doubtful he will come tomorrow," Mrs Gardiner added. "'Tis the Sabbath."

She proved right on this, a merciful reprieve.

He did not come on Monday.

Elizabeth was astonished at the disappointment she felt at his absence. Had she truly not believed her own words? What had she expected? That he would attempt to call for two or three weeks, accept rebuff after rebuff by his social inferiors, before he forgot about her and went on with his life?

Yes, foolish girl, she mocked herself. She had believed he might try for a bit longer than he had—but why should he? He was Mr Darcy of Pemberley, nephew to an earl, of vast fortune and numerous properties. She was Elizabeth, of nowhere in particular. He had come to this realisation sooner, even, than Colonel Fitzwilliam had predicted.

That man—I will not *call him a gentleman—must be satisfied now.*

But later in the afternoon, her uncle sent word requesting her presence in his study.

"Yes, sir? You wished to see me?" she asked, peeking her head into the room.

"Elizabeth, please—come in and be seated. Yes, shut the door behind you, there's a good girl."

He seemed unusually distracted.

"Is something the matter?"

He scratched his head, his jaw clenched. A stack of documents lay before him; he stared at the papers as if he wished to toss them all into the fire. "I have heard from Mr Darcy today," he said, meeting her eyes at last. "Or rather, not from him directly. From his solicitors."

"What? But why?"

He shoved contemptuously at the mass of papers. "This. This is a threat of a suit for breach of promise."

"What?" Elizabeth could only repeat the question stupidly, unable to make sense of it. "*He* is suing *me*? Why? This is impossible!"

"Not you, *per se*, but your father and I, for withholding you from your promise to contract a marriage with him."

"It is ridiculous! He has suffered no reversal from any of it! In fact, he will go on, it is to be presumed, to marry some fat-dowered miss who will increase his already immense fortune in a way I never could have! He cannot have a leg to stand on!"

"He does not claim his damages are financial, but that his deepest feelings have been wounded. You, he claims, have broken his heart."

"*His* heart?" She shook her head incredulously. "It is all ridiculous, is it not? *I* was the one who was humiliated on my wedding day, before a hundred witnesses! He cannot do this, can he?"

Mr Gardiner sighed. "Unfortunately, yes, he can."

She folded her arms. "Let him, then! I shall tell any judge in the nation what he has done!"

"Actually, you would not. Neither you nor he—the ones closest to the situation—would be eligible to speak. Truthfully my dear, the winner of such matters is often determined by which barrister best entertains the jury. Besides, it is doubtful Mr Darcy wishes to go to trial. It is extortion, plain and simple. Either you agree to one private conversation, or he will proceed to embarrass you—and himself—in a court of law."

Elizabeth could not, for a moment even, understand him. "He is suing me to-to *speak* to him?"

"Rather, he is threatening your father and me with punitive legal action if you do not. Well, let him, I say. Let him embarrass himself."

She shook her head. Mr Darcy was behaving ridiculously, but she would not add to it. There was a part of her—a part which she was sure she must *never* encourage—that was flattered at the lengths to which he would go to have his conversation.

"No, Uncle. We shall not allow it to come to that."

"You do not have to speak to him, Lizzy. You never need speak to him again. He does not deserve your time, no matter the threat."

"I know it, and I am most thankful for your protection. But let us be reasonable, if he will not be. I shall listen to what he has to say, and then I shall tell him we do not suit. It might be good for me to have…to have some sort of complete finish to the whole matter. His explanations were interrupted, and I do wish to know exactly how responsible he is for Jane's unhappiness. I do not like that it was Colonel Fitzwilliam who had the last word on it "

It was all true, and yet, she knew it would hurt. But what did that matter? She hurt now. She would hurt tomorrow. She might as well face this conversation he was determined to have, and sooner than later; it would be the last one, the final injury. Maybe then, she would be more successful in laying this love she held for him to rest.

CHAPTER THIRTY-TWO

Mrs Gardiner waited with Elizabeth in the blue drawing room—chosen, Elizabeth knew, for its soothing colours. Elizabeth had chosen likewise easy colours for the stitchery on the handkerchief she embroidered as a gift for her uncle. Unfortunately, she seemed incapable of making a single stitch in its blank whiteness.

Mr Darcy would be here at any moment, and Elizabeth's fingers would not comply with her brain's chosen design, resisting any such quieting. She might as well have chosen red thread, for an embroidery of flames.

"Lizzy," her aunt said, softly, "you are too sensible a girl to refuse a man simply because you have been warned against him by your father and uncle, I know."

"Aunt! My reasons for refusing Mr Darcy have nothing at all to do with *them*, and you know it. How could any consideration tempt me to look favourably upon a man who has destroyed the hopes and broken the heart of my beloved sister?"

"I do not doubt Jane's feelings for Mr Bingley. However, that gentleman has allowed, practically required his friends to influence him. Such a man, one who does not know his own mind, may not have been the ideal she believed him to be."

"He is young, to be sure," Elizabeth argued, "but also too modest to doubt the opinions of his older, more successful, and supposedly wiser friend. You did not see Jane with him at Netherfield as I did. I never saw a more promising match, on both sides."

"Do you not believe that, were you to agree to marry Mr Darcy, you could set that particular situation to rights?"

"That is the whole point, I think," Elizabeth said sadly. "How did he mean to keep them separate? I have thought of little else. He said nothing at all of our expected marriage to the Bingleys. He intended that we should collect Georgiana and go directly to Pemberley. I believe he had some idea of removing me from Longbourn and leaving it all behind—everything he hates about who I am and where I come from—including Jane, and all my family. I believe it never occurred to him that I might object. He does not know me, not really. I did not know him, not at all. We narrowly escaped a match of the worst sort of convenience, one that would have made us both miserable."

Mrs Gardiner took Elizabeth's cold fingers in hers. "No one ever really knows the man they marry, not until one lives with him, day in and day out. Every female who has ever married is due the surprises—not always delightful—of learning to intimately live with and love a man. It is the same for men. With loyalty and forgiveness as a binding glue, that living and learning can become an adventure. As free-thinking humans, we are never doomed to remain the same man or the same woman we were yesterday."

"Aunt Gardiner, are you suggesting I should disregard all his opinions, including his prejudice against my family—which is actually a prejudice against *me*?" Elizabeth was shocked at this notion, but her aunt smiled.

"Perhaps Mr Darcy did err, even greatly. However, he has now imperilled his very reputation and all his dignity, in trade for a few minutes of your time." She gave Elizabeth's fingers a final squeeze. "Use it well."

Elizabeth was surprised when her aunt shut the door behind her, closing her in with Mr Darcy. But perhaps she should not have been; he had required privacy, and she was hardly in any danger from him—she had no doubt that Mrs Gardiner was just beyond the door, alert and attentive.

For a few moments there were no words between them.

She would not lie to herself—she was thirsty for the sight of him, memorising his face, his features. Then he seated himself beside her on the settee, sighing once, deeply. It seemed he struggled with what to say, but she had no such trouble.

"Miss Bingley wrote to Jane after they closed Netherfield. It was quite clear that she had no idea of there being any marriage between us. You did not tell them, any of them, anything about it, did you." It was not a question, but a tiny part of her still hoped he would deny it.

"I did not," he replied stiffly. "I could see that Bingley's partiality for Miss Bennet was beyond anything I have ever witnessed in him, but she remained clearly unaffected."

"And you know this how?" Elizabeth demanded, astonished. "You have not been acquainted with my sister for long, and half your acquaintance, she was very ill."

"If I have been mistaken in her disinterest, I apologise. It was not obvious to me."

For a moment, Elizabeth wanted to protest. How dare he make such assumptions! But her conscience raised objections. "Perhaps it would not have been, to you. Jane is always very careful, very ladylike. Some of that, as you must be able to guess, is to avoid comparison to our mother, and my younger sisters as well."

"Yes," he acceded, and there was something in his tone which added a silent 'Amen' to that agreement.

"Still, it was not *just* that you did not see it—also, you did not *want* to see it. You did not *try* to see it. You could have, simply, *asked* me regarding Jane's feelings. You did not want to hear my answer. You did not *want* to face the snide remarks of the Bingley sisters upon learning of our engagement. You have judged my family unworthy of the connexion—and yet, for yourself, you think I should be happy to have a man such as your cousin consider me the dirt beneath his shoe. I can imagine how his father would regard me."

"Neither of us was anxious to listen to the Bingley sisters. You do not trust that I can protect you from the earl?"

She gave a little huff of frustration. "Can you not hear

yourself? You hate my family, who has never done anything at all requiring you to be 'protected'—but I am to overlook yours, because—why? They are my betters? Even Mr Collins, who—"

Darcy reared back. "Oh, Mr Collins, yes, do let us discuss him. Has he asked you to marry him?"

For a moment, she could not process what seemed to her a complete non sequitur. "What has that to do with anything?"

"He has, then?"

"Yes. But that has nothing to do with why I will not marry you."

"I think it has everything to do with it. You wish for someone perfectly safe, whose feelings would never stir yours. You would remain in control, always. There would be no risk, no gamble, and you would become the heroine of your family in doing it."

Elizabeth stood, unable to stay still in the face of his wild assumptions. "You are being perfectly ridiculous. Tell me truthfully—did you expect that I would sever all of my family ties once I married you?"

He would not meet her gaze, not even when he stood as well, facing her, and her last hopes sank. When he spoke, his tone was laced with sarcasm. "Should I bring your mother to the earl, and listen to her explain where her wedding ring has been? However—"

"You have said quite enough, sir." She could not continue listening to his excuses. It was all as Colonel Fitzwilliam had asserted; she might call the colonel cruel, but she could never label him *wrong*.

"Is this a dismissal?" Mr Darcy asked, pacing away from her. "Will you not listen to me? Are you going to *marry* him?"

Sorrow speared her, but she clung to dignity. "Please accept my best wishes for your health and happiness."

He whirled back around to face her again. "Elizabeth! That is all you have to say? Truly?"

She took a deep, shuddering breath. *In a few moments, it will be over.* She nodded, unflinching.

His eyes narrowed, boring into hers, his gaze piercing her, as he moved within inches of her, his very presence overwhelming. She could see the intricate folds of his cravat, the glistening of the jewel at its centre. He was furious, and yet, she was not at all intimidated; instead, she felt powerful, that she had been able to provoke him so thoroughly.

"Then know this," he said, "if you will instead choose your ham-handed cousin as husband: whenever he kisses you, when he clumsily touches you, each time he leaves you, perfectly content himself whilst you lie awake, unsatisfied, wondering why you feel nothing except impatience— remember then. You could have had me."

Her anger returned then, and it helped. *The sheer, unmitigated arrogance! How dare he! He does not know me at all!*

"Know this!" she retorted. "When you take to wife some diamond of the first water, celebrated in the papers for her ice-cold perfections, when you leave her frigid bed—remember then: you could *not* have had me."

He stared at her, fury and frustration fighting for dominance in his handsome visage.

"If I had known the day I met you that you would rip my heart, nay, my *life* in half, destroy my plans, my very peace of mind, if I had *known* that day..." He shook his head as if he could not think of barbs vindictive enough to hurl at her, and it was with effort that Elizabeth stifled the sobs wanting to break free.

But his expression smoothed, and turned suddenly bleak.

"If I had known the day we met of the havoc you would wreak upon my life...yet, I would not change it—not one minute of it. I shall never be sorry to have loved you, Elizabeth. Only sorry that I failed to show you how much." He reached out, and she thought he might take her into his arms, while she stood frozen. Instead, he gently pushed aside a strand of her hair fallen across her cheek, the tips of his fingers barely grazing her skin.

He leant closer; his lips grazed her forehead, then her cheeks.

Her anger disappeared, and all that remained was despair. A tear slipped out, and then another. He kissed those, too, taking the droplets into himself.

Their mouths met, softly, reverently. She could not help it, would not stop it—it was to be her final kiss, hers alone, from the last man she would ever love. Although her lips clung to his, she would not reach out in an embrace. Although she tasted his sorrow, his misery, he did not move his body any closer to hers.

At length she forced herself to take a step back, before she forgot everything she knew to be true. "I know you cannot like or respect my family, but they love me, and at my lowest moments, they have rallied round me. I understand your feelings, for I can neither like nor respect your family. I am trying, as hard as I can, to do what is right for both of us." She did not bother to correct his assumptions about Mr Collins. What did it matter? He had a beam in his eye when it came to his own family, and a prejudice when it came to hers. It was a mismatch, plain and simple. Still, a silly part of her wished he would argue.

He only looked at her. Then he nodded once, bowed low, and turned away, leaving her alone in the blue parlour—a colour that she would now forever hate.

CHAPTER THIRTY-THREE

"I hate to leave you at such a time," Mrs Gardiner said, her voice laced with concern. "I would never have accepted the invitation had I dreamt you would not go." The Gardiners were all to depart for a long weekend at the country home of one of her uncle's friends, some thirty miles distant. Elizabeth had flatly refused to accompany them.

"You accepted the invitation well before the end—or, the second end of my little romance was any consideration," Elizabeth replied. "I promise, I shall not be crying in my soup. I simply long for a quiet time of reflection."

"We should not leave you alone here."

Elizabeth found a laugh. "Here alone, except of course for your housekeeper, cook, and a half-dozen servants?"

"My girl, you know what I mean," Mrs Gardiner said, a little sternly.

"I assure you that I am completely safe—and especially safe from any excursion requiring shopping, entertainment, or people in general. Please, Auntie. Just this once, allow me to forgo your very kind invitation."

Inside her heart, Elizabeth was screaming to be left alone. The idea of four days without having to paste a false pleasantness upon her face, to simply be left to her own misery, was almost an idyllic notion. It had been two days since she had seen the back of Mr Darcy. It felt like two years.

"Elizabeth, I hesitate to say this, but best I give this advice now rather than always wonder whether I should have spoken. It is obvious you are desperately unhappy. It seemed clear to me that Mr Darcy genuinely cares for you. I do not believe it is too late to change your mind. I can have your uncle send him a note, asking for him to come and talk once more upon our return. Your conversation with him did not last very long —I cannot believe you both said everything you meant or hoped to say."

Oh, if only! How she wished for one more chance! *'I shall never be sorry to have loved you, Elizabeth.'* But it would do nothing except make things worse.

She tried to explain aloud what was in her heart. "Learning that Mr Darcy deliberately *concealed* our engagement from the Bingleys—not simply waiting to reveal it—was very hurtful. However, once I discovered his reasons for missing the wedding, I immediately looked for excuses of why it made sense. He did not like to exacerbate Miss Bingley's feelings, I told myself. A few moments later, however, I learnt that he *purposely* separated Mr Bingley from Jane. I asked him, Aunt, whether he had expected me to give up my family entirely upon our nuptials. He could not answer. He could not even look at me, and then he made a snide remark about the foolishness of introducing Mama to his uncle, the earl."

Mrs Gardiner patted her niece on the shoulder with some sympathy. "Very unkind," she murmured.

"I know Mama is not...refined. She would be no more comfortable in company with an earl than he would be in company with her. Yet, Mr Darcy's own sister behaved monstrously, and I would be expected to guide her! Should she once again run off with a villain, the polite world would say it was *my* influence! I can assume the colonel would certainly encourage her to despise me. Should I surrender the family I love for a family who will hate me? It seems irrational. I think that in the pleasure of beginning to know Mr Darcy, in the beauty and newness of my feelings, I imagined him into the man I wished for, rather than truly seeing him for the man he is."

Mrs Gardiner sighed. "Oh my dear, we all do that. The first year of marriage generally opens our eyes to those flaws new love blinds us to. It does not mean that what—*who*—is left behind is less worthy of every affection, and that a stronger love cannot build on that less-than-perfect foundation."

Elizabeth bit her lip. How she wished it was a simple misunderstanding! But his family, plainly, hated her; Mr Darcy, plainly, was mortified by a connexion even to Bingley for Jane, who was so good, so gracious, so kind, and whose birth was better than Bingley's own.

"I am sorry. I just cannot," she whispered.

Mrs Gardiner gave her a long look, patted her shoulder

again, and with another sigh, left her niece to check on the progress of the packing of the children's trunks.

Elizabeth closed her eyes, and wondered how long it would be before she would find her smile. *Will I ever be happy again?*

She straightened her spine. *Yes, I will.* As her mother had said, she was not one to lose her entire world over a man. By the time her aunt and uncle returned, she was determined to have these feelings packed away, attic-bound, the door to their memory firmly shut and locked. Nevertheless, she would take these few days—to grieve, to remember, and to mourn what might have been.

Three days after her brother returned from his call upon Miss Bennet, Georgiana sought out Mrs Annesley in a chamber where they would not be overheard. She might be making a terrible mistake, and not all her hard-won wisdom could tell her whether speaking to her companion was a good idea.

Her original notion had been to escape the house unnoticed, taking a hackney coach to the address on Gracechurch Street that she had memorised. Her time with George had taught her one useful thing—how to catch one of those breakneck vehicles racing along the streets of London carrying passengers this way and that, those smelly, often rickety carriages which barely stopped long enough for a lady to gather her skirts and leap inside. She knew she could get to Miss Bennet before anyone discovered her absence.

But discover her absence they would—and they all would

believe she had run off again. If she was ever to earn Fitzwilliam's trust, she must at least *try* to curb her impatience and play by his rules. *Sort of.* Nevertheless, she held no great hopes of gaining Mrs Annesley's cooperation in this matter, and if it caused significant delay, her brother's life might be ruined.

"Mrs Annesley, I need to pay a call upon Miss Bennet, and I wonder whether you would accompany me. I do not wish to inform Fitzwilliam of it."

The older woman raised a brow. Georgiana knew the rules —until further notice, all excursions required her brother's explicit permission.

"He has barely touched his plate in two days. He is grieving and upset, and it is all my fault. I cannot do *nothing*, yet he would never agree to my speaking with Miss Bennet. I know, for I have asked him." She said the words all in a rush, afraid she would not be allowed to explain. "I simply wish to apologise to her for my part in him missing their wedding, and assure her that I do not intend to be—to be undisciplined and unmanageable and-and a hellion. He told me she has no dowry, and he made her feel the differences between her family and ours by his own actions, that she cannot respect either of us, and that she will never forgive him. But even if it does not help and comes too late, I need to do this. I cannot live with myself until I do. It is...it is the *right* thing to do, despite Fitzwilliam's express disapproval."

Mrs Annesley regarded her for a long moment. Then she stood. "I shall ask for the carriage to be brought round."

Georgiana's eyes widened in surprise. "What-what will you tell my brother?"

"Not a thing. I daresay a stampede of carriages could blunder around the square for hours before he would notice, in his current mood," she replied. "You had better change your dress—I expect the blue walking dress would be ideal for paying a call—and wear your boa to protect from the chill. However, if she will not receive us, you must accept it is out of your hands. Perhaps you could then write a letter instead, but that is all the interference I can condone."

A little bewildered by her companion's easy acceptance, Georgiana made haste to change. It was not until they were seated in the Darcy carriage headed for Cheapside, having departed the house without trouble, that she dared ask about it.

"I did not believe you would indulge me in this request without Fitzwilliam's permission, not for any reason."

Mrs Annesley met her gaze directly. "After your elopement, your brother would have been well within his rights to terminate our agreement, and let it be known to all the polite world that he found me incompetent and careless. I *lost* you, and no excuse was sufficient. Instead, he held himself equally to blame. He refused my offer to depart immediately, and instead sent me to Pemberley to await your return. Not one man in a hundred would have been as generous and gentle as he was with me. I shall do whatever is necessary to support his happiness, even should he dismiss me for it."

Guilt again struck Georgiana. She had never, not for one moment, spared a thought for Mrs Annesley's fate, had her elopement been successful. It had never crossed her mind that her actions might leave the older woman destitute.

"I am sorry," she said quietly. "How is it that you do not hate me?"

"How would hatred assist either you or Mr Darcy?"

It was a very practical response, and Mrs Annesley was a very practical woman; Georgiana tried to imagine feeling that way about someone who had treated her so ill, and could not. Except, she had, of course. George had been vile. And Davis, too. *I let them both bully and manipulate me.* But this was different.

She thought of how Mrs Annesley had also helped her discover the Gracechurch Street location from the Bingley sisters. In almost everything, Mrs Annesley complied with society's dictates and expectations; yet, it seemed she evaluated her options and based her decisions, not upon authority or 'the rules'—but upon her own conscience. Perhaps some believed women could not have a code of honour. But Mrs Annesley did.

"I hope," Georgiana said, "that I shall become like you when I grow up. If I ever do."

Mrs Annesley smiled.

CHAPTER THIRTY-FOUR

Elizabeth spent the morning wondering what had been in the letters Darcy had sent her, wishing she had not left them behind in Mayfair. It had, undoubtedly, been the right thing to do—but had she not, she would have been able to hold in her hands the proof that once he had loved her. For days like today, it might have been a comfort.

"Excuse me, miss." The Gardiner housekeeper interrupted Elizabeth's stare at a book in which the words refused to form into coherent sentences. "But you have a letter."

"Oh, thank you Mrs Miller." Elizabeth accepted it. Her heart raced, a part of her she could not prevent wanting to see her name written across the envelope in a firm, masculine script.

Of course, it was nothing of the kind. It took her a moment to realise who had written, for the handwriting was remarkably ill—so much so, that it had been missent elsewhere, and reposted. *It is from Jane,* she realised, mildly curious about her sister's loss of penmanship.

Although Elizabeth was not sorry to have stayed home, it did not mean she was pleasant company for herself and could not appreciate a good distraction. She had been disappointed not to have received word from her family earlier this week, for generally her sisters—especially Jane—wrote so often. *I am happy for the interruption.*

Penned some five days ago, the first part of Jane's letter contained an account of all their little parties and engagements, with such usual news as the country afforded. But her eyes halted suddenly on Jane's handwriting where it deteriorated most abruptly, and it took her some moments to make out what it said.

> Since writing the above, dearest Lizzy, something has occurred of a most unexpected and serious nature; but I am afraid of alarming you—be assured that we are all well. What I have to say relates to poor Lydia. She slipped out in the middle of the night—

At this most inopportune moment, Mrs Miller interrupted again.

"Excuse me, miss, but you have callers. Miss Darcy and Mrs Annesley are come, and beg most urgently for a moment of your time."

Elizabeth could hardly understand her. *What? Miss Darcy? Now?* Hardly knowing how to act, she gave a wave to the housekeeper that could have been one of refusal or acceptance. As for her own eyes, she could do nothing except hastily discover what in the world had happened to Lydia. Vaguely, she was aware of the ladies' entry into the parlour, but nothing would or could make her stop reading. However, once she had finished the page, she dropped it in her lap, closing her eyes and covering them with both hands, wishing she had never read a word of it.

"Oh, dear Miss Bennet, I can see we have come at a terrible time," the older woman said. "Is there anything we can do for you? Can we call your maid, or your housekeeper?"

Elizabeth opened her eyes to stare at them blankly. "No. No, I thank you," she replied, endeavouring to recover herself. "There is nothing the matter with me. I am quite well. I am only distressed by some dreadful news which I have just received from my home—in Hertfordshire."

"We shall go now," the older woman said. "We should not have disturbed you."

But Miss Darcy knelt directly at Elizabeth's feet. "Please, Miss Bennet...you do not know me, except as the girl who has ruined, perhaps forever, my brother's happiness and caused you great distress. But I pray, if there is anything at all I can do to help, in any way, you must please allow it. My brother's physician is most renowned. If Fitzwilliam says the word, Mr Hadley will make haste for the country."

It took a moment, in Elizabeth's chaotic state of mind, for her to truly understand the offer. How to explain? Her instinct was to make an excuse and let the elder woman take Miss Darcy away. Still, this young lady who beseeched her so earnestly reminded her far more of Eleanor than any wild, spoilt heiress. She was clearly hoping to make amends for her past behaviour, even though the consequences were not all her fault. There was also this: Miss Darcy, of all the people she knew in the world—and, it was to be presumed, her discreet companion—would understand.

"Miss Darcy, it is not illness. My youngest sister has eloped. She left in the night, and it was several hours before her note was discovered. To Scotland, it said, but she did not name her bridegroom. We know not who he might be, but there *is* a regiment stationed nearby, and my sister has been… has been enamoured of the attention she has received, from more than one of the officers." She choked on a sob, and Miss Darcy's companion handed over a delicately stitched handkerchief. It was some moments before Elizabeth could continue, but the women waited patiently, expressions of compassion upon both faces.

"My father went to its commanding officer, Colonel Forster, to see who might be unaccounted for, but as of the time of my sister's letter, they have been unable to tell, for more than one man has recently disappeared, and apparently none of them told anyone anything."

"What efforts have been made to recover her?" the companion asked, plainly hoping to redirect Elizabeth's thoughts into a more positive vein.

"Colonel Forster has sent men after those who are missing. None, apparently, went north. They were traced as far as London, but few clues remained thereafter. They could be still in town, or they could have scattered across the countryside, or gone abroad. In the absence of any trail, Papa does not know how to act. My sister says he might come here to search himself but…Jane feels that, of the men who are missing…

none of them is of the sort who can support a home or family. Or who would try."

At her words, Miss Darcy's big brown eyes, so like her brother's, filled with tears. "I am so sorry," she said. "I am grieved for you, and for your family. How-how old is she?"

"Fifteen," Elizabeth said, the word emerging in a whisper.

Miss Darcy closed her eyes as if in remembered pain, but when she opened them, they were filled with a new resolve. "But you must be wishing to be at home with your sister, with your family."

At this, Elizabeth could not prevent a few more tears of her own to escape. "Yes. My aunt and uncle have gone away. Not for long, but it will be a couple of days before their return. It seems so selfish to wish them back from their visit, but oh, how I wish they were here!" She covered her face with the borrowed handkerchief.

But Miss Darcy reached for her other hand. "My brother's coach-and-four can be made available to take you home—it can be here within an hour if you like, and make as good a time as the mails. It is the very least our family can do for yours—it is our fault you are in town instead of with them. Please say you will accept this small favour. I beg you."

The last thing Elizabeth's pride wanted was to accept any aid at all from the Darcys, but desperation drove her to consider it. Their mother had taken to her bed, Jane said. The house was in an uproar. An overwhelming desire to be with them, to help Jane, to comfort them all, filled her. In the absence of her uncle, she might even have tried to have one of the servants hire her a carriage. This would be much easier, and besides...what had she to be proud of?

"Thank you." She forced the words from her throat. "I can be ready within the hour."

"Miss Bennet needs you."

Darcy had been startled by his sister's sudden entry. Now he could hardly understand her words, watching numbly as she went to the closed drapes and shoved them aside. Pale winter sunlight streamed into the gloomy study.

"I can barely see in here," she complained.

"What? What do you mean?"

"It is as black as a coal digger's grave in this room. I am allowing in some light."

"Coal digger's...no, not that. What about Miss Bennet?"

"I said, Miss Bennet needs you. Mrs Annesley and I called upon her this morning. She had just received a letter from home. Her youngest sister has run off with a man, just like I did, except no one has found her. She wants to go home—Miss Bennet, not the sister, I mean. I offered that we should take her. She has accepted."

"She-she did?"

Georgiana rolled her eyes, visibly impatient. "Yes! Her relations are from town, and she has no other recourse. We must not allow this opportunity to pass!"

Darcy knew then that this could not be Elizabeth's preference. However, there was no question but that he would do anything, anything at all to increase her happiness. Elizabeth had chosen someone else, but what did it matter? He was hers, and would put himself at her disposal, whenever he could—always.

He stood. "I shall take her, of course. But do not expect that this will change anything."

Georgiana put her hands upon her hips. "Well, it will not if you intend to wear that day-old cravat, and arrive coatless and bearded. Do clean yourself up, Fitzwilliam! And hurry! I told her we would be there within the hour! You must have your things packed!"

"We? Packed?"

"You can hardly travel with her alone, and Meryton has inns, does it not? You *do* intend to offer to assist in finding her sister, do you not? We should plan on at least one night, I think."

Befuddled at his usually meek sister's officious manner and bewildered by the unlooked-for opportunity to be near Elizabeth once again, Darcy obediently called for his man.

CHAPTER THIRTY-FIVE

E lizabeth was waiting on the portico with her trunk when the gleaming carriage, pulled by four perfectly matched horses, arrived at her uncle's property. Beside her waited Betty, the older maid who had—with not very hidden reluctance—agreed to accompany her.

A robust-looking coachman with a kindly smile refused the help of her uncle's footman, hefting her trunk himself; it was not until she and Betty had followed him nearly to the vehicle that Mr Darcy emerged from the coach, stopping her in her tracks.

Without waiting for his servant, he pulled down the steps, turned to her, and bowed. "Would you prefer I ride on the box with Frost?" he asked politely, as if he regularly gave up his comfortable seat in his fine coach.

"Oh—oh, no, of course not," she replied, stupefied by the sight of him. She had not expected it in the slightest—had, in fact, wondered if he would honour his sister's impulsive invitation, perhaps sending a hired carriage instead. He was immaculate, as usual, and far more handsome than any man had the right to be. "I-I thank you for this favour. It is beyond anything I could ever have expected."

He gave her a sober nod, opening the coach door more widely. "My sister insisted upon coming along," he said quietly. "Unless you object."

Within the carriage, Elizabeth saw Miss Darcy's eager expression, her obvious desire to do something—anything—to fix what was irretrievably broken. Sighing, she turned to Betty; at least it would save the maid a return journey on the post. "It appears we shall not need you to accompany us. I thank you for being willing to go. Please ensure my aunt sees the note I left for her immediately upon her return."

The relieved-looking maid agreed happily and hurried back into the house. With a mixture of dread, a despair she could not prevent, and an anticipation she could not help, Elizabeth took Mr Darcy's proffered hand and slipped into the carriage beside Miss Darcy.

Darcy had believed he knew exactly how beautiful was his Elizabeth, but now, her lovely dark eyes swollen with tears she kept from falling by some act of strong will, her soft skin pale with a vulnerability he had never before seen, he realised how weak was his memory. The pictures he had preserved in his mind were of eyes flashing with temper, chin stubborn, or the dreamy look she wore after being thoroughly kissed. But she had a thousand looks, and it would take a lifetime to catalogue them all.

She would not meet his gaze now; he could not stand for her to be embarrassed.

"I am sorry to hear of your sister," he said, feeling that only by broaching the subject directly, could he mitigate any awkwardness.

Her cheeks turned pink.

"I do hope you are not mortified by us knowing," Georgiana said boldly. "In fact, if you would like to know all of the stupidest reasons in the world for why she might have chosen to elope, please, just ask me to name them."

Elizabeth looked up, perceptibly disconcerted. Then her eyes closed briefly before she opened them again and turned to Georgiana. Darcy bit his tongue, wanting to tell his sister to keep her mouth shut, that she was embarrassing Elizabeth—that they *both* were. But Elizabeth spoke before he could find the right words.

"I fear your advice would not help much with Lydia. You are repentant, while Jane said that my sister's note treated the whole thing as a great joke. It does not concern Lydia at all, that her unmarried sisters are now ruined—she probably did not think of it, nor would she care if she did. When Lydia gets an idea in her head, nothing will do but that she follows where it leads. She is spoilt and selfish and…" She paused, taking a hiccupping sort of breath. "And she is fearless and self-assured, and would defend me to the death, if it was in her power to do it. You, Mr Darcy, have had a narrow escape."

The tears she had been trying to prevent overflowed, he saw, as a single tear tracked its way down her cheek. She swiped at it, as if annoyed. He handed her his handkerchief, trying to think of how to protect her words without further embarrassing her.

"Your cousin, Mr Collins, will break your engagement?" Georgiana asked.

Darcy flushed at the brash question but said nothing; he wanted to know the answer to it more than anything.

"I am not engaged to my cousin," she shot back, sounding incredulous, looking at him in disbelief. "I *never* said I was engaged to him!"

He opened his mouth to reply, but she did not wait.

"Do you really think that I would fall in love with you and then agree to marry another man within a few weeks? Oh, of course you do. You believe I wish to be the 'heroine of Longbourn' or some such nonsense. *Thank* you for your opinion of me."

Both ladies stared at him with identical expressions of outrage.

"He also thinks that you hate me for making a laughing-stock of you on your wedding day," Georgiana said helpfully.

"What? That is most untrue, Miss Darcy!" She turned back to face him. "How could you tell her that?"

He sighed. "I never said that, Georgiana. I told you Miss Bennet could neither like nor respect my family, and after the way she has been treated, I could not blame her."

"I did not mean your *sister*! Not at all! I could not assume that she would be happy to have me in her familial circle, however, with Colonel Fitzwilliam to influence her. I expect the rest of your family supports his actions. Can you tell me they do not?"

"What did the colonel do?" Georgiana wondered aloud.

"He received your brother's message that he would be unable to marry me on the date we had designed—and why. There was also a letter for me included, that he was asked to deliver. He did not give it to me. He did not explain a thing. He simply left Netherfield, left ugly remarks about me to the neighbours, and left me to my humiliation."

"The beast! Why did you not tell me what he had done, Brother?"

Darcy scrubbed his hands across his face. "You are correct. I should never have been so careful of him," he said, feeling another thick wave of resentment towards his cousin. "In retrospect, I see I ought to have chosen my words to you much more carefully—I never meant for you to take those words to mean Miss Bennet referred to you. I did not want to utterly ruin Fitzwilliam in your eyes, Georgiana, although he is ruined utterly in mine."

"Oh, he ruined himself in my eyes long before this—when he told me I was no lady and never would be, that I had spoilt my whole life, that I must be naturally bad and would be lucky if any of my family would agree to see me again, and that you would have to use half your fortune to find a man who would take me."

"He said what?" Darcy choked.

"I am completely unsurprised," Elizabeth said, taking Georgiana's hand. "I hope you told him that his words plus a shilling are worth a dish of beef."

"No," the younger girl sighed. "I just sobbed and begged him for forgiveness."

Darcy looked at her, aggrieved. "You have never begged *me* for forgiveness."

"Well I did not *mean* it. I just wanted him to stop talking."

He saw it then, a tiny sparkle in Elizabeth's eyes of warmth, of humour. The foibles of human nature did not upset her, they amused her. She did not expect perfection; in truth, a life of it, for her, would be very dull indeed.

He felt his lips curve upwards, smiling at her—the feeling strange for its complete lack of familiarity. He did not believe he had smiled, truly, since he had left her at Longbourn, what seemed so very long ago.

CHAPTER THIRTY-SIX

Elizabeth had not meant to smile back. She was doing her best to remember all the reasons why she had chosen to walk away from this relationship, all the reasons why it was a terrible idea. She had felt every one of them quite reasonable a few hours past.

Yet, here he was, dropping everything in his life to escort her home to a family grieving a runaway sister. That thought sobered her again, pointing out just how justified *he* had been in looking down upon the Bennets of Longbourn.

He does not treat you as though he looks down upon you, came the thought, unbidden.

Certainly his sister did not, and he seemed to treat *her* with a mix of bewildered chagrin and obvious affection.

"I know my cousin behaved unforgivably towards you," that sister said now, appearing thoughtful. "The colonel is slow to anger, but has a terrible temper once he truly gets riled. You would really have to meet my aunt in order to understand why he must have done it."

Even Mr Darcy gave her a reprimanding look at this statement. "I do not believe Lady Matlock, at her worst, would condone his behaviour towards a lady," he said sternly.

"No, of course not. She adores rules, and he, clearly, broke every tenet of good behaviour. But almost every time he is with her, somehow, at one point or other in every conversation, she brings up his marital prospects and goes through a long list of acceptable brides. You *know* she has preached the gospel of marrying well to him almost since his birth. It must be ingrained in his very nature by now, although for me, it seemed to have had an opposite effect. Every time she lectured *me* upon suitable husbands, it only made me like George better. Not that I blame her for my bad decision," she added quickly. "Still, the idea of marrying someone who lacks a prodigious dowry must seem the most alarming of notions to our cousin."

Mr Darcy rolled his eyes. "My circumstance is not the same as his. One would think he could tell the difference."

"I do not mean that you should excuse him—only that his panic, in the face of my elopement, makes sense to me."

"Panic? The man has fought in Spain. I hardly think he *panicked*."

It was Miss Darcy who rolled her eyes this time. "Of course he did! All of his bluster to me, when he rarely blusters, and never before at *me*? I could see he had worked himself into a state. Every time he mentioned what the earl might do or think of me, he grew more rattled. He probably thought he was saving you from Matlock's wrath."

Mr Darcy scrubbed his hands through his hair, ruining his untouchable image as he regarded Elizabeth once more. "His decision to leave you to face an empty church was abominable, regardless. I have cut the connexion."

Elizabeth started at this news. Never had she dreamt that he would do such a thing. He had done it, moreover, even though *she* had cut her connexion with *him*.

'My temper would perhaps be called resentful. My good opinion once lost is lost forever.'

He had said that in her hearing, it was true, and apparently, he had *meant* it.

"You did not," she said, shaking her head.

He frowned. "Of course I did. Why would I maintain any sort of kinship with a man who would hurt you? I can only regret that my own treatment of your sister led to his belief in the rightness of his actions. It was very lowering to realise that my blindness towards her feelings, and hence yours, caused me to trample upon them. I ought never to have interfered with Bingley in any fashion."

Elizabeth found herself speechless at his admission.

"I *told* you so," Miss Darcy said, looking altogether satisfied.

"So you did," Mr Darcy said, nodding sadly at his sister. "So you did."

And Elizabeth's first doubts about her decision to refuse his second proposal began to seep into her mind.

Georgiana had hoped—despite warnings from both Mrs Annesley and Fitzwilliam that putting the two of them in the carriage would solve their troubles. Briefly, when they were laughing at her—although she did not mind *that*—and her brother had admitted his own errors, she had thought it might be the beginning of some kind of new accord.

But they had both since lapsed into a silence that neither seemed able to break. The carriage rolled onwards at a brisk pace; Georgiana began to worry that her brother's sturdy team was eating up the miles much too quickly, with fewer changes than was usually required.

Why was conversation so difficult? She had always been bad at it, never knowing what to say and when to say it, and often choosing poorly. She had lapsed into shyness simply as a protective means of minimising her own mistakes. Now, she was realising that Fitzwilliam was not so good at it either. She could tell that his mood was somewhat easier now, the set of his shoulders less tense, but likely Miss Bennet only saw his sober expression. As she considered it, she decided it must be a Darcy flaw. Perhaps it was why her brother gravitated towards Colonel Fitzwilliam and Mr Bingley, both so gregarious and—usually—socially adept. Come to think of it, her entire family was flawed, and in more ways than one.

"Well, this is a pickle."

Both Miss Bennet and Fitzwilliam turned to her simultaneously, and she flushed—but there did not seem to be anything for it but to say aloud what she had been thinking.

"I wanted to assure Miss Bennet that Colonel Fitzwilliam is not representative of our family. Unfortunately, he is often, actually, of easier temperament than his father. Lady Matlock is equally arrogant, if usually better behaved. Viscount Ridley is not terrible, but he despises confrontation and would never stand up to both his father and brother, if it came to a row. As for Lady Catherine de Bourgh, she would be so furious at losing Fitzwilliam to you, Miss Bennet, when she has so long dreamt of him for her daughter Anne, she is unlikely to be very welcoming at all."

Miss Bennet glanced at Fitzwilliam, looking more curious than appalled by the family's bleak showing. "And how would Miss de Bourgh feel?"

"Oh, she would probably ignore you, but it would not be personal. She ignores most everyone, unless one is a horse." Georgiana shook her head. "In retrospect, it is not at all remarkable that I ran away. It is surprising that I did not do it sooner."

Miss Bennet smiled at her, reaching over to squeeze her hand, although Fitzwilliam closed his eyes and shook his head in disbelief. But Miss Bennet turned back to him.

"I understand why you have been, at times, mortified by *my* family's behaviour. I simply cannot comprehend your conclusion that my sister, Jane, was not good enough to be a potential bride for Mr Bingley."

It was Fitzwilliam's turn to flush. "It is not that she was 'not good enough', not at all. You cannot believe I would think that. You and your sister have always demonstrated the highest standards of conduct and propriety. I simply wanted Bingley's wife to love him for who he is, and not for what he brings to the marriage."

Georgiana stared at him. "You cannot believe that the sister of the woman who has refused you for the most refined of motives, would marry Mr Bingley for wealth alone, can you? Would your sister Jane do that, Miss Bennet?"

"She would never."

"Georgiana," Fitzwilliam said through clenched teeth, all his briefly improved mood vanished. "Stop helping."

"Oh, do keep on, Miss Darcy. I find you absolutely fascinating."

"That was sarcasm, was it not?" Georgiana said in a small voice. *This is why you should not speak!* she lectured herself.

Miss Bennet sighed. "It was. I apologise. It is a bad habit of mine."

"You were provoked," Fitzwilliam said. "And, if I could be allowed to finish what I meant to say, I wrote to Bingley after we spoke the other day, and told him that I had discovered I was entirely mistaken in Miss Bennet's feelings about him. I apologised to him for my error, as I will to you, now. I have not seen him since I left Netherfield, and have no idea whether his feelings for your sister held true—that is the other reason I had for caution, you see. In the past, he has fallen in and out of love so easily. I thought him too young to know his own mind. I still believe it, but it is not my responsibility to think for him. I overreached."

It was Georgiana's turn to sigh. It was not the passionate apology on bended knee that she would have preferred, but at least it was respectful. Unfortunately, Miss Bennet appeared bewildered, rather than impressed.

How much more time do I have to bring about a reconciliation? She feared they would have to drive to Wales in order to get these two to reunite.

Her brother turned to stare out of the window, instead of

into Miss Bennet's eyes. Anyone could see that his former betrothed was confused and vulnerable. Perhaps novels did not always provide the right guidance, but no hero worth his salt would look away from his one true love, instead of *at* her. What kind of books did Fitzwilliam read? Farming journals?

She remembered Mrs Annesley saying that she would do anything for Fitzwilliam's happiness, even should he dismiss her for it. *I broke them. I must mend them*, she thought, with desperate resolution.

"Miss Bennet," she said, cringing inwardly at what she knew Fitzwilliam's response would be to her next words, "my brother has not been happy for one minute, I daresay, since he left you at Longbourn. The last few days since your final conversation, he has not been eating or shaving or even bathing, really."

Fitzwilliam's head snapped back to hers. "Georgiana!" he hissed. "Be quiet, now!"

"Oh, what is your dignity worth? You could not care less that Miss Bennet's sister eloped with a blackguard, but you have yet to *tell* her! Your desk blotter is inscribed with a hundred renderings of her name, because she is all you think of! You are unhappy without her, desolately, desperately so, but she cannot know it because you will not *say* so!"

"I do not want her *pity*, foolish girl! As you have so *oblig-ingly* pointed out, we belong to a family of selfish characters who will do their best to make her life a living hell, at least at first. What woman would knowingly choose it?"

But at this, Miss Bennet drew herself up. "You do not believe I can handle myself amongst difficult 'characters', is that it? Your memories of my own family have faded, have they?"

Georgiana felt her first stirrings of hope.

He looked at her incredulously, opened his mouth, and Georgiana's worry flared, along with her eagerness to be useful. "Fitzwilliam," she said, interrupting whatever he had meant to say, "before you speak, now would be the perfect time to kneel at her feet."

He rolled his eyes, openly as frustrated with her as she was with him. "Life is not a silly novel, Georgiana!"

Miss Bennet gave him a withering look. "Do you mean novels wherein the protagonist would do anything for his friends? Or the novels in which the hero never loves by halves, but commits unreservedly to his passion? *Those* novels?"

She sounded sarcastic again, but there was something about her expression that made Georgiana's breath catch.

Fitzwilliam looked at her for a long moment. "Miss Bennet...I dare not hound you."

"You apparently did not feel this way when you threatened your breach of promise suit."

"I was desperate. I would never have gone through with it. But my sister is perfectly correct, if a trifle over-informative. I have not had a moment's respite from my regrets. If I could turn back time, I would do everything differently—including announcing our engagement, to the Bingleys and to anyone else who would listen, from the moment you agreed to it."

Her eyes had grown...soft. Did he see it?

"You hurt me," she said. "I thought you never would."

Georgiana bit her lip, but Miss Bennet was not finished.

"My aunt says, however, that it is possible my expectations were a trifle too high."

"Your expectations were perfect. It is *my* behaviour that was low," Fitzwilliam countered immediately. "I would give anything for the chance to make it up to you. Or to try. Is it possible you might find forgiveness in your heart for my wretched performance? I fear no one could be so kind."

"Well," Miss Bennet answered soberly, although a dimple showed. "I agree that it is a risk. If you believe I could reverse my every decision against loving you, body and soul, merely out of some misguided sense of compassion, it *would* be unwise to ask. You might only make a great fool of yourself." Her eyes were positively twinkling now. Had he noticed *that*? *Oh, Fitzwilliam, do not spoil this opportunity! Should I give him another hint?*

However, he knelt as best he could in the small space before Miss Bennet with no hesitation whatsoever. "Already I have made a great fool of myself before you, too many times now to count. I can promise to be your fool for always, if you will agree to take me—I *have* noticed, you do like to laugh."

CHAPTER THIRTY-SEVEN

Elizabeth looked down onto the face of the man who had humbled himself so deeply before her—not to mention having done so with his young sister as an audience. It took so much courage to debase himself like this, whereas she had hidden behind teasing and sarcasm, not daring to believe his love was real. He was braver than any man she had ever known.

"Oh, my dear," she said, placing her hands upon his cheeks. "I have been listening to my fears, have I not?"

"It was quite reasonable for you to have them, considering all you have been through. I can but assure you that I will be here to fight any battles with you. I shall send my family to the devil, if I must."

"But that is just it—I do not *want* you to have to give them up, just as I do not wish to surrender mine. I promise you, I shall make allowances for your family's behaviour, set my own boundaries upon their influence, and refuse to be intimidated or ashamed by our differences. Can you do the same for mine?"

"I can," he promised, looking at her steadily. "Selfishly, I relegated your family to the periphery of your life. I only thought of myself, and I am sorry for it."

She smiled at him. "It may be some time before we introduce Mama to the earl, if we ever do. I do not mean that we should bring her to live at Pemberley. Besides, she would not like it. She loves her home, and her neighbours, and her place in life. It is why she has been so desperate to keep it."

He regarded her seriously. "She will be angry with me, will she not? Now that her hopes for a possible match between you and Mr Collins will be permanently crushed?"

Laughter broke free. "My darling, I am so sorry. You have misunderstood. Mr Collins married my sister, Mary, just after Christmas. Mama will never be required to leave Longbourn, and I assure you, there was never *any* prospect of a match with me."

"Oh. Ohh," he said, shaking his head in some chagrin. He glanced up at his beaming sister. "Georgiana, I suppose you may begin breathing again, now that it appears I did not muck up my entire proposal as you feared I would, and have gained you the sister you have always wished for. Perhaps you would trade seats with me, however, so that I am not required to crouch here the rest of the distance to Longbourn."

The younger girl quickly bounced—there was no other word for it—into the seat facing, so that he could sit beside his re-betrothed.

"Oh, yes," she said, looking radiant. "You must call me Georgiana, and may I call you Elizabeth? I have always wanted a sister, and never dreamt my brother would choose so well. Are you certain your older sister is set on Mr Bingley? Do you have other, unmarried ones? My cousin, Viscount Ridley, is unwed. He is not so kind nor so sociable as Mr Bingley—but then, he has no sisters, if that makes up for anything. It would be much better for everyone if we could stuff the Fitzwilliam family circle with Bennets, I think."

Elizabeth smiled at the impetuous, engaging girl. "Jane's feelings for Mr Bingley are too strong to be easily dissuaded, I believe. You may call me Elizabeth, of course, Georgiana. But..." She frowned suddenly, as she was abruptly reminded of all her worries and fears for Lydia. When she spoke, her voice was sober.

"First, we must find Lydia. I do not think you can overestimate what we will face when we reach Longbourn. My mother will be *very* upset, and not very quiet about it. Jane's letter said that Lydia had teased Kitty with clues regarding the, er, romance, while refusing to name the man involved. Kitty confessed what little she did know after, but my parents are very displeased with her, and she in turn is distraught. My father will be impatient and, um, not pleased to welcome you both while we are so troubled. In short, Longbourn will be a scene of chaos and despair, and...and I wish you would not see it."

Darcy took her hand in his much larger one. "I am certain that ahead of us are many scenes I would rather *you* did not witness. Would you accept my company now as an earnest payment on my intentions to stand beside you, always, in the future, no matter what prospects it brings us?"

Relief flooded her, cooling her embarrassment over what

they would face at Longbourn. "I would," she replied softly, setting her other hand atop his. "But Georgiana, we must not overlook you in our desire to not be parted. I cannot stress how…eccentric you will find my family. Perhaps you could let me off at Longbourn and take rooms at The George, in Meryton. It is a well-known inn to travellers in these parts, with very good accommodation. I could send a note over after I have prepared my family for the surprise."

But Georgiana looked at her reprovingly. "Elizabeth, I *eloped*. The only thing the man I thought *I* loved left *me* with was several highly descriptive curse words and a hitherto unknown skill for picking pockets. Do you think I would sit in judgment? Do you think they will say anything that will shatter my 'delicate feelings'?"

Darcy covered his face with his free hand and groaned. "Georgiana, perhaps these revelations could wait until after I secure my bride?"

She sighed loudly. "I did not mean to say all that aloud. Miss Ben—I mean, Elizabeth, for most of my life I have been perfectly behaved, and I-I said as little as possible in company and made very few social *faux pas* because of it. Regrettably, my brief adventure seems to have loosened my tongue to an unfortunate extent. I will get right to work on governing it again, I promise."

Elizabeth looked over to the man who sat beside her now, holding her hand, shaking his head. She scooted closer to him to lay her head comfortably upon his shoulder, appreciating his strength and solidity and the comforting beat of his heart.

"Oh, I do not know, sweetheart. Somewhere between 'remaining a diffident shadow in company' and 'eloping with known criminals' there must be a happy medium. You have been very useful today, as your honourable brother must confess."

He promptly wrapped his arm around her, snuggling her in more tightly to him in unabashed affection. "Elizabeth is probably right," he admitted.

Elizabeth shut her eyes. There were several miles left until they faced the tumult at Longbourn, and for these very few precious minutes, she could afford to rest from worrying about Lydia, Mama, Papa, Jane, and Kitty. For these relatively few moments, she could sit within the sheltering arms of the man she loved, and who loved her, and find peace.

CHAPTER THIRTY-EIGHT

Longbourn was not at all the asylum Elizabeth had expected. For one thing, as she entered the drawing room with Darcy and Georgiana trailing, it was occupied already—by Jane and Mr Bingley, with Kitty a gloomy-looking chaperon.

"Lizzy!" Jane flew into her arms in undisguised joy. "Oh, Lizzy, I am so glad to see you." Her eyes widened at the sight of her companions. "Why! Mr Darcy!"

Mr Bingley jumped up to greet them. "Oh-ho Darcy, what is this? Greetings, my friend! I have not seen you in an age. And Miss Darcy! I swear, you are an inch taller every time I see you!"

He spoke to Georgiana, Elizabeth noticed, as if she were still in the nursery. So much for Miss Bingley's assurances of a forthcoming marriage between them.

Darcy shook Mr Bingley's hand, and Elizabeth almost smiled at how quickly he brought up their engagement. "Miss

Elizabeth has agreed to marry me," he said. "She has been staying with her relations in town, but I brought her home just as soon as—" He halted mid-sentence, as if suddenly unsure what his friend knew of the situation.

"About Miss Lydia, yes," Mr Bingley said, abruptly sobering. "So very unfortunate." He shook his head sadly, but quickly brightened. "But this is much more welcome news. I congratulate you! I am so happy for you both!" He shook all their hands, repeating his congratulations, while Jane stood quietly looking in perplexity from Elizabeth to Darcy, and Kitty watched in equal bewilderment.

Elizabeth smiled at them all. "Georgiana, I would like to introduce my sisters. Jane, Kitty, this is Miss Darcy, who will be my new sister soon."

"But…but I thought we hated Mr Darcy!" Kitty blurted.

"All is to be forgot. It was just a dreadful misunderstanding," Elizabeth said forcefully, hoping they would hold their questions. "Mr Darcy will talk to Papa and explain, but nobody hates anyone, and we will be marrying. Soon, I hope."

"As soon as the banns can be called," Darcy agreed.

Mr Bingley looked puzzled at this interchange, but never one to be over-curious about details, and visibly gladdened by the news of his friend's connexion to a family he was well on his way to making his own, he asked no potentially mortifying questions. Elizabeth and Darcy were soon seated on one settee, Jane and Mr Bingley on the other, while Kitty and Georgiana had taken the chairs nearest the fire. They appeared to be having a slightly stilted but not unfriendly conversation.

"Is there any more news?" Elizabeth asked, as soon as everyone was resettled. "About Lydia, I mean."

"Nothing good," Jane sighed, her expression turning bleak. "One of the men was found in-in a gambling establishment in town. He was alone, and knew nothing of any elopement. The other two have not yet been traced, but they are now checking passenger lists at the port for likely possibilities."

"Has no one checked the routes to Scotland?" Darcy asked. "Is your father gone to do it himself?"

Jane flushed, but tried to explain. "All signs of the men led south. No one believes Scotland to be their destination. The entire company has been interviewed, and everyone agrees that an actual marriage is unlikely in either case. Papa is going to Uncle Gardiner—soon, he said, to search in town."

No, a capture would have been unlikely, Elizabeth realised. *Nevertheless, Darcy would have left no stone unturned, while Papa has almost given up.* At that moment, Darcy gave her a quiet smile and reached for her hand; he had removed his gloves upon entering the manor, as had she—so now she could feel, skin to skin, his strength and warmth. It helped.

"How does Mama fare?" Elizabeth asked Jane.

Jane sighed, glancing once at the solemn Darcy, obviously still bemused. "She is better, these last two days, than at first." Her eyes flickered to Mr Bingley, and Elizabeth understood that it was his presence that had somewhat calmed their mother. "She is still very worried, and very sad, of course. Mary is upstairs with her now. She has been a great help."

"Mary is here?" Elizabeth asked, surprised. "With her husband?"

"Yes. He has walked to the village to watch the choir practise, but he should be back soon."

"Somehow, I did not think Mr Collins would offer to be… helpful at a time such as this."

"Oh, well, he had a lot to say at first," Kitty suddenly interjected. "But Mary makes him discuss Bible verses about loving his neighbour and being an example of the believers every time he says something hateful. I do not know whether he has learnt not to say stupid things about Lydia, or whether he is tired of hearing Scripture, but he is much quieter about it all now."

Darcy squeezed Elizabeth's hand, just as she glanced at him—half-expecting censure.

"It can take some time for men to learn not to say stupid things. Perhaps I should speak to your father soon?" he asked under his breath. That was when Elizabeth realised he was not thinking about Lydia much at all, but of their own future. She did not want to leave her sisters, no matter how distressing the subject under discussion. But it was time to face her father.

Mr Bennet glanced up at the intrusion into his book room, with an expression of irritation. "I asked not to be disturbed—what? Elizabeth!" He quickly stood, and she ran to him.

For a few precious moments, she basked in his comforting embrace. "I have missed you, Papa," she said earnestly.

"The house has been excessively absent of sense since you departed," he grumbled. But then shaking his head, he let out a gusty sigh. "Perhaps it is one of the reasons why Lydia left. She has always known how to step on my last nerve, but since you moved to town, my patience for her nonsense has been lacking. I fear I was too stern."

If you were, Papa, it was too little, too late. But what good does placing blame do now? "Oh, Papa," Elizabeth said sympathetically. "Lydia has always been who she is, and I do not believe a few lectures would have changed it. Will you go to town?"

"Yes, I know I must, and I shall. Colonel Forster was so absolutely convinced he could trace the miscreants with all the resources available to him that I delayed! But he has been unsuccessful in finding anyone who has your sister. Perhaps your uncle will have ideas that he does not." He looked so miserable, Elizabeth's heart broke for him.

"Papa, I must tell you—Mr Darcy has come back."

He frowned ferociously, but she quickly explained what had kept him. "I must have your word that you will not tell anyone about Miss Darcy's unhappy experience. Mr Darcy would not consider inventing a weaker excuse to explain to you his absence, for nothing else accounts for his cousin's erratic and unconscionable behaviour. But he has vowed to help us discover Lydia. If anyone can, it is he."

"It is a regular epidemic of elopements!" Mr Bennet cried, astonished. "What is in the novels you females read these days?"

"I do not think Lydia has read much of anything," Elizabeth replied forlornly.

"What of the nasty things his cousin said of you? Lizzy, are you certain you are making the correct decision?"

"Mr Darcy is very angry with Colonel Fitzwilliam. He had instructed him to explain to me Miss Darcy's situation before we went to the church for the wedding. Unfortunately, the colonel was so mortified by Miss Darcy's elopement, and not knowing us at all—well, he chose to flee instead. I do not know if he and Mr Darcy will ever reconcile."

Mr Bennet frowned his incomprehension, but then his shoulders slumped. "It was wrong, very wrong. But I suppose…had there been any way to prevent Lydia's shame from becoming public, I would have wanted to take it. I do not think I would go so far as to leave a bride standing at the altar, and his spiteful words to Goulding—meant, I suppose, to cover his motives—were ungentlemanly in the extreme. He could, simply, have sent a message over to us without explanation, and at least saved one humiliation. Yet, we all make idiotic decisions in moments of distress. Here I have been stewing over Forster's ineptness without leaving for town to search for Lydia myself. I ought to have gone at once," he admitted glumly. "I hope to never meet Colonel Fitzwilliam again, but I suppose I understand him."

It was a convoluted reasoning, but Elizabeth could see his point. No one behaved perfectly in every situation; Darcy, attending a long-ago assembly where he had not wished to be, had once spoken thoughtlessly, and but for an accidental eavesdropping on the Bingley sisters in Netherfield's library, his carelessly spoken words might have continued to influence her initial poor opinion of him.

"You are kinder than I," Elizabeth said. "The colonel's selfish sacrifice of my feelings in defence of his own is a breach of honour, in my opinion. I do not intend to waste any great sentiment upon him, however. Mr Darcy may forgive him, or he may not. As for myself, I shall be polite and respectful, nothing less, and nothing more."

One corner of her father's mouth tipped up. "We shall see how that goes for him." But then his expression flattened again. "He wrote to you. Mr Darcy, that is. Thrice. I did not give you his letters, but returned them to him unopened. I thought you had been hurt enough, and I feared those letters were full of self-justification. I apologise for adding to your injury."

Elizabeth nodded. It was in the past, and he had meant well. "At least you did return them, so that Mr Darcy knew I had not received them. He was very determined that I should."

"You are entirely resolved to have him, Lizzy? Mr Bingley is back, and it seems he will stand by Jane. Even your ridiculous cousin Collins means well, and tells me we shall 'present a united front of family honour'. Mary might make something of him yet—I have underestimated her, it seems. What I am trying to say is, if you are marrying Mr Darcy to cover your youngest sister's sins, it is unnecessary."

"I love him, Papa," was her simple reply.

He examined her expression for some moments. "Well then," he said at last. "Send him to me, and go and share with your mother the good news. It might be restorative enough to help her to leave her bed at last."

CHAPTER THIRTY-NINE

Since Bingley had reopened Netherfield, Darcy was not required to stay at The George, but instead took advantage of his friend's grander accommodations. His conversation with Mr Bennet had been brief, but when he had offered to leave with him in the morning to return to London, opening his own home to him if Mr Gardiner remained absent from town, helping him to take up the failed search for his daughter, there had been genuine gratitude in the older man. Bingley had also offered to accompany Mr Bennet, of course— but it was obvious he doubted the younger man would be of much use. Darcy doubted it too but was glad to have him along regardless, and though the thought of separation from Elizabeth was physically painful, especially so soon, it could not be helped. Nevertheless, he worried a little over his sister, who had accepted the Bennets' invitation to stay with them at Longbourn.

He could not always understand Georgiana, and feared

leaving her here. Was it wise? While he wished her to learn to emulate Elizabeth and her elder sister, he was not so certain of Miss Catherine's influence. There was also the fact that Miss Lydia had so easily escaped her parents' protection, and in her fragile state, Mrs Bennet would not be much help with supervision. He trusted Elizabeth, of course, but did not want her to have to take a disciplinary role in Georgiana's life. Not yet, at least.

He had once believed his young sister to be possessed of an extreme natural diffidence; now he was unsure whether he had always misjudged her character or whether Wickham had corrupted it. What had possessed her to choose the man... twice? Most of all he wondered...*will she ever do it again?* Was she easily swayed by a pretty face and charming manners, with no judgment whatsoever? She was repentant, in that she had done everything possible to reunite him with Elizabeth— and he owed her for it. *But...has she learnt anything of wisdom from her mistakes? What more can I do?*

His inability to supply answers to these questions kept him from his sleep.

He and Bingley arrived early at Longbourn the next day, as they all wished to get on the road. Elizabeth looked bright and lovely in the morning light. How he hated to leave her! Mrs Bennet's dark circles attested to her lack of sleep; still, she was up and dressed—apparently for the first time since Miss Lydia's flight—and greeted the men cordially, insisting that they sit for a meal. Darcy seldom ate much in the mornings, and did not wish to do so now—thinking it much better that they be on their way. Yet, she had gone to some trouble to see that an abundance of breakfast food was available, and he would not insult her by refusing her table.

His impatience was eased tremendously when Elizabeth took his hand beneath the table linen, squeezing, and he felt the softness of her skin upon his own. Abruptly, he wished nothing more than to sit beside her all day, and wondered how he would ever find the strength to depart.

They had not been sitting long, however, when a woman hurried into the breakfast parlour—she was vaguely familiar, but at first, he was so astonished by her singular appearance that he could not begin to recognise her. For one thing, she seemed to be wearing some sort of loose silk nightgown which did not begin to fully contain her generous figure; her wildly-dressed hair was wrapped in cloth rollers, and she looked for all the world like a woman who had been startled from her bed. For another, she was sobbing noisily and in incoherent distress.

"Frances! Oh! Frances!" was all he could discern of her words.

Georgiana's eyes were so wide, he could see the whites all the way round. Mr and Mrs Bennet, the bewildered servants—and the table in general—stared at the weeping woman in shock. Only Elizabeth rose and went to the woman.

"Aunt Philips," she said gently, patting her shoulder. "Please, you must sit and calm yourself. Mrs Hill, please bring Mrs Philips a fresh cup." With such soothing and directives, Elizabeth soon had her aunt seated, wrapped in a blanket, and a semblance of order restored.

When she had her calmed and sipping her tea, Elizabeth spoke carefully. "Aunt, please, tell us what has happened."

Mrs Philips's lower lip trembled, and it appeared she might burst into tears again, but a few words of assurance from Elizabeth helped, and she looked to her sister. "It was George all along, Frances. I am so sorry. I never dreamt he held the slightest *desire* to elope. He certainly did not seem the type who would consider it."

George? The name, although a common one, caused a cold streak of dread to shoot down Darcy's spine. From a regiment? Had Wickham joined up, hiding *here*, almost beneath Darcy's very nose? Had he heard of Darcy's failed wedding to Elizabeth and targeted Lydia in response to his loss of Georgiana?

"George? George who?" Darcy said, so sharply that all eyes turned to him.

"George Philips," Mrs Philips answered at once, obedient to his tone. "My husband's nephew. He took him on recently as his clerk, with the hope that one day he will take over the practice—he is a very clever young man."

"Lydia went away with George Philips?" Mr Bennet cried, incredulity in his voice.

Tears leaked down Mrs Philips's cheeks, and in some relief, Darcy handed her his handkerchief. No one could possibly be as awful as Wickham. Elizabeth's young sister had at least a chance for happiness.

"Yes. He had told us he needed to go to town to take care of some personal business, and so his absence, at the same time as Lydia's, did not alarm us. He has never betrayed any special preference for her, nor she for him. Did you ever see it, Frances?"

Mrs Bennet could only shake her head, speechless.

"I had never considered the possibility, nor had Mr Philips! But he did not go to town. Instead, he took her to Scotland! They just arrived home, the foolish children. I asked George what in the world he was thinking, and he said creating such an adventure was the sole enticement he could offer Lydia to prove he is not dull." She blew her nose loudly.

"Lydia...is married?" Mr Bennet asked weakly. Mrs Bennet still gawped in shock.

"Yes, and over the anvil," Mrs Philips cried. "I apologise, my sister. I know that you would much rather have planned Lydia's nuptials. An elopement was *not* ideal, and so I told her. I know she took ten years off your life with her antics, but the silly girl is so happy to be married—she thought she never would be, you see—she probably won't listen to us complain about it for a fortnight, at least. They will have to live with us, of course. It will be some time before Mr Philips is ready to hand over the reins, and before George can afford his own place. There won't be much money in the beginning, although, as I said, George is a clever lad and good with a shilling. He will be able to care for her—eventually. In the meantime, I shall teach her how to reap what she's sown—you needn't think I won't take on the responsibility. It was my idea to bring him here, and I'll own it." She blew her nose again before addressing Mr Bennet.

"I know George is not what you wanted for her, but it would be foolish to contest the marriage now."

Mr Bennet turned away, but not before Darcy saw the tears in his eyes. "What I wanted? I wanted her safety. Just that." Leaving them all where they stood, he slipped into his book room and shut the door behind him.

"Oh! Mr Bennet! Always with his books, even at such a time as this!" Mrs Bennet cried, a bit foolishly. "Matilda, we must plan a dinner for them. Oh, my dear Lydia! I must speak to Mr Bennet about new clothes for her! You will bring them both to dinner tonight, with Mr Philips, too. Come upstairs with me, dear. You have left the house in your night-rail again. You may borrow my blue."

The sisters bustled up the stairs together, Mrs Philips hissing in a noisy whisper, "Sister! Mr Darcy is at your breakfast table?"

"Yes! Oh, Matilda, soon I will have four daughters married!"

Darcy gazed at Elizabeth, seeing the amusement gleaming in her eyes, and the relief. She did not care that her aunt was silly; like her father, she only cared that Lydia was safe.

"Come, walk out with me," he said. "I see the weather is particularly fine." It was a grey, drizzly sort of morning with fat, dark clouds that appeared as though they would spit rain at any moment.

"Oh, yes," she said, smiling up at him. "Let me don my coat, and we shall go out and enjoy the sunshine."

CHAPTER FORTY

lizabeth wanted Darcy to kiss her.

It was not merely desire—although there was plenty of that. They had been torn apart by life and circumstance and even their own flaws; she had believed that, due again to the choices of others, they faced separation. Suddenly their future stretched out before them, and whatever adversity they faced, she knew they would face it together. She wanted connexion and closeness. She wanted the man she had agreed to marry.

But she walked beside him in the damp morning air, saying none of those things. Was there a vocabulary for such desires? How, exactly, did one express them? It seemed impossible to simply blurt them out, baldly. Still, she tucked her arm in his, and in some mysterious translation, he seemed to interpret the language—at least to the extent that he moved in closer still, until his body warmed her all along her side, matching his stride to her shorter one.

Could it be that he wanted the same things, but also lacked the words?

"It is a great relief about your sister," he said solemnly.

"Yes," she agreed, not really wanting thoughts of Lydia to intrude on this interlude.

He glanced down at her. "You are not pleased with the match?"

Elizabeth considered. "I am unsure how to answer that. On the one hand, George Philips is reliable and will be a good husband to her, I think. Whether she is ready to be a good wife to him is another question entirely. I believe her too young and too spoilt to easily settle into the responsibilities of marriage. On the other hand, my aunt will be good for her."

"She will?"

Elizabeth could not prevent a smile. "I know you think she is rather silly, and so she is. Still, she will expect more of Lydia in the way of responsible behaviour than does my mother, who seems to think Lydia is approximately eight years of age. Also, my aunt is extremely persistent—she will not surrender to Lydia's tantrums as Mama does, yet she is very patient. Papa will never allow Lydia to live at home again, so likely it will all work out for the best. In time."

He seemed to accept that, and changed the subject to those much more pleasing—those having to do with their future life together. "The weather in Derbyshire will be cold, and Pemberley is monstrously difficult to heat. I usually remain in town after Christmas celebrations are past. However, I am anxious to show you the old pile, much of which is in need of refurbishing, and of course, you cannot begin to do any redecorating until you have seen the place."

They made plans then, for a journey to Pemberley to spend two or three weeks, and then a return to town before Easter. He told her of his imperious aunt—not altogether a surprise, for Mary had written extensively on the subject of Lady Catherine.

"Mary says that the behaviour Lady Catherine expects, even demands of her husband is the exact opposite of those attributes she most wishes to encourage. It is very confusing for Mr Collins."

"Is he the type who must drift with the course of every passing breeze?"

"Oh, I suppose many of us are. It takes a great deal of courage to create one's own direction. She says Mr Collins's greatest desire is to please those around him. He never could satisfy his own father, who seems to have ignored him for much of his life before dying unexpectedly. Now he is caught between pleasing his wife and pleasing his patroness. It is not an easy spot to be in. Mary is clever, however. We shall see whom he listens to." She paused. "There is a favourite verse she has marked in the family Bible. Remind me to show you one day."

He nodded. "I came here, you know—to see you. You were not here, having already moved to town. Collins defended you most vigorously, and made obvious his low opinion of me. Since I did not at that time realise that you had not received my first letter, I thought him courting you. When you said he had asked you to marry him, I drew all the wrong conclusions."

Elizabeth giggled. "I think Mary strongly encouraged him to ask me. She believed it the honourable thing to do."

He frowned, and she knew it had reminded him of their separation and her hurt and his cousin's betrayal. It was not what she had intended. But when he spoke, it was of none of those things.

"What do you think of Georgiana?" he asked.

"I find her delightful," she replied promptly.

"Delightful," he repeated, as if he had never heard the word. "Puzzling, inconsistent, difficult, moody—these are the attributes that come to my mind."

"Helpful, loving, romantic, remarkable, courageous—these more accurately describe her, to my way of thinking. She is one who creates her own direction—or who tries."

He paused, smiling down at her. "I love the way you see people," he said lowly, and she just knew he was about to kiss her. But the sudden sound of voices halted him in place.

"Miss Darcy! Oh, I am sorry. I did not mean to upset you. Do come back!"

"Return to the house, Kitty. I shall go after her," Mrs Bennet ordered loudly.

They turned to see, off in the distance, Georgiana striding away from Kitty and Mrs Bennet speeding after her departing figure. Darcy sighed heavily.

Elizabeth took his hand. "Perhaps a bit moody as well," she said, laughing, and pulled him after her mother and his sister.

Darcy quickly lost sight of Georgiana and Mrs Bennet, but Elizabeth seemed certain of the likeliest way.

"Which direction?" he asked, as they reached a turning point in the path.

"If Mama caught up to her, she would lead her to the hermitage, where there are benches nearby."

He increased his pace—for who knew what a woman like Mrs Bennet would say? What had Miss Catherine said to distress his sister? Without meaning to, Elizabeth's impractical mother might make everything worse, and he desperately wanted peace between their families.

They soon came upon the two ladies, sitting near a small decorative hermitage, their backs to Darcy and Elizabeth's approach.

"I wish I had not!" Georgiana sobbed. "I wish I could take it all back, but I cannot. I cannot undo a thing!"

"Why would you want to?" Mrs Bennet asked.

Elizabeth laid a hand upon his arm, halting him in his tracks. He looked over at her, almost desperately. Georgiana, it seemed, was in a confessing sort of temper—and the woman she might confess to was not known for her discretion, not to mention that she often behaved as silly as a feather pie.

"You would never understand," Georgiana said, tears of hopelessness in her voice.

"Was it a man?"

His sister nodded. "Catherine was telling me about how all of her sisters have married or will marry so happily, and I do not know if I can ever have that for myself, because of all my stupid mistakes."

Mrs Bennet began patting Georgiana's back, rubbing in a circular motion. "Whatever happened, I know one thing—all will be well," she said softly. "*You* will be well. It might not seem like it today, but you don't need an idiot man in order to be happy. You will be happy again."

"Are you sure?" Georgiana choked out the words miserably.

In the next moment, Georgiana was wrapped tightly in Mrs Bennet's embrace. "Oh, of course I am. My sweet girl. My poor, sweet girl," Mrs Bennet said, while Georgiana sobbed within the shelter of her motherly arms as if her heart would break.

Elizabeth grabbed Darcy's hand again, leading him away from the scene. It was not until they were beyond the hearing of the others that she spoke. "Sometimes," she said, "a girl needs nothing in the way of wisdom or advice. Sometimes, she simply needs a mother's embrace and reassurance. Mama is good at that."

"Very," Darcy agreed, feeling quite foolish. He had misjudged. Again.

"And sometimes," Elizabeth continued, a little hesitantly, "a girl needs a very different sort of embrace and reassurance." She looked up at him from under her lashes, so lovely she took his breath away.

Darcy was a foolish man, but he was not stupid. Taking her into his arms, he attempted to show her, with every fibre of his being and every ounce of his affection, just how willing he was to meet her every need.

CHAPTER FORTY-ONE

February 28, 1812

I t was *not* usual for a wedding to be so well attended. The breakfast afterwards, yes—and most of the neighbourhood would participate in that event, too.

Elizabeth sighed at the sight of the crowded pews as she peeked into the nave, feeling as though she was put on display for the entire world. It was Darcy's fault, really. Had he not failed to show up for their first wedding ceremony, their second try at nuptials would not have caused such a stir. At least half the attendees probably hoped to witness another dramatic non-appearance.

She peeked again into the nave; Bingley stood before the Bennet family pew, waiting for the bridegroom, passing the time by engaging in quiet conversation with Jane. Darcy was conspicuously absent.

The vicar, Mr Palmer, appeared in the vestibule. "Miss

Elizabeth, perhaps you and your father would like to await your bridegroom in a more private chamber? It is chilly out here." He hesitated. "If you would like, you could come around the north side and enter that way."

He is terrified of history repeating itself.

"Yes, that is an excellent idea," Mr Bennet agreed immediately.

So is Papa.

"No," Elizabeth said firmly. "Mr Darcy will either come, or the world has stopped spinning on its axis, or he is already at heaven's gate, awaiting entrance. Nothing but death or the end of the world would stop him, I promise you."

At that moment, the church doors were flung open, and Darcy barrelled through, his hair disarranged and cheeks red— as though he had run all the way to the church. She caught a glimpse, several yards behind him, of a tall, thickset older man struggling to keep up.

"Elizabeth," Darcy gasped, reaching for her hands. "I am so sorry to be dela—" He paused mid-sentence to look at her, really look. "You are astonishingly beautiful." Tugging her towards him, it appeared as though he might take her into his arms right then and there—had not Mr Bennet insistently cleared his throat. Darcy resumed his explanations instead.

"My uncle turned up at Netherfield just as I was leaving for the church."

"Your uncle?"

At that moment, the doors opened again, the older man reaching them. "You did not need to run from the carriage as if your hair was afire," he grumbled at Darcy, puffing for breath.

"Thanks to your younger son—yes, I did," Darcy snapped

back. He appeared to gather himself, straightening, but leaving one hand firmly clasping Elizabeth's. "Mr Bennet, Miss Elizabeth Bennet—moments away from becoming Mrs Elizabeth Darcy—Lord Matlock. Matlock, Mr Bennet, Miss Bennet."

Elizabeth curtseyed as best she could with Darcy's hand clutching hers; he did not seem inclined to let her go. Her father acknowledged the introduction politely, but she could see his confusion. "Colonel Fitzwilliam's father," she murmured by way of explanation.

Mr Bennet stiffened.

"Let us get the ceremony underway," Darcy said. "My lord, if you will accompany me."

"Pleased to meet you," the earl said genially, ignoring his nephew, and as if a church full of people were not waiting just beyond the doors, probably all straining to hear what the commotion was about. Of course, he was an earl, and likely accustomed to making the world wait. "There is a quiet little churchyard just beyond these doors. I wonder, Miss Bennet, if you would favour me with your company for a brief walk?"

"Now?" Mr Bennet and Darcy exclaimed in unison.

"Now," the earl said, distinctly unperturbed.

"It is out of the question," Darcy said.

"You cannot be serious," Mr Bennet chorused.

Elizabeth could see that Darcy and her father were disinclined to accommodate him, but there was something in the earl's expression—earnest, grave, with eyes so like Darcy's own—that sparked her curiosity. Other than Georgiana, there was no one else here from Darcy's family, although he had written to them. She had felt they were united in their disapproval, and probably this was nothing more than a chance for Lord Matlock to give her an earl's set down. Her courage, however, rose to the challenge. She had never before met this man; she would give him a chance to be civil.

"I shall do it," she said, speaking to her bridegroom, "unless there is a specific reason you wish me not to do so, other than the unfortunate timing of this conversation?"

"The earl can *wait*," Darcy said decisively.

"A few minutes of your time only, madam," the earl said, facing Elizabeth, obviously sensing her as the more malleable party.

She turned to Darcy, smiling up at him. "Perhaps, sir, you would await me inside, near Mr Bingley—where my neighbours will all stare at you in obvious enquiry, wondering if this time *I* have abandoned *you*?"

Mr Bennet's brows rose almost to his hairline in astonishment. "Lizzy," he murmured, "perhaps now is not the moment to indulge your unique sense of humour?"

Elizabeth did not blame her father for the protest, for Darcy was frowning ferociously. But as she looked into his eyes, trying to read them, his expression smoothed. "I suppose that is only fair," he said, softly touching her cheek. He turned to the earl. "I give you ten minutes, no more, before I come to fetch her. And if you say anything at all which she finds objectionable, you will never speak to her, or me, again. Am I understood?"

Matlock nodded impatiently—unmistakably bridling, unaccustomed to chastisement by anyone at all.

Reluctantly, Darcy let go of his bride and stalked into the

church. A torrent of gasps and whispers from the congregation accompanied his entrance. Elizabeth turned to her father. "Papa?"

He sighed, gave the earl a suspicious glance, and withdrew his pocket watch. "Oh, do choose this moment for your country stroll," he said to them both with no little sarcasm, seating himself on the bench. "I am quite at leisure."

The earl offered his arm; Elizabeth took it, and walked out with him into the weak winter sun.

For a minute or so, the earl was silent; Elizabeth was determined that he should be the first to speak.

"You must be at a loss, Miss Bennet, to understand the reason for my insistence."

"I have been unable to account for it, sir," Elizabeth concurred.

"And yet, at almost the moment of your wedding, you agreed."

"You are soon to be my uncle. Duty and respect obliged my agreement. At least this once."

He grunted. "Say what you think, do you? Probably what Darcy likes about you, contrary lad that he is."

Elizabeth had no answer to this; Darcy was the least 'contrary' person she knew.

"His mother was my favourite person in the world. On her deathbed, she begged me to look after him. He made it difficult, however. Has his own ideas about everything he does, from where he would gain his education to how he ought to invest his money, to how *I* ought to vote on this bill or that in the House of Lords—he is the least governable man I know."

Although he said this in a grumble, there was pride in his voice. Elizabeth could not do more than nod. They walked a little farther before he spoke again.

"He is at loggerheads with my youngest son. They have been the best of friends most of their lives, but Darcy says Richard behaved towards you in an ungentlemanly manner, failing to inform you of Darcy's compulsory absence upon his wedding day, leading to the further postponement of your marriage. Richard agrees that this is what happened, but declines to provide his reasoning for such dishonourable conduct. Both tell me to ask the other for the entire truth of the matter, but neither will reveal the whole story. I am asking you for it."

Both of them protect Georgiana. It is good of the colonel to refuse to defend himself, for her sake. It was the first kindly thought she had had towards Colonel Fitzwilliam since she learnt of his actions on her first wedding day.

"I am afraid that I am unable to help you with that," she answered evenly.

He glowered, but it simply made her want to smile; it was Darcy's glower, exactly. The earl wore the fearsome aspect for a few more moments, but seeing its lack of effect, he gave it up in a sigh.

"The older I get, the more I see of myself in Richard," he said at last. "I have been strict—very strict with him. I did not want him waiting around, hoping his elder brother would die before he had a life of his own. My wife and I have empha-sised, again and again, the need for a certain exactness of standards in his bride. I suspect he did not find your birth well enough for Darcy's expectations. None of his business, of course," he was quick to add, "and his situation is not Darcy's. He should not have involved himself in the matter. He ought to have remembered that duty, honour, and gratitude for the many ways Darcy supports and assists his family demand our defence of his decision, and so I have reminded him. When I was a younger man, however, without a right understanding of the Darcy stubbornness, I might once have made the same blunder."

He looked at her with some anticipation, as if hoping he had hit on the truth and that she would confirm it.

"You will have to ask him his motives," she said simply, and the elderly man's face fell, his shoulders slumping.

At his obvious dismay, something within her let go of her anger. It was in the past; she would not think of it again. The last thing she wanted was for the earl to keep poking at the old wound. If Darcy ever wished to renew his friendship with his cousin, she certainly would not fight it.

"I recommend, however, that we, none of us, dwell upon it," she said. "Families are imperfect. They err. I will, doubtless, make my own mistakes in the future. If we acknowledge what we have done wrong, and vow to do better in the future, we surely can move past them. I am willing if he is, and so you may tell your son."

His palpable relief at her words told her they were the right ones.

"Well then," he said, straightening, smiling, and turning her about. "Well then. We had best get you into the chapel before Darcy comes out here to drag you back indoors. I still must have a word with your father. Come, Niece. Let us hurry you now to your bridegroom."

And this was how Elizabeth found herself escorted up Meryton's church aisle with her father on one arm and the renowned Earl of Matlock upon the other. It made her final wedding day a sight that few in attendance would *ever* forget.

EPILOGUE

June 26, 1817

Invitations to the ball commemorating Georgiana Darcy's wedding, held in Matlock's grand ballroom, were among the most highly coveted of any event in 1817. Her bridegroom, Lord Whitney, was a jolly, earnest young man of good character who adored his bride.

Colonel Richard Fitzwilliam remained at one end of the ballroom, surrounded, as usual, by a cadre of his mother's friends who had appointed themselves responsible for his still unwed state. For once, he was awaiting the same thing they were, and knew by a herald of whispers when the moment arrived.

Mrs Darcy entered on the arm of her adoring husband, to murmurs of appreciation at the beauty of her sapphire blue silk gown, and wonderment and speculation about the others in her party. Willingly enough, the colonel performed the office expected of him.

"The girl in the pink gown is Mrs Darcy's younger sister, Miss Catherine," he answered and, because the old hens would love the titbit, added a knowledgeable aside. "She is betrothed to the man who holds Pemberley's living—Tilney, I believe is his name. Bingley and his wife, Mrs Darcy's sister, are entering just behind them, with Bingley's youngest sister bringing up the rear —she married old Sutherland, you know, but still hovers ceaselessly around the Darcys. Oh, and here come Mrs Darcy's parents —Mr and Mrs Bennet, of Longbourn estate in Hertfordshire."

"Oh, we all know *their* names," Mrs Acton-Smith replied. "Who can forget how Mr Darcy placed announcements of his marriage in *The Morning Post, The Morning Chronicle, The Morning Herald, The British Press, The Evening Mail, The Courier, The Globe,* and *The Sun.* Am I forgetting any?"

The ladies all tittered appreciatively, and he smiled along with them.

"Does she not have relatives in trade?" asked Lady Buford, with snide undertones.

"She has very wealthy, very powerful relations, and is a great favourite of Matlock," the colonel replied with chiding asperity. "Her father is a gentleman, and *you* may choose to take Mr Darcy to task for those connexions, but *I* shall not."

At the other end of the ballroom, Elizabeth and Darcy watched Mr and Mrs Bennet join the first set—a country dance.

"How in the world did your mother ever convince your father to attend a London ball? I never thought to see the day."

"Neither did I," Elizabeth replied. "Of course, never did they expect to be invited to an earl's entertainment. It is not Papa's idea of a perfect evening, perhaps, but he refused a future of forever listening to Mama's disappointment if she had missed it. Look how happy she is!"

Her mama was indeed sparkling with smiles—most all of them, it seemed, for her husband. What was even stranger to Elizabeth, was her father's returned smiles towards his wife.

"Not everyone need be the greatest wit in the country in order to be valued and valuable," Darcy remarked. "Loyalty and devotion mean much."

"I think they were very angry at each other for a very long while," Elizabeth said softly. "Mama did not bear a son, and she wanted Papa's love regardless. Her nerves, her complaints, her refusal to allow anyone to discipline Lydia—these were her weapons. Papa responded by withholding affection and firing off sarcastic remarks she could seldom understand. In every argument, I took his side, without stopping to think how my judgments hurt her. Of course I was not Mama's favourite —why would I be? But at the bitterest moment of my life, she offered only her love."

Darcy reached for Elizabeth's hand; she knew he understood of what bitterness she spoke. "I shall always be grieved you had to experience that moment. I am grateful your mother was good to you at a difficult time."

"I have an excellent family," she agreed. "Slightly eccentric, perhaps, but loving and supportive."

"I know," he replied ruefully. "I have read your family Bible."

She grinned up at him. "Did I ever tell you of the time Lydia brawled with the Harrington girls in the streets of Meryton because they dared insult me?"

The entire family had worried about whether the new Mr and Mrs Philips could be happy together for longer than a few short months. No one had counted upon the tenacity of young Mr Philips. He was ambitious and determined, and after investing in one of Mr Gardiner's riskier schemes, he had earned enough for the pair to move from the Philipses' home to build their own. In furnishing it, in combing London antiques markets with a clever eye for price and design, Lydia found true joy, and not long afterwards she and her husband opened a shop—Philips & Philips Curiosities and Collectibles. The shop proved popular, and as word spread, the area attracted other such merchants. Meryton was gradually becoming a destination itself, instead of a mere stop along the way to better places.

"I do not believe you have ever mentioned that particular tale. It might be best not to repeat it in Jane Elizabeth's hearing."

Their young daughter would probably be escaping her nurse and sneaking out of the earl's nursery any moment now in order to catch glimpses of the dancing, while her elder brother remained obediently in his bed.

Once the receiving line had been dispensed with, the earl was quick to seek them out from amongst his other guests. Matlock had done his best to mitigate the damage caused by his younger son's actions—he very much depended upon Darcy's influence and intellect, and if he ever had learnt of Georgiana's one-time misadventure, he had opted to pretend otherwise. Nevertheless, Elizabeth did not believe for a moment that he had been thrilled by Darcy's choice of bride. In private, the earl and countess were always civil, but they had not truly warmed to her until the children had begun to come along. They were excessively formal, and excessively preoccupied with public opinion. Whatever her own parents' flaws, she could not imagine being raised by Matlock and his wife instead.

Her eyes sought out the colonel. He had been well-nigh ostracised by his parents and elder brother—only recently had he begun to truly be welcomed back into the family circle. Nevertheless, he had done his best to mend fences; Georgiana held him in good standing, he never forgot Elizabeth's children's birthdays, and he in turn was a great favourite with them.

The earl saw the direction of her look. "Lady Matlock has decided it is long past time for Richard to marry. I believe she favours the daughter of Sir Percival Biddlesby. He is a good man. A baronet, you know."

"She is a child in her first Season," Darcy said, incredulous, glancing over at the young lady in question, a thin, wide-eyed girl, whose head was overwhelmed by a crown of white roses, and who avoided everyone's gaze.

The earl shrugged. "He has had plenty of time to choose one more to his liking, and he is not getting any younger. May as well marry her now while she is willing," he said carelessly, and, hailed by another of his guests, disappeared into the crowd.

"What he means is that Biddlesby fears the girl has not taken well with the *ton*, and Matlock has need of her settlement," Darcy growled. "It would be a disastrous match, and only my aunt and uncle could fail to see it."

Not for the first time, Elizabeth felt sorry for Colonel Fitzwilliam. She had attempted, over the years, to bring about a rapprochement between the two men, but Darcy's anger was as deep as his hurt. They were always civil, but the breach was a wide one, and seemed all but impossible to overcome.

"When you think of it, we actually owe Colonel Fitzwilliam a great deal," Elizabeth said in confiding tones.

Darcy raised a brow. "How so?"

"Thanks to his misjudgment, the earl extended himself to curb any possible incivility from the rest of your family. Our first years could have been full of bickering and infighting; instead, I had the benefit of public acceptance and private courtesy."

"Nothing excuses Fitzwilliam's actions towards you."

"We do not have to excuse his *actions*—but the man himself ought to be given the opportunity to prove he learnt from them."

"You have been kindness itself towards him."

"I shall continue to be kind. He had my forgiveness the first time he visited the nursery and allowed our son to use him as a cavalry horse for a solid two hours. I am speaking of friendship—yours and his."

An exultant, excited Georgiana and her new husband descended upon them then, and all private conversation was impossible for some time. In fact, it was not until the first waltz of the night that Elizabeth had opportunity to express more of her opinion.

"Colonel Fitzwilliam is surrounded by women who want him to marry their daughters and granddaughters. He is too polite to fend them off, and requires a friend's assistance."

Darcy obligingly looked, and could not resist commenting. "Matlock is correct, in that he could have married elsewhere before this."

"He could marry one of the women who has his parents' approval, you mean."

Darcy frowned. "Probably. Dash it, he never can bear to cross his father, and yet he could not possibly want one of the earl's cronies as a father-in-law."

"I agree, and have given some thought to the matter. I believe he would do well with my good friend, Sarah Bentley. There is certainly nothing objectionable about her. Her father, or her young brother, will inherit Lord Hampton's title, and her dowry is magnificent."

"Oh, there are a few things they could object to."

"Her conversation is not always…typical, I suppose, but I find her very interesting. Refreshing. Typical people are often so dull, and she is more than strong enough to withstand the, er, affections of Lord and Lady Matlock."

He looked down at her with some sternness. "It is not like you to play the matchmaker."

Elizabeth shrugged. "Everyone could do with a little help now and again. Remember how useful your sister was to *us* at a critical juncture. I only wish you to perform the introduction."

"That is all?" His aspect was most severe.

"Oh, well, perhaps you might hint, in the most delicate way possible, that it would mean a great deal to you if he took the introduction seriously. A step, even, towards redemption. Friendship."

Lady Buford pursed her lips, murmuring to Colonel Fitzwilliam, "Just look at that. Mr and Mrs Darcy are arguing! Right in the middle of the dance floor, at his own sister's ball. Perhaps the bloom of his inexplicable fascination for her has *finally* faded, do not you agree?"

Colonel Fitzwilliam glanced over in the direction the old shrew was nodding, to where Mr and Mrs Darcy performed the simple, uncomplicated steps of a waltz. He saw what Lady Buford saw—the imposing form of Darcy, his expression harsh and unyielding as he gazed down upon his wife, who unmistakably was speaking to him of matters far too serious for a ballroom.

"I do *not* agree," the colonel replied. "Watch a few more moments longer. You will see."

Sure enough, as Lady Buford stared, Darcy suddenly twirled his wife in a rapid, twisting spin, expertly weaving through dancers less skilled, her laughter floating to them over the heated air of the vast chamber. For a moment, as they came to a halt very close to where Fitzwilliam was standing, Darcy dipped her nearly to the floor and held her there, poised and perfect, his lips close enough to almost—but not quite— scandalously touch hers, her smile brilliant enough to exceed the brightness of the many glittering, crystal-laden chandeliers.

"They are making a spectacle of themselves!" Lady Buford scolded in a near-shriek of disapproval.

Darcy's mouth descended the rest of the way, in a passionate kiss sure to send all the Lady Bufords into a dead faint; the colonel could not hide his grin, and did his best to distract the matrons away from the sight. One would never guess Mr and Mrs Darcy had been married half a decade, the parents of two children, instead of new lovers caught in that first heady steam of a fresh romance.

"Fitzwilliam?" Darcy hailed from behind him, causing the colonel to start in surprise and turn around. Darcy *never* singled him out for his attention. Not any longer.

Darcy was grinning at him in a carefree way that Fitzwilliam had never thought to see again; Mrs Darcy's eyes were shining. "I hate to see you standing about in this stupid manner. You had much better dance," his cousin proclaimed.

"Me?"

"Are there other Fitzwilliams here?" Darcy kept his wife's hand in his, managing, even so, to draw his cousin farther away from the crowd of too-interested onlookers. "I would consider it a personal favour if you were to bestow your attentions upon a particular young lady."

The colonel steeled himself. He had seen his father talking to Darcy earlier, and with this overture, his intent became clear. The earl had applied pressure. There would be forgiveness, or at least acceptance, if Fitzwilliam capitulated. "I suppose," he began, "that you desire I should ask Priscilla Biddlesby for the next set."

But Darcy frowned. "Do you believe I hate you so much as that?"

"You have every right to," Fitzwilliam replied quietly. "It would be a fitting revenge. For the rest of our lives, you will be with the uncommonly lovely Mrs Darcy, whilst I endure… poor Priscilla."

"Oh, Colonel," Mrs Darcy said, very sympathetically, giving her husband a meaningful look.

"Great gads, man, what an awful imagination you have. No, Mrs Darcy has a friend she swears you would like, to whom we thought to introduce you. I do not hate you at all, I find. I suppose…I *have* forgiven you without truly realising it. Shall we, on the occasion of dear Georgiana's wedding, let bygones be bygones?" He held out his free hand.

Fitzwilliam did not hesitate, but gripped it tightly. His throat closed around his gratitude, and for a mortifying moment, he was in danger of bursting into tears right there in his father's ballroom.

"I should like it above all things," he managed at last. "And if her friend has anything approaching the graciousness of Mrs Darcy, it would be an honour to meet her."

"Very good," Darcy replied gruffly, with emotion in his own eyes.

"Come with us then, Colonel," Mrs Darcy said gaily. "I have a prescience that there is more than one happily-ever-after in the works this night."

And like Darcy before him, Colonel Fitzwilliam cheerfully followed where she led.

ALSO BY JULIE COOPER

A Match Made at Matlock

A Stronger Impulse

A Yuletide Dream

Irresistibly Alone

Lost and Found

Mr Darcy's Abducted Bride

Nameless

Seek Me: Georgiana's Story

Tempt Me

The Bachelor Mr Darcy

The Perfect Gentleman

The Seven Sins of Fitzwilliam Darcy

ANTHOLOGIES & COLLECTIONS

'Tis the Season

A Match Made at Matlock

Affections & Wishes: An Anthology of Pride & Prejudice Variations

Fitzwilliam Darcy, Hero

For Love Apart

Happily Ever After with Mr Darcy

Obstinate, Headstrong Girl

Otherworldly

ABOUT THE AUTHOR

Julie Cooper lives with her husband of forty-one years in Central California. She spends her time boasting of her four brilliant and beautiful children, doting on her four brilliant and beautiful grandchildren, and cleaning up after her neurotic Bichon, Pogo. Somewhere in between the truly important stuff, she peddles fruit baskets and chocolate-covered strawberries for a living whilst pressing penitent Mr Darcys on an unsuspecting public.

ACKNOWLEDGMENTS

Much appreciation is due Jessie Lewis for her insightful editorial chops, as well as Katie Jackson for hers. Thanks also to Lisa Sieck, for kindly reading this before submission, even though she had to read with one eye closed during the angsty bits. It should be noted that I would never have figured out love in the first place without Dennis Cooper. Last but never least, Sarah Cooper, who wanted Darcy ditched at the altar at least once in his many variations…here you go.

Made in the USA
Las Vegas, NV
04 January 2025

15800813R10184